A Perfect Arrangement

Kate Murphy

ISBN: 979-8-218-86495-8

To those friends, partners, and family
that feel like sunshine & help us grow.

1

It's not that I don't believe in happily-ever-afters. What I don't believe in are whirlwind romances. Passion so strong, it rips the roots out of your carefully crafted routine. Take it from someone whose own life cartwheeled away from her; risk is for long-term investment portfolios, not love.

"How's it look, Lizzie?" Jessie swishes her skirt so it catches every ray of sunshine. She beams, her smile the only thing brighter than the gown's glare. Jessie's an exception to the rule—she's getting her real, honest-to-goodness happily ever after today, like she always planned. Clark might seem boring, but he is as stable as they come.

"Dazzling. You look like a shooting star," I say. She's glowing. And she feels farther away from me with each passing minute.

My best friend has always been the fairytale princess, ever since we were enrolled in ballet and decked out in tutus. At her sixth birthday party, Jessie wore a ballgown and made her mom bedazzle our roller skates.

Meanwhile, the sparkly Converse worn by the wedding party feel overly saccharine on me.

"Not my intended look, but I'll take it." Jessie grins. "Can't believe I didn't get an 'out of this world' pun from you."

"What if I tell you that your asteroid looks stuffed in that dress?" I counter.

She laughs, laser-whitened teeth throwing more light. "You always know the right thing to say." I force a bright smile her way, until she turns her attention back to the troupe of bridesmaids.

My best friend's wedding is in some ways like *My Best Friend's Wedding*, except I'm not technically in capital-L love with Jessie. I love her in a platonic, my-forever-person way. She's stood by me at peaks of happiness and pulled me out of pits of sadness. She is the first one I call with any news.

Maybe the reason we grew into either side of the same coin is because we were inseparable as kids. She's the light to my dark, the sparkle to my shadow. I have band t-shirts for every one of her sequined dresses. While Jessie gained semi-influencer stats on social media, I stopped using mine in a show of solidarity against tech monopolies.

Simply put, we've spent our lives together. Except lately, it's like we've stopped growing up and started growing apart. The cloud of discontent dulling my Converse's shine could have something to do with the fact that I planned on getting married this year, too. But I've learned that's what happens when you expect life to be predictable; it leaves you floundering.

Clara leans on my shoulder in a move that looks a lot like swooning but is aimed at taking the weight off her swollen ankles.

"Jessie looks stunning," she says, smiling at our mutual friend.

"It's true. You look amazing too," I reply, subtly shifting so I can help take more pressure off her.

Pregnancy, Clara has told me more than once, is more a pain in the legs than a pain in the ass.

She snorts. "Honestly, I'm lucky there was enough fabric left in this dress to cover my ass, thanks to this little monster." She tenderly rubs her belly despite the harsh word choice.

Clara and Jessie did gymnastics together as kids and stayed close. Shockingly, I'd only met Clara a handful of times before the wedding festivities started, but we've been the odd women out in this group, which makes for a special brand of trauma bonding. To be friends with Clara is to experience pragmatism sprinkled in hot pink confetti —she's clearly over the patriarchal bullshit but also a firm believer in true, all-encompassing, head-over-heels love. She keeps me on my toes.

The rest of Jessie's bridal party are from her college, Texas A&M. Three of the bridesmaids got engaged at the same time and are now carefully spacing out their weddings so they can be part of each other's ceremonies. I've been regaled with stories from two bachelorette parties so far, both varying versions of, *it was so fun,* and *you should have seen how many free shots we got! Her fiancé would lose it if he knew she rode that mechanical bull in a dress.*

Jessie and I have already gone through much of life in different places, but we grew off separate branches of the same tree. We've always been able to tap back into our roots, even while far away.

After college, Jessie moved to the 'burbs and I moved to the city to live out my big-girl career aspirations. Honestly, I couldn't stand the thought of going anywhere that resembled our hometown. Even so, we faithfully spent at least every other weekend attached at the hip. Luckily, her soon-to-be hubby, Clark, is amenable to our giggly sleepovers after one too many margaritas. He's even so kind as to leave a fresh pot of coffee and always offers to get bagels for us when we inevitably wake up hungover.

I chew my lip and watch Jessie's mom secure the length of buttons on the back of the dress with a hook. Each latch seals my friend's fate, locking her into a path that veers away from the one we've been living together for as long as I can remember.

I can't help but feel like life's dominoes were lined up unfavorably while I wasn't looking, splitting my life from the direction that it was supposed to follow. The direction that aligns with Jessie's. It suddenly feels too hot in this sun-drenched, sparkling room.

Clara waves a hand at my cleavage, ripping me out of my own head. "But enough about me, there is something I *must* tell you. Lizzie, your tits are looking positively fabulous in that dress."

I choke on a laugh. "Oh, wow, thanks? Um, yours look great too."

Did I mention I really like Clara?

"Pfft, right? It's just one perk of the tiny demon. Also, my hair is growing approximately seventeen times faster than usual.

Which is cool, except it's happening to *all* my hair if you catch my *I'm-talking-about-my-pubes* drift." She glances down and frowns while I try not to snort. "I do love this dress. Mint green is our color." Clara winks. "I could live without the toe-pinching sneakers, but I guess they're better than heels. Or sweaty ballet flats. Man, those things stink."

"Agreed. I pocketed some Band-Aids for tomorrow's blisters," I say. And then, because I am feeling out of sorts and a bit hysterical, "I'll share them with you if you tell me what growth hormones you're using on your bush."

Clara cackles so loudly, everyone in the room looks our way. She keeps laughing without telling them why she's losing it. "Lizzie, I always knew you were the smartest, sexiest little cookie of us all."

On the first day I'd seen Clara in fifteen years, she pulled me into a bone-breaking hug and sighed. "Lovely to see you again, you beautiful bitch. I'm with child."

While my twenty-nine-year-old self is not ready for a baby, Clara's got her shit together. She's the one who wrangled all the girls at the bachelorette party, made sure our tabs were paid, and handed out morning Advil. She's dependable, reliable, and has the foulest mouth of anyone I've ever met. I only met her partner at the dress rehearsal, but he seemed relieved to fall into Clara's orbit, too.

"Okay, ladies! Time for a toast!" Jessie squeals. The attendant hands me a glass of champagne and brings over sparkling cider for Clara. She rolls her eyes and fake gags.

"You've all made my big day amazing so far," Jessie continues. "Each of you is so special to me. You helped shape me into who I am—" *gentle touch to her mom's shoulder* "—and are always supporting me in who I want to be."

Jessie starts to cry, prompting panicked looks from the makeup artists but she's the daintiest crier in the world. A few tears slip cinematically down her cheeks, and she dabs them gently with a tissue before they threaten her dress.

"I love you. Thank you for being here for me." She raises her glass. "Now let's party."

Everyone cheers and shoots their champagne. I take a swig

for liquid courage. Bubbles go up my nose and burn my eyes.

After additional prodding and zipping and stuffing tissues in bras in case of ceremony tears, we file into line and head outside.

"Goddamn swollen feet," I hear Clara whisper at her size-too-tight Converse. My own shoes wink sunlight back at me as we step into the world.

I'm paired up with Clark's teenage brother, Nick, for our walk to the altar. When Jessie matched up the couples, I wonder if she realized she paired the shortest and tallest members of the party. My 5'1 self next to Nick's 6'4 gangly limbs looks ridiculous. My dating profiles say I'm *fun-sized* but I imagine I look like a toddler being escorted up the aisle. Since my current life probably looks more like Nick's than my fully adult friends, I guess it's an appropriate match.

As we take careful steps, I avoid making eye contact with anyone. My mom is here, of course. While we were growing up, she was like Jessie's mom, too. Jessie and I flew back and forth between each others' houses like ping-pong balls. In high school, our parents kept each other's favorite snacks on hand. Cheez-Its for Jessie, square pretzels for me. We were a package deal.

Like a magnet, my eyes find Mom's. Her small frame is perched on an aisle seat. She chose a light brown wig for today, cropped short. She gives me a thumbs-up and a smile. Melancholy thoughts rise to the surface of my mind like tiny bubbles. I will them to sink back down. Champagne has a way of making me sentimental, and I must have polished at least half a bottle while we were getting ready.

The ceremony is undeniably beautiful. I give thanks that it's outdoors, a spring breeze playing with the free pieces of Jessie's updo as she glides down the aisle.

I sniffle during the vows, thankful for bra tissues. If nothing else goes right today, at least I don't mess up the ceremony. I take the bouquet without dropping it, fluff her veil, and don't make a face even when one of the guests has a sneezing fit in the third row.

After the ceremony, we're shuffled out for pictures. As Maid of Honor, I am the moon to planet Jessie. I hover near her, squashing problems like bugs before they can get too close. Then I'm being positioned on one side of Jessie, with Clark and Nick on the other.

"I never thought I'd hate having photos taken of me but have we been doing this for hours or what?" Jessie hisses at me through smiling teeth.

I stretch one arm and then the other, a baseball player warming up for batting practice. "My arms hurt from holding this goddamn flower bouquet. Did they fill these things with lead?"

"Please, stay still," the photographer says briskly.

"Oops, sorry. Will do," I call back. I drop my voice again and mutter, "Whatever happened to acting natural?"

Jessie tries to stifle a laugh, which makes me snort, and soon we're hunched over into a chuckling heap.

"Ow, my ribcage." Jessie is holding her side and half hyperventilating. "I can't laugh in this thing."

"They don't build those whalebone prisons like they used to," I sputter.

We are hysterical now, hands on knees. The photographer snaps a few candids and tightly turns to direct the groom and his best man. I can feel her trying not to roll her eyes.

Once we recover, Jessie looks at me. Tears sparkle in the corner of her eyes. "Lizzie, thank you. I know it's been a lot with your mom this year, but I needed you here."

I swallow the melancholy and give her the chipper response I know is required.

"Oh my god, of course. This has given me something positive to focus on. I love your love." It's not a lie. I do love her love, I just wish her life would slow down and wait for mine to catch up.

"I miss you. I feel like this whole wedding has been a whirlwind." She squeezes my hand. "After this is over, we can have an *Elf* movie night," she says.

"In May?" I ask.

"Yup, in May."

"Okay, frozen wine slushies in lieu of hot chocolate." I raise my pinky in promise, but the photographer is back in our business before Jessie can loop her own finger around mine.

"Bride! This way, please!" The photographer waves a friendly-yet-demanding hand.

I distract myself by watching the colors of the sky and earth meld as the sinking sun fuses the two.

When the reception rolls around, I am not ready to walk out on the dance floor and bust a move, as is required of the wedding party. Nick and I decide to take a shot in solidarity beforehand.

"To prosperity!" Nick says.

"To making it through tonight with both false eyelashes intact!" I counter.

We clink glasses and throw them back. Despite being underage, Nick slugs his like a pro and calls for another. The tequila burns all the way down my throat until I feel it fizzle in my empty stomach. Did they offer us food all those hours ago in the bridal suite? I can't quite remember.

"You ready?" He asks. He's a good sport, willing to dance around the ballroom without shame. Ah, to be nineteen again.

The heat of the tequila in my system has me eager to get this over with.

"Hell yes, let's show 'em what we're made of," I say, leaning hard into the fake it 'til you make it ideology.

The rest of the wedding party makes their way out. Ken and Rachel do a TikTok dance, Camilla and Cleary chest bump in the middle of the dance floor, and Roger pretends to reel in Clara like a fish. Then it's our turn.

There's nowhere to hide, but I know we've made a good choice when the crowd starts laughing. Luckily, Nick was also a fan of *The Office,* so it was easy for us to agree on The Scarn. We make new friends, tie some yarn. Then we mosey off the dance floor and line up to welcome in "for the first time as a Mr. and Mrs."

"Hey, that wasn't too shabby!" I poke my elbow into Nick's ribs with real enthusiasm. "Now I can save the rest of my terrible dance moves for the part of the evening when everyone is wasted, and it no longer matters."

"How do you know when that is?"

"My usual threshold is when 75% of the women are dancing barefoot, despite the risk of broken glass."

"I'll catch you out there to Scarn it up later, then." Nick smiles, fake bows, and heads towards the other groomsmen.

It's not until I turn around to head to my table that it happens.

I notice Lionel, laughing at a table across from my own. My breath catches. Of course there was a chance he would be here. It is his cousin's wedding, after all. I was just banking on the fact that he'd still be on tour in Europe, too busy with his musical career to fly home.

To be fair to Jessie, I avoided asking her questions— I didn't want to make it weird since he's Clark cousin and I didn't want to seem like I still cared. Because I shouldn't. Because I was the one who broke it off. But seeing him in the bronzed flesh for the first time since we split, I realize that it does matter. I cough a few times to get my breathing under control but end up sounding like a dying pterodactyl.

"You alright? You look like shit." Clara materializes next to me, which is pretty impressive since what used to be a tiny bump now looks like she's smuggling in a watermelon. I asked her if that was normal for four months. "Absolutely not. Lucky me, this bad boy's sitting right on my bladder."

She prods me now, looking me up and down. Particularly at my face, which I know from previous experience must be bright red.

"Yup, overcome with emotion," I whisper. The music changes for the first dance. I peel my eyes away from my ex-lover, almost fiancé and turn to look at my best friend. Every eye in the room is drawn to Jessie, like flowers opening to the sun.

She and Clark do that epic scene from *Dirty Dancing*. They look picture-perfect, even though I know it took months of classes to make this a seamless reality. Both of their smiles light up the floor (maybe I need to invest in that goopy whitening toothpaste Jessie recommended Freshman year when we were jokingly applying to be on *The Bachelor*). I'm over the moon happy for her, but the not-so-nice part of me burns a little green.

By the time they get to the lift, everyone is cheering and screaming, myself included. Although if my screams were isolated, they would probably sound like those of a wounded animal. Thank the universe for crowds.

Clark lifts Jessie effortlessly over his head, spinning her so the entire room can admire her beauty like a bird in flight. Then everyone is seated for dinner. Clara sits next to me, passing me her glass of champagne while chatting away.

"Savor this for me, please."

"Thanks."

She follows my eyes, boring holes at the side of Lionel's head. I'm trying not to look, I swear, but it's impossible to avoid from this angle. My heart rate spikes. Is he with that blonde girl seated next to him? She's even shorter than I am, a tiny human with a pixie cut. She's beautiful, and she looks nice, like she'd compliment your shoes and mean it.

"Who's that?" Clara asks conspiratorially. Normally, I wouldn't air my grievances to anyone but Mom or Jessie. But Clara was my partner-in-crime for the bachelorette. She helped me make custom bride bingo cards and pick out my outfits every night. Even though she's expecting a baby and owns her own consulting firm (aka is worlds away from my messy life) she and I gravitate towards each other.

Screw it. It's exhausting carrying all this anxiety on my own.

"That's Clark's cousin. And, regrettably, also my ex." Cue swig of the champagne.

"Oh shit. That's how Jessie and Clark met!" Clara's eyes spark. I can see her placing Lionel in the family tree, inserting him into the story of Jessie's happily ever after.

Clara squints in his direction. "Oh *shit* shit, is he engaged now?"

"No, we only broke up a year ago and…" And then I see it. The big, shiny diamond on the pixie's left ring finger.

"Oh. My God." I turn away quickly, before my face glows hot enough to Mount Vesuvius them where they sit.

Clara's eyes go wide.

"Oh. Balls. Fuck. Fuckballs. He got engaged a year after you broke up?" My skin is a thousand degrees, and my ears must look as if they've been dipped in red paint.

"Guess so." I gulp, trying to keep tears from rising up. I feel them get stuck above my collarbone, all the hurt lodged like cotton in my throat.

"Oh man. I'm sorry, Lizzie." Clara's forehead scrunches and her eyebrows arch in. "Fuck that guy. He has weird hair anyway." She turns to her fiancé and plucks up his flute of champagne.

"Hey! Clara, what are you…" James turns from his conversation with another plus one to wonder if his wife is drinking.

"It's going to a good cause, I promise." Clara turns away from him without further explanation, holds the offering out to me, and nods.

"Drink up."

I'm grateful for her hand on mine. Her gentle touch is the only thing grounding me, keeping me from shattering into a thousand tiny shards.

I nod and solemnly gulp down the champagne in one go, letting the bubbles tickle the backs of my eyes. It's better than tears.

Then I pick up the second glass in front of me, and polish that one. With a brain in panic mode and a stomach empty of all but beverage, I make a very conscious, very stupid decision; I am going to drink until I stop feeling like my heart is being repeatedly slammed in a car door.

I squeeze Clara's hand as she mutters, "What a dick." Then the food is served.

2

As I fork down my herb roasted chicken and fingerling potatoes, I stare at the centerpiece and wish a portal to hell would open underneath my chair. I'd rather dine with Satan than think about Lionel's life leaving mine in the dust.

From the second I ran into him picking songs from the old-school jukebox at a dive bar, I thought Lionel was sexy. His disheveled hair and crooked smile made him approachable. And he had that geeky, frazzled energy of someone hyper-obsessed with a certain part of their life. Lionel's obsession happened to be the violin.

I stood patiently, waiting to queue up ABBA while the man in front of me clicked through song options. Jessie elected to stay at the bar, gently tapping her hot pink nails on the countertop while ordering us a round of vodka sodas.

When I turned back to gauge the jukebox progress, a man with dark hair and the longest eyelashes I'd ever seen stood smiling in front of me.

"I believe it's your turn, m'lady." He gestured to the jukebox with a bow. "Although I'd love to stick around and see what you pick."

"No pressure though, right?" I joked. Jessie and I had been hit on in plenty of bars; I didn't need some random man's judgment of my musical taste.

"None at all. I'm Lionel."

"Lizzie." I stepped up to the machine and selected ABBA before adding a few extra songs, including *Untouched.*

Lionel raised his eyes. "While not my favorite song, the

opening of the violin feature draws you in." I stepped closer, so I could hear him over the noise of music and crowd.

"Yup, I definitely like this song because of the violin. Not because it reminds me of my deep seeded teenage angst," I replied.

"If I buy you a drink, can I bear witness to said angst?"

I accepted the drink and spent the night learning a ton about the violin. While my life was predictable, Lionel's was so goddamned interesting. I always erred on the side of caution, building a stacked resume of internships and locking down a high-salary investment job. Lionel went to college for music but dropped out to spend more time with his band, determined to make it in music.

Jessie hit it off with Lionel's cousin, Clark, after he bought her one of every snack-sized chip bag to sample. She cheerily chattered about zodiac signs while Clark looked enthralled and terrified, like a beautiful, rare butterfly had landed on him.

After a night of taste-testing chips and trading off jukebox picks, Lionel asked for my number. I went to his next gig and afterwards, he kissed me against a brick wall in the rain. Once my best friend started dating his cousin, it felt like all the puzzle pieces had miraculously fallen into place. We were carving out the life I'd always wanted; I had a cool and talented boyfriend, and Jessie and I would get to spend every holiday together.

I was happy to follow along in the groove of Lionel's life. We didn't hold hands very often, but I decided I didn't need to be a hand-holding kind of gal. We had a lot of sex and we talked about Big Picture things, like the vast expanse of the universe and why Bugles were made to fit perfectly on human fingers.

I knew I'd always come second to music, but that was fine. I had Jessie and my mom. I didn't need the undying affection of a partner. It almost seemed excessive to ask for more.

Lionel and I lived together for a year, which was quite convenient since we were on different schedules. He'd sleep in late so he was ready to play gigs at night. I would get up early and trek to my office downtown. Sometimes I'd go to his shows and sit at a tiny table reserved for me. The most intimacy we had was when he was on stage and I was in the crowd. When our eyes connected, he'd light up, like we shared something special. If I could trap these perfect moments in amber, I was sure I'd be able to point to them as evidence of the magic between us.

It was snowing the morning I awoke to Lionel chatting excitedly on the phone. Which was strange, since this man was definitely *not* a morning person.

"Lizzie!" I was settled in the living room with a cup of Earl Grey, reading the news on my phone. Some new crypto currency was booming, making a bunch of college kids rich.

"What's up?" I looked up to see Lionel wearing his exuberant face, one that only ever bloomed to the surface when the band finally nailed down a new song or he got a surplus of streams. Something musical, then.

"It's happening."

Lionel bounced on his heels. He always did this dance when he couldn't contain his excitement.

"What? Jeff Bezos died?" He hated Jeff Bezos, especially after the moon trip. I mean, who among us?

"No, goof! We're going on tour! They signed us!"

"Wait, what!?" I put down the phone. "I thought that wasn't going to happen for, like, another year?"

"Things moved more quickly than we thought. They saw our streaming and social numbers and felt like they had to jump now. We leave in a month." He grabbed my hands and pulled me up, only splashing a little Earl Grey onto the white carpet in the process.

Here's the thing about Lionel; it is hard not to get wrapped up in his enthusiasm. He has the most expressive eyebrows, and his face takes on this shiny "can you believe our luck!" glow that's basically irresistible. Lionel's excitement was a wave that always swept me off my feet. Which is how we ended up living where he wanted to live, hung out with his friends, and ate at the restaurants he insisted we try.

"Holy shit, one month? What are we going to do about the lease?"

We'd just signed this apartment for another year. I started calculating the cost to bail, assuming we even could. There was no way we'd get the deposit back.

He frowned at me like I didn't understand. Like I was a big storm cloud, coming to rain on his parade. "We'll figure that out, that's small potatoes, Lizzie. Don't you see? We're going on tour! In Europe! Eurotour!" He thrust both fists in the air.

I didn't want to be a Debbie Downer. Europe could be fun! I loved architecture. I loved pastries. I could do Europe. So, I stood and we held hands and hopped around the living room. I called out of work, and we drank mimosas and talked dreamily about getting married to make customs easier.

Lionel was never one for details. Luckily, details are my strong suite. I got us out of our lease. I arranged the travel. I rented a storage unit for our furniture. I put in my notice at my job and typed up a budget.

I let the idea fill me with yearning for places I'd never been. I saved up enough money to carry me through at least a year. Working a numbers job in the city with a boyfriend who only frequented dive bars was a recipe for a solid savings account. Everything was going *smoothly*.

"You're the best, Lizzie. I could never do this without you," Lionel said. And I believed him. I believed I was a key piece of his life, of his goals.

And then Mom got her diagnosis. Breast cancer, caught early but still daunting enough to scare the ever-loving shit out of me.

I snap back to the present to look over at my mom, seated beside Jessie's mom. She's rapid-fire talking, fingers dancing in the air like she's painting the most beautiful picture. Mom's always been a fast talker, scrambling words together to get them out more quickly. Dad used to say that when she was excited, she spoke in cursive. Even after they got divorced and he landed a new job in California, he'd sometimes FaceTime just to catch up and watch her excitement manifest.

I couldn't leave my mother alone through chemo. She and my dad were still friends, but that didn't change the fact that she was divorced and my brother's life made it impossible to move home and help her.

In the end, Lionel didn't even put up a fight. I told myself afterwards that I should have seen it coming. His dream was in

Europe, whether I was there or not. And my reality was back in Windstone, Massachusetts. I didn't ask him to stay. Even if I did, I knew he still would have gone.

I probably could have groveled to my job. They would have understood the change in plans, would have made concessions for me. Maybe I could have worked remote from my mom's place by the ocean. But my heart was bruised in too many places and, in truth, I was exhausted by the soullessness of staring at a screen. So I moved in with Mom and tried to stay bright and upbeat through the nightmare of chemo, a double mastectomy, and finally, remission.

Since we broke up, Lionel texted a few times to see how my mom was doing. A part of me wondered what would happen when the tour ended. Maybe he'd beg me to join him, tell me he couldn't go on with his life on the road if I wasn't there. In all our conversations, I was sure he'd never mentioned a girlfriend, never mind a fiancé. A teeny piece of me was still waiting for Lionel to come through my life like a tornado, pick me up and sweep me in a new direction again.

While Lionel thoughts creep into my head like a sickly fog, I forge ahead with my drinking plan. I like Clara the best of all the bridesmaids, but Clara can't drink. And my mom, post-cancer, also doesn't drink.

Since drinking by myself seems tragically sad, I invest my time into making new friends. Camilla is one of the picture-perfect Texas A&M gals. Her hair is big (very Texan, in my very East Coast opinion) and she smells faintly like honey. On the bachelorette party, she was the only one of us who agreed to ride the mechanical bull—in a dress, nonetheless. She did an impressive job, honestly She's a big personality, but she's also the perfect drinking buddy for tonight.

"Hi Camilla! How was your wedding?"

Between the bridal shower, the bachelorette, and our group text I've learned that there are a whole variety of questions to get a bride talking.

"It was absolutely phe-nom-inal!" She squeals. She's already quite a bit more intoxicated than I am, reflected in her volume and the emphasis on each syllable.

"Ah-maz-ing!" I mirror. "Let's do a shot to celebrate!"

"What a great idea, let's do Jägermeister since I've officially married into Germany!"

I don't think that's how it works, but I say nothing. At least it's an open bar, so my wallet won't hurt even if my gag reflex does. We order two Jäger bombs and sloppily cheers before dropping the shots into Red Bull. The bartender gives us an oily smile, says "Enjoy, ladies," and winks before helping other guests. Gross.

Camilla throws it back like a pro. I choke mine down, trying to seem unaffected. Then I pick up the drink I was sipping before (a red, fruity number) and do my best to wash away the too-sweet Red Bull laced with the essence of forest.

At this exact moment, as I'm making my sputtering recovery, Lionel walks over. He's cool as a cucumber, standing as if the room belongs to him. I forgot that was part of his draw, how he commands a stage even when he's not on one. Damn him.

"Lizzie, hi." He eyes the shot glass inside the pint glass and raises his eyebrows. I very, very, *very* rarely do shots.

"Lionel. Hey. Fun night, right?" I toast him with my double-empty cups.

I feel a little bit of sticky Red Bull on my cheek and try to lick it off. Very graceful, Lizzie.

"Yeah, super rad," he says. It seems like he is completely unaffected by seeing me here. Which makes sense, since he knew I'd be part of Jessie's bridal party. We'd originally been invited to her wedding together, after all.

"I didn't expect to see you here."

"Wasn't sure I could make it, honestly." He chuckles as if to say *isn't it wonderful that I made it after all?* Oh yes, so wonderful, I hope my face says rather than *I wish a big slit would open in the earth between us and swallow me whole.*

And, suddenly, the pixie girl glides up next to him. She puts a delicate hand on his arm. It looks so routine that I cringe.

Lionel turns to her and smiles. "This is Fayette, my fiancé." He speaks the words into reality and it's like falling onto a cactus. A thousand tiny pricks everywhere, and I know I'll have to pull the spines out one by one once I am alone.

"Please, call me Faye."

I reshape my grimace into a smile. At least, I hope that's what my face appears to be doing.

"So lovely to meet you. Congratulations," I say, a bit too loudly. Camilla, who has been gesturing to a waiter, turns around and re-enters conversation. Bless her heart, I think. Are you allowed to use that term without irony?

"Hi there. I'm Camilla. Wow, you look like a dream. Where'd you get that dress?" she says.

"This was my mother's, it is vintage. It is lovely to meet you both." Faye smiles, tipping her head in our direction. If she wasn't the fiancé of my recent (a year counts as recent, right?) ex, I would want to be her friend. Even as it stands, I want her to like me.

She has a lilting French accent that strokes my cheek as she speaks. Why couldn't she have a smoker's voice? Or mild B.O. I'd take any flaw to make me feel a smidge better, but she is utterly perfect.

As I'm about to make an excuse to walk away, Camilla steals my exit strategy. "Well, it fits you like a glove. Ya'll excuse me, I need to use the ladies' room." As if someone sprinkled fairy dust, she's gone.

I turn back to the happy couple. "Nice to meet you, Faye. Are you French?" I ask stupidly. I wonder if she'll think I'm not cultured enough to know a French accent when I hear one.

"Oui. From Cannes, originally. Though, much of my family lives in the States now." She smiles, all warm glowing cheeks. Her little head looks perfectly made for a beret.

"I met Lionel in Paris after a show while visiting my aunt. When we realized my family vacationed a few hours away from Lionel's hometown, I knew it was fate." She smiles at him demurely before turning back to me. "Are you living here?"

"Mhm," is all I can manage while I sip my drink and wish I could drown in it. It's better than telling them I'm the almost thirty-year-old still living with their mom.

I need to extract myself from this conversation. I should have followed Camilla, but now it's too late. I fiddle uncomfortably with my glass. I wish my mom would notice and rescue me, but she's deep in conversation with some man I don't know.

As if he can hear my prayers, a server manifests. "Can I take that from you, ma'am," he asks in a voice like caramel, rich and smooth. He gestures at the drink in my hand. I hadn't realized I emptied it while standing with the lovebirds. I nod, and unfortunately turn to look at a very tall, attractive, blue-eyed man.

"Thank you."

"More Sex on the Beach?"

"Excuse me?" I turn my body towards him, my face already hot. I wonder if all the men in this building are trying to piss me off. Have they ever tested this water for unusually high levels of testosterone?

"Your drink. Would you like another? Or I could get behind the sticks and mix you up a Piña Colada? A Mai Tai? Tropical is my specialty." His eyes glimmer wickedly. *He's poking fun at you,* my Jäger-affected brain registers. Teasing me in my time of need? What a dick.

Now that he's brought it up, drinking a Sex on the Beach at a wedding, rather than on vacation, does seem relatively embarrassing. Am I twenty-one?

"No. I think I'll have some water for now. Thanks," I say as sternly as I can manage.

"Of course, I'll be right back with that." As Lionel opens his mouth to order another drink, the man walks away and disappears behind a group of loud-talking dads in suits.

Lionel frowns. "We're going to grab a drink at the bar, but we'll see you out on the dance floor?" He cocks his head like he means it. Faye smiles politely.

Yes, because there is nothing I'd like more than to dance with my ex-boyfriend and his fiancé at my best friend's wedding.

"Sure thing!" I say, a bit too cheerily.

"Bye bye," Faye waggles her manicured fingernails.

Once they step towards the bar, I beeline for Clara. She's been watching wide-eyed from the dance floor. I may be running, but I have too much pent-up frustration to care.

"You should have rescued me!" I whisper-yell when I finally make it there.

"I didn't know what to do!" She throws up her hands in an I-was-helpless gesture. "But how was that?" She's bopping to a Miley Cyrus song, her fiancé holding her water glass next to her. I nod at him, and he raises the glass in mock-salute.

"It was terrible. Why does she have to be so pretty? And French! Shit," I say.

"French! Damn. Maybe she has terrible morning breath. Or runs over small animals for fun. Or her hair clogs the shower drain like, *every* time. You never know, there could be something!"

"Doubtful." I sigh.

"Well, your tits are ten times better than her tits. And I'm not just saying that, I mean it!" Clara nods, like her word is final. "And her vibes are off. She's too fucking perfect."

I can't help but laugh. "Jesus, Clara. Instead of craving pickles, has pregnancy manifested as a swearing addiction?"

"First of all, tits isn't a swear. And second, I was like this before I was inseminated."

James turns around, exasperated. "Clara! Please stop telling people I inseminated you like a farm animal."

She slaps his hand lightly. "Well, you did! I'm not saying you turkey basted me, but this didn't get in here by itself."

She turns back to me. "Anyway, all I'm saying is, you two seem super different. Not just because of the obvious rating difference between tits. He clearly couldn't find someone else like you so he had to go for something not remotely close. So that's good, right?"

"Ugh you're no help."

Once Lionel and Fayette leave the bar, I find Camilla looking fresh from the powder room. She drags me over to take a shot of tequila. The two of us, plus her husband (Jeremy? Gerald? At this point the drinks have demolished my ability to retain new names) continue on in this dance-drink-dance-shot manner until I am sufficiently intoxicated by way of too many different types of alcohol. Everything seems a little fuzzy, but at least I don't wish I was dissipating into the earth.

Jessie is making the rounds and finally stops to dance with us. She saddles up next to me and drops it low while I wiggle. It's like we're twenty-one again, in our first club and drunk off well drinks that used to go down like water. Those were the days when we refused to wear a jacket, not wanting to pay the $5 coat check even though it was 15 degrees outside. I savor the feeling of being carefree with the person who has known me through all of my ugly phases and watched me pee in unspeakable places.

The more drinks I have, the faster the night moves. Mom leaves on the first shuttle—we're sharing a hotel room, so I promise to be quiet when I come in. She kisses my forehead and I decide to save a recap of today's drama for breakfast.

I skillfully avoid Lionel and Fayette until the end of the evening, when they wave to me as they go. Whoops, I didn't realize I was staring. I feel the urge to run away, but I stand there with a smile plastered on my face and wave back.

It's got to be close to midnight when I take one final shot of tequila, and the uh-oh moment happens.

I will admit to barfing many times in my life. I'm no stranger to the harsh light and the disgusting reality of leaning over a toilet in a public restroom. But in the last three years, I haven't (not once) drank enough to merit puking. At least this time, there's a bridal suite with a semi-private toilet.

I hike up the bottom of my long dress. My shoes were abandoned long ago, and I rush over the geometric patterned carpeting in the hallway to the suite's bathroom.

The door connecting the bridal suite and the room where the groomsmen got ready is open, but I know from experience that I only have seconds before I'm forced to vomit into my hands. Or worse, all over the floor. I run to the bathroom and slide (an ump yells saaaaafe in my head), reaching the toilet in the nick of time.

Puking in any public forum is hot and harsh and downright soul-sucking. This is no exception. Once I've exorcised my demons, my eyes sting with tears and my throat burns like I've chugged a bottle of hot sauce. I have gone from righteously carefree to much too drunk. My elbows are propped on the toilet bowl, head in my hands, when I hear a timid knock.

"Uh, hi there."

I raise my leaden head to see Sex on the Beach guy loitering in the doorway. Son of a bitch.

A part of my brain recognizes that I should probably be nervous that this very large man is alone in the bridal suite with my very drunk self, but all I can manage is anger. He's leaning against the doorframe, like he has nowhere better in the world to be. I wipe my eyes with the back of my hand, realizing too late what that will do to my makeup.

"What do you want?" I manage to sound pretty indignant for a girl who was head-deep in a toilet bowl mere seconds ago.

"To make sure you're alive," he says. I can't tell if he's worried or amused by my predicament.

"Why, so you can have the pleasure of murdering me with embarrassment over my drink choice?" Maybe all those words come out a bit too slurred, because he looks a little confused. And even more concerned. I try again.

"Did you follow me here?"

"You didn't see me packing up in the other room? Those fruity drinks must pack a punch," he says.

My stomach somersaults dangerously and I groan. "Please don't mention the drinks."

"How about some water?"

I nod. He disappears while I sit on the cold tile floor, trying to get my bearings. The "YMCA" blares through the speakers in the other room. The bass thumps in time with the headache that is gently starting to pulse behind my eyeballs.

"Here." The man has manifested next to me again. He could have been gone two minutes or twenty. He holds out a glass of ice water and, like he's doing a magic trick, a hair tie slides out of his sleeve.

"I thought you might need this too."

"Are you saying my $125 hairdo hasn't stood the test of time?" I squint up at him. The lights are very bright so it's hard to tell if he's looking down in an 'I want to murder you' way or with sympathy.

"I think it hasn't stood the test of tequila." He shrugs. "Whenever my little sister came home drunk and puked, step one was always get everything out of the way with a hair tie. So now I consider it an essential part of the puking process. Is that wrong?"

"I'm glad your little sister has prepared you for your grand gesture of rescuing a sad, barfing bridesmaid."

I don't want to be the sad girl at the party, but here I am. Puking in a bathroom and dumping my feelings out to a stranger.

"Seemed like you were the life of the party." He raises his eyebrows and I realize his face is unreadable. It's impossible to know if he's teasing or being serious. Or maybe the alcohol has numbed my ability to read emotions.

"You should see my dance moves when I'm not otherwise incapacitated." As if on cue, I dry heave.

"Is there someone I can go get for you?" He sounds concerned, but in reality, he probably wants to get the hell out of here. Whatever his job is, the description certainly doesn't include caring for severely dehydrated women.

I think of mom, already tucked into her hotel bed. Then I remember that, even if she was here, I would never let her worry over me. This is my own fault, and I will deal with it solo.

"No, thanks. I wouldn't want to break up a booze-fueled version of the Cha-Cha-slide. I think I need another minute in case there's a round two." I hiccup.

"Okay." He plops down onto the floor next to me, criss-cross apple sauced on the tile, and leans back against the sink counter so he's facing me. Without him hovering like an evil overlord, I can finally observe him. Square jaw, blue-gray eyes but one has little flecks in his pupils that make it seem like they're twinkling. Only when a slow grin spread across his face do I realize I am most definitely checking him out.

"So," he says, "do you come here often?"

"If by here you mean the bathroom, yes. Several times a day." I hiccup again.

"You can go back to the party. I'm sure you have a lot to do." I try to look him in the eyes without watching those little dots dance.

"I'll stay here if that's alright. It's a solid hideout. It's less about the food now, and more about the booze anyway."

We talk some more, my mind too loose to hold on to long threads of conversation. I accidentally tell him that I grew up thinking cartoon Simba was hot. He laughs so hard, he snorts.

"Wait a second. You were sexually attracted to a *cartoon lion?*"

"Teenage Simba is objectively attractive. He has a nice jaw line!" I burn behind my airbrushed makeup, hoping he doesn't associate my compliment with *his* jaw line. Luckily, he seems too caught up in my young animated romance to care.

"What, like you've never been attracted to a cartoon before?"

"I save those intimate secrets for second dates." He flashes a dimple at me, and I realize that, at some point in this conversation, I've gone from scowling to smiling.

From afar, we hear the DJ announce the last dance song. How long have we been spit balling in this bathroom?

"Seems like that's our cue. Are you going to be alright to take a shuttle home?"

"Oh, yes. There's nothing left in me. Not even my dignity," I say as I take the hand he offers. He pulls me off the ground effortlessly, even though I am doing very little to support my own weight. I take a step and stumble slightly.

"Easy there. Can I help you to the van?" Normally, I would vehemently refuse help from a broad-shouldered, good-looking guy. But he seems genuinely concerned, and I'm genuinely exhausted, so I concede. I lean on him until we get closer to the throng of wedding guests heading for the shuttle and then give myself a few steps of space.

Clara is waiting. She's changed into Crocs.

I look down at her feet. "Crocs" is all I can manage to slur.

"Dogs were barking. Do you know how much your feet swell when you're prego? Or when you've been absolutely annihilating the dance floor? These shoes are *the best*." She shakes her head and laces her fingers in mine. It feels very nice, but presumably it's so I can't wander off again.

"Where have you been?"

Then she looks at the man who has ushered me out, giving

him the most obvious up and down I've ever seen. "Oh, never mind. I see what you were up to." The smile that stretches across her face makes me want to die of embarrassment.

"If by *what I was up to* you mean tossing up a buffet's worth of food and a swimming pool of drink then yes, you hit the nail on the head," I groan.

"Shit, you puked! It seems like you did have enough champagne for both of us, good for you. Gotta get an open bar's worth. Thank you for taking care of her," she says to Sex on the Beach man.

I forgot he was there for a minute. I turn to him and ask something like "Won't you get in trouble for being MIA?"

He replies with something like "Me? Trouble? Never. That's your job. Bye, Nala."

I scowl at his joke but wave anyway and stumble up the shuttle's steps. That's my last memory of the night before I fall asleep on Clara's shoulder.

3

I wake to a head full of radio static, but what forces me out of bed is my stomach. She is *angry*, and demands my full attention despite it being 7 a.m. My mom, always the early bird, is already up and watching the news on the hotel TV with closed captions. Even with a bass drum pounding in my skull, seeing Mom curled up triggers a small pang of joy in the deepest part of my chest.

"Hey there, sweet stuff!" She chirps.

I wave and run to the bathroom to pee. Once that's taken care of, I can focus on my head feeling like an anvil.

"Ugh, I'm never drinking again." I flop back onto the bed, landing on several pillows and sheets strewn about from a restless night's sleep.

"Whatever you say. I've heard that one before." My mom laughs the self-righteous laugh of someone who isn't dying of a hangover. It may be my own actions that brought me to this point, but I envy her.

I lay with my arm flung over my eyes, blocking out the light and hoping the pressure will stop the spins.

"I saw Lionel last night," she drops casually. She doesn't say anything else, the silence ballooning inside my already aching head. The problem with Mom is she's patient; she knows it's a matter of time until I crack like an egg.

Sure, why not relive this upsetting reality when I'm already in physical pain. I groan.

"Yup. And I met his fiancé. She's *French*." I say, doing my best French impression to emphasize the point. As if my day after drinking anxiety isn't already making me feel like a weirdo,

I now have to worry about my interactions with my ex and his flipping fiancé. I remember everything that happened, but my brain seems to have line item vetoed most of what I said. Was I weird? Did I make it awkward?

"Fiancé?!" My mom screams, eyes round as coasters. "He came and asked how I was doing, but he didn't say anything about a fiancé."

I know she feels guilty that things ended between us because of her. Even though that was a huge factor in the end of our relationship, I would never admit it out loud. We barely talk about her cancer, like if we speak the words it'll be summoned back. The end of that relationship is one more layer of the cancer onion that I hope to never peel back.

"Mhm. She's got a big ol' ring." I massage my neck, hoping it makes this ache in my head, and now my chest, cease.

"Hm. I never got the impression that Lionel could commit to anything other than his career." She says this so matter-of-factly, it startles my wrung-out brain.

"He always said we'd get engaged," I remind her. I can hear myself get defensive, even though Lionel's not mine to defend.

"He always said things you wanted to hear."

"Jesus, Mom. You're picking now to bring this up?" I snap and immediately regret it. "Sorry. My head is simultaneously so heavy and light, I can't figure out what to do with it. I think it's scrambling my emotional regulators."

"Speaking of scrambled, I'm going to get some breakfast. You need some quiet time, I think." She jumps out of bed–of course she's already fully dressed.

"I'll bring a book and hang for a bit so you can join me if you feel any better." She kisses my head. "I put some Advil next to your bed." And then she's gone.

I sleep for another half hour and, mercifully, the sleep and meds have dulled my headache to a manageable throb by the time I awake. Unfortunately, a clearer head gives me space for all sorts of questions.

How long after we broke up did they get together?

How long after they started dating did they get engaged?

Does he love her more than he ever loved me?

How in the hell did Jessie forget to tell me all of this?

Last night I was too gone to speculate about Jessie's knowledge of the engagement. She might not have known that Lionel was engaged, but she would have known he was bringing a plus one. There's no way she would forget to share something like this with me. Right?

I'll have to ask her at breakfast.

I check my messages. Clara's pops up first.

Clara: *Are you alive?*

Lizzie: *Yes, barely. Thanks for getting me home.*

Clara: *NP, I've been there before. You were in quite the state. Praise be that Adam found you.*

Lizzie: *Adam?*

Clara: *Lol you really were messed up huh?*

Lizzie: *Ughhhhhh*

Clara: *James is in bad shape too, he's still sleeping. Threw up this morning. Come get breakfast and we can rehash.*

Lizzie: *Rehash my brown out over hash browns. That has to be a limerick, right?*

I start getting dressed and let the film reel of regret play. Why did I drink so much last night? (I know exactly why). But now I pay the price in half-glimpsed conversations and alcohol-dulled memories. I hope Jessie had fun. I hope I didn't say anything dumb. Who the heck is Adam?

One pair of leggings and an oversized Pink Floyd T-shirt later, I'm in the hotel lobby. My mom is nowhere to be found. Judging by the sparkly sunshine out the windows, I'd guess she has ventured outside to read.

Clara is sitting in a corner on her phone. She waves and gestures to the chair across from her. A couple of the other bridesmaids nod at me from their two-tops. At least they're struggling too. I take comfort in the fact that I am not the only one who partied a little too hard.

The smell of eggs triggers instant nausea, so I hit the carb station and grab a plain bagel, not bothering to toast it or grab silverware. Armed with black coffee, I maneuver over to Clara's table.

"Hello, sunshine."

"Ugh." I plop my plate on the table, then drop my head into my palms. "Please tell me you have a magical hangover cure. Today's Lizzie is paying the fun tax."

"I wish I had one, but I am definitely not hip enough to be a witch. If you ever find one though, let me give it a test run on morning sickness too." She pats my hand on the middle of the table. "Eat. That bagel will help sop up all the booze."

"Okay, tell me everything that happened. How embarrassing was I?" I brace myself for the truth, knowing that Clara is as filter-free as I'm ever going to get.

"Oh don't even, you weren't embarrassing at all. It was very fun and you were such an excellent dancer."

"Shit. Please tell me I left the shopping cart and the sprinkler at home," I moan.

"Nope, those were on full display. You also schooled me in the ways of the traffic cop." She mimes a whistling and waving through traffic. I'm embarrassed of my other dance moves, but not the traffic cop. That one is pure gold.

"Bury me now so I don't have to live the rest of my life with the knowledge that people I've known since I was born didn't stop me from sprinkling."

"No, it really was incredible. And you weren't the messiest, not by far. Cheryl broke *three* glasses on the dance floor. Three!" She nods towards one of the very hungover bridesmaids. It looks like we all got hit by a collective bus named tequila.

"The only one to witness the less fun repercussions of your drinking was Adam. And I swore him to secrecy."

The memory of a man bringing me water and a hair tie blooms in my sluggish mind.

"The hair tie guy!"

"Last night after we left you were calling him Sex on the Beach, but that seems like a way more appropriate title for the light of day." She sips her decaf coffee and watches me shake my head.   Leave it to Lizzie. That's what Jessie and I used to say when I put my foot in my mouth big time. It happened a lot in high school.

"He was quite enamored with you."

"He spent the whole night laughing at me! Besides the water

and hair tie thing. He purposely embarrassed me in front of Lionel and Fiona." I throw my hand over my eyes, trying to forget the run-in with my ex and his shiny new faerie bride.

"Fayette. But close. Maybe she also turns into an ogre at sundown."

"Whatever. Beautiful pixie princess." She does remind me of a princess, full of grace and good manners. I bet she knows exactly when to use the array of tiny forks at fancy restaurants. "Hair tie guy made fun of me for my drinks and my cartoon crushes. And he was going to dump me on the shuttle!" I try to let the embarrassment I feel morph into indignation, but the memories make me cringe.

"If we're sticking with the Shrek theme, maybe Adam's like an onion. You know, layers." Clara shrugs. "Also, he did return you safely to me. He said, and I quote 'make sure she gets home safe' when you weren't looking."

"He probably wants a medal for his good deeds. Or maybe he's a small man with a hero complex, if you know what I mean."

"I don't think anything about that man is small, at least not from the outward appearance," Clara winks devilishly. "But either way, I had a fun night. You're coming to my baby shower." She picks at the wrapper of a mini muffin, pulls it off, and shoves the entire thing in her mouth in one bite.

"Clara, you don't have to pity invite me. I'm sure everything is finalized!" I get this very awful feeling of everyone watching me out on the dance floor, feeling bad for me. I try to wipe it away with a big bite of bagel.

Clara's baby shower is, like all of Clara's chosen activities, non-traditional. It's going to be an all-gender inclusive costume party. Everyone's supposed to come dressed in pairs or groups like their favorite children's character duos.

"It's not a question! Nothing is finalized; don't you know me at all?" She snorts. "I have my work life so together that everything outside of that is a whirling vortex of mayhem. I want you there. And I already talked to Jessie about having you as her plus-one since it's a group costume party. Listen, I promise Lion and his princess won't be at that one," she says through a mouthful of muffin.

Jessie did mention Clara's shindig of a baby shower. Clark has a conference (he does something with inner ear technology and August is the hot month for ear conventions, who knew?) so Jessie and I had tentatively talked about me going as her plus-one. Getting an invite from Clara herself still gives me butterflies. I feel my heart get all fluffy at the blooming of a new friendship.

"Okay, count me in."

"It won't be quite as splendid an affair as this." I laugh, since the current splendid she's pointing to consists of a lot of flip flops and droopy eyelids.

"Well, you know what I mean. But I'll make sure the staff is stacked with hot bros to rescue you from your puke-fests."

"You know how to win a girl over. By the way, where's Jessie?" It's taken me this long to realize that the woman of the hour is not in sight. We've met for breakfast after every single wedding we've ever been to. Sure, it's the day after her own wedding. But I happen to know Clark loves a strict timeline and a free breakfast buffet more than anyone.

"She didn't tell you? Their original flight tomorrow got canceled, so they booked one for tonight instead," Clara says.

I tap the front screen of my phone and punch in my code, wondering if I missed her text in my morning haze. But my last text from Jessie is from before the wedding.

"She must have forgotten to tell me in the rush." I try not to feel sad that our tradition won't carry on.

Jessie and Clark are doing the magical Italian honeymoon thing. I still had all the notes on prime beach spots from once-upon-a-time when I was planning a European move. I offered to help plan their trip, but Jessie told me not to stress, that they were hiring a travel agent. I forgot that marrying Clark means Jessie's life now included amenities like travel agents and first class flights. In hindsight, my recommendations may have been too budgety for them anyway.

"I'm sure she'll remember and shoot you a message tonight. I heard second-hand from her brother anyway. Decaf coffee is a joke." Clara frowns and sets down her mug.

"Doesn't it taste exactly the same?" I ask to distract myself from the fact that it'll be weeks until I can ask Jessie about the Lionel stuff, since I can't dish while she's on her honeymoon.

"I guess so, but it doesn't have that zing to it, that metallic buzz of caffeine. I can taste the deceit."

"Have you tried herbal tea?" I sip my own coffee (likely my first of three today) and wonder how I'd cope with no caffeine.

"Tea, Lizzie? You want me to drink *tea* instead of the lifeblood that is coffee?" She shakes her head. "I'd rather my water break in the grocery store in front of hot deli guy than have to go coffee-less for nine months. This pregnancy thing ain't all it's cracked up to be."

"The deli guy at Market Basket isn't that hot!" I laugh.

"He's just not your type," she dismisses me with a wave. "I love a man who can handle his meat."

"I can accept that. Cutting the cheese does present its own problem though."

"I never said I needed a classy man. Plus, do you know how often pregnant people fart? If I am an accurate case study, then it's *a lot.*

"Before I forget. And look, I know you're probably too hungover to deal with this now but I have to tell you before it leaves my brain and floats out of my head forever. James' company might have an opening soon. I know it's smaller than you're used to, but he said he'd be happy to hand over your resume when the position starts accepting applications," Clara offers.

"You're right, I am way too hungover for this conversation right now. But tell James I'll think about it." My stomach goes queasy from more than sour alcohol. Thinking about the future does that to me lately.

"I will. Now, eat more carbs before you barf all over my new favorite pair of sweatpants. Look, so stretchy!" She pulls the waistband of her pants as far as they'll go, then proceeds to butter *and* cream cheese the rest of the bagel for me.

"I know we are only several months into our relationship, but I love you," I tell her.

"I know you do. Now eat."

4

I've never met a pun I didn't like. I sometimes wonder if that's how life led me to my job at Green With Ivy, Windstone's local greenhouse. I stare longingly at the glass facade while waiting for Zed, the owner and my boss. It's past my shift start and he still hasn't arrived.

I chew my thumbnail and listen to "Let the Sunshine In" while trying not to think about Flaynel (Lionel and Faye's couple name, obviously). Their relationship has dug into my brain like a worm, wriggling and stirring up the unpleasant thought that I am replaceable. Normally, Jessie helps extract my thought parasites, but she left for her two-week honeymoon, and I don't want to bother her with my moping.

Lately, I've had plenty of time to ponder how strange it is that when your life falls to pieces, everyone else carries on. Even after everything changed for me, Lionel kept making music, my bi-weekly rowing class kept rowing, the kids I used to babysit got a new nanny (according to Facebook). The sensation of being unnecessary digs into the soft place between my ribs.

At least all that change also meant freedom from stressful days at my job as a portfolio manager. I didn't realize how much I hated office life until I was free from it. I needed a job, more for my sanity than anything, while Mom was going through her treatment. Zed's a family friend who hooked me up with flexible hours so I could bring Mom to her appointments.

The transition from long hours and sterile office space to sunshine, water, and serenity of a green space is the best thing to happen to me in the last year. Making things grow other than the portfolios of already rich people brings me a lot of joy. It helps that I get to wear any and all manner of comfy pants.

The pay is decent enough that I don't have to dip into my canceled Eurotrip savings and, for the first time in my life, I enjoy going to work. At least, when I can get into the building. I tap on my dashboard and contemplate how I'd be inside already if I had my copy of the key that Zed was supposed to bring last week. In typical Zed fashion, he left it in one of the endless number of zipper pockets in his hiking pants.

Finally, ten minutes past the hour, Zed's Prius pulls in next to me. Zed's what I can only describe as a cool hippie dad, minus the kids. He and his husband go on week-long camping trips in the White Mountains and are living their child-free dream. There's a high probability that they do shrooms on the weekends.

Windstone has plenty of cash to blow on landscaping and lots of people happy to take on a part-time gig, so Zed's little greenhouse is a goldmine during the right seasons. I know because I'm the one who tags all of the plants and balances the books. Guess I'll never escape finding *some* use of my finance degree.

"Lizzie, good morning young padawan." Zed bows to me, which I'm not sure is traditional in the *Star Wars* universe but I roll with it.

"Morning, Zed." I bow back. "How was your weekend?"

"Excelente. Truly superb. Chris and I did a meditation session on Saturday that blew my mind. You've got to try it sometime. I have a business card in here somewhere." He rummages around his cupholder, which is full of receipts and straw wrappers. I wait patiently, now twelve minutes behind my morning ritual by no fault of my own.

"Ah, can't seem to find it. I have to clean this mess out."

"No worries, you can hand it off later. Or tell me about it and I'll find it on Google."

"You youth and your tech!" Zed says as if he's sixty years my senior. In reality, he's probably in his mid-fifties.

Despite his quirks, Zed's a great boss. A few months ago, he offered to put me through a florist design course. *The Blooming*

Florist Workshop sounded a little too reminiscent of a puberty talk for my liking, but who was I to complain when it was on Zed's tab? Plus, with Jessie knee-deep in the wedding weeds, I had a surplus of free time.

In the realm of DIY, I'm more likely to end up a Pinterest fail than an Instagram success. But I realized after the first few sessions that floristry is part art, part organization. I've always excelled at the latter, and surprisingly I have a knack for arranging flowers. And, to my greater shock, I *like* it. I love how the combination of texture and color can work together to create something unique from plants you've seen at every baby shower, wedding, or party.

The hope is that these new skills will carve a space for me in the greenhouse, since not every New England season is prime plant season. I'll do everything in my power to prevent another small slice of happiness being stolen away from me. I shake my head firmly, expelling the thought before I bring that negative energy near my delicate plant babies.

"Here's that key I promised you, kiddo. Sorry for the delay." Our last lock broke when Zed forced the wrong key in and broke off the tip. I suggested a keypad that was deemed "too high tech." So, key it is.

I try out my new key and get the side door unlocked. I'm greeted by the heavy, metallic smell of freshly churned dirt and Daisy, our unofficial mascot and pest control helper. She zips over to greet us, meowing up a storm. She happens to be the noisiest cat I've ever met. Seriously, her screams rival any toddler. I reach down to pet her, but she arches her back and then weaves between Zed's legs. He's her food source.

"C'mon then Daisy. Let's get you fed, girlie." Zed pats her head and she trots after him to the office. I get to work on the plants.

The greenhouse gets hot by midday, but in the early mornings it's heaven. The air is heavy with moisture and the earthy smell of soil. I take a deep breath as I walk between the aisles, reveling in the vibrancy and texture. Spiky spines of cacti, soft petals of peonies, pointed fans of palms. Identifying plants from rows away is like solving a perfectly logical puzzle. Being here is its own type of meditation.

Zed shadowed me the first couple months, showing me how to care for each plant type and letting me ask all manner of question. He's one of my favorite people; not overbearing, approachable, and open to feedback. He started this greenhouse on his own in his twenties. It's easy to think of at least twelve people I used to work with who could use a lesson in leadership from the plant hippie.

My Wednesday morning routine includes inventory. I count our supplies of pesticides, soil, and fertilizer. The finite, tactile numbers and accomplishing this task puts me in a good mood. When that's done, I walk to one end of the rows upon rows of plants and begin to care for them. My mind stops spinning as I water.

By noon, the sun is a fireball. I take frequent water breaks or risk dropping dead. I'm sure my corpse would be dutifully eaten by either the ants or by Daisy. We get a few customers, but most people are vacationing on this unusually hot week, spending their days toasting on the beach.

I'm wrist-deep in dirt, arranging succulents to display in the "low maintenance plants" section. The dirt is lighter than I expect, even though I've done this before. This soil is special, made to drain moisture since succulents hold water in their leaves. I close my eyes, feel dry earth between my fingers and the sun radiating down on my head. I'm imagining I'm somewhere like Utah or Arizona, the sun setting and turning the sky all the colors Kacey Musgraves imagined in *Golden Hour*, when a purposeful "ahem" pulls me out of my reverie.

There is a very tall woman with the longest, most toned legs I've ever seen standing at the end of the aisle. Maybe it's because I am actively surrounded by so many plants, but she reminds me of a palm tree. She smiles at me tightly, lips closed.

I must be gaping because she clears her throat, frowns a little, and says, "Sorry if I startled you."

I switch my brain from plant mode (I swear I'm not crazy but sometimes I talk to the plants; Zed encourages it, says the noise stimulates growth) to human mode and try to remember my manners.

"No problem. Can I help you with something?" I brush the light soil off the front of the apron I wear for planting.

"I'm wondering if you do floral arrangements. Like for weddings." She smiles tightly at me again. "Centerpieces, bouquets, all of that."

I try not to roll my eyes as she stares down her nose at me. I work in a greenhouse. I understand what floral arrangements for weddings are.

"Yes, we do. Let me grab Zed, he's the owner and will be able to give you a better idea on what we offer."

She continues as if she hasn't heard me. "It's imperative that edible flowers are included as well."

I picture a group of bridesmaids in sparkly dresses very subtly nibbling at their bouquets. In my imagination, one purple petal gets stuck and makes it look like a bridesmaid is missing a front tooth in all the wedding photos. I cough into my hand to keep the laughter in. Maybe I have been spending a little too much time alone with the plants.

The woman continues, "This is one of the highest profile weddings of the season. It's going to quite a big deal. The bride is very into supporting *local economy,* so we wanted to go with some place small that still has the capacity."

She says the words *local economy* like my tiny pea brain might not understand. It's times like this, when I'm being condescended to because I'm on the other end of a customer service interaction, that I would like to scream about the injustices of the capitalist power structure. At least this isn't the bride we'll be working for.

"Sure thing, like I said, let me grab Zed. If you'd like to wait by the fountains, he'll meet you over there." I gesture to a spot in the middle where there are some fountains filled with water lilies surrounded by benches. It's a lovely place to wait, but also far enough away that the sound of running water will drown out my conversation with Zed.

I head to the office and let the doorframe catch my weight when I get there. I forgot how exhausting it was talking to sentient beings who can talk back.

"Knock, knock."

"Not now, Satan. I'm busy. Nah, I'm kidding. Come in." Zed is wearing tiny spectacles that make him look like Gepeto. I'm momentarily tempted to get him an accordion for his next birthday.

"So, there's a very palm-tree-esque woman outside."

"Palm tree like? What do you mean?" Zed's confused, but intrigued. He loves an oddity.

"Hm, well she's tall and imposing. Her attitude makes it seems like, given the chance, she wouldn't provide enough shade to shield you from a sunburn. And she but might drop a coconut on your head if she feels like it. If I had to describe her as a coffee order? Skinny white mocha latte with soy milk and extra shot of espresso."

"Oh, thanks Lizzie. Your description really clears things up." Zed rolls his eyes. "Plus, we shouldn't be stereotyping our rich customers." He winks, so I know he's joking.

"Aha! You're the one who called her rich." I smile. "Can you go deal with her? Unrelated to palm trees, she has an extraordinarily specific idea of a flower experience. I'm sure she'll want quotes on what will definitely be a custom package."

"Sure thing, kiddo." Zed stretches as he raises himself from his chair. I shake my head. I know Zed doesn't actually view me as a kiddo, he views himself as ancient. Ironic when he's done more rebirthing rituals than any other person I know.

I decide I'll watch this exchange from the safety of the ferns.

I carve a round-about path through the front of the store so that I end up in a spot that's barely visible, but where I can still hear. You'd have to be looking to notice my brown curls popping out from the foliage. Lucky for me, I got over dying my hair blonde after college, although I've never thought of my au-natural hair as being useful for camouflage. As soon as my face is in the plants, I have to shove down the urge to sneeze. I've never been great at eavesdropping. My body regularly betrays me.

I grab the clippers from my apron and busy myself with trimming the dead leaves, just in case Zed turns around.

"Heya, nice afternoon we've got here. How are ya?" Zed has entered the chat.

"Hello. You're the owner?" I can hear the eyebrow raise in the question. Zed is dressed in his usual corduroy overalls, with his hair in its graying faux-hawk. I guess if you don't spend half your week with him, he's probably an odd sight.

"Yup. What can I do ya for?"

"My name is Lauren Crawford, of Everlast Wedding Planners." Before I can blink, she extends a hand in Zed's direction. Zed looks at it like she has offered him a fully skinned chicken. He's a vegetarian. After a delay, he handshakes. Lauren Crawford doesn't miss a beat.

"I'm here on behalf of a client. The couple would like to use you for all their floral needs, provided your work matches the services they are looking for. Bouquets, garlands, centerpieces. And they want to incorporate edible flowers into the meals and drinks. Is this something you're equipped to do?"

Her clipped tone of voice is driving me slightly bonkers. I realize I've plucked almost an entire leaf of the fern bare. Whoops. I pick up the plant and tuck it into the back of the pile, then wipe the dirt on my pants. It'll be fine there until it bulks up again.

Zed, for his many eccentricities, has a buttload more patience than I do. I suppose he also has the business to think about. He nods enthusiastically.

"Yup-a-doodle. Sure can handle that. We'll need to go over specifics, like what flowers you had in mind, number of tables, all that jazz before I can get you a quote. Why don't you step into my office and we'll run through the deets."

"Excellent." She raises a slender, French-manicured finger as if to say *but wait, there's more!*

"The big thing is, the wedding is taking place in August. The couple is very anxious to tie the knot, so we are making this happen on a shortened timeline." She seems severely pissed off by this, in the way that only the extremely wealthy can. It's all crisp t's and m's in shortened timeline, annunciated like it's a filthy concept.

"Three months to pull this together? Jeez. Well, let's see what we can do." I can hear the surprise in Zed's voice, but also the excitement. He loves a challenge, and this may be the *Iron*

Chef version of floral arrangements.

Lauren nods and follows Zed into his office. I duck lower while they walk towards the corner. Unfortunately, being in stealth mode throws me off balance. When I try to steady myself, I knock over a cart of pothos.

Bemused Zed and starchy Lauren turn to see if the greenhouse is imploding. Instead, they glimpse me covered in dirt and tangles of vines through the gaps in the plants.

"Need some help there, Lizzie?" Zed asks.

"Nope. All good. Thanks a bunch." I grunt and try to extract myself without destroying the plants that are draped over me. I'm glad my face is covered in dirt so no one can see the heat radiating from my cheeks.

"Alrighty then." They head into the office, and I set out to clean up the mess I've made.

5

Zed plays it cool for all of five minutes after Lauren leaves. Then he runs to the front door and flips the sign to *on lunch break, leaf a message.* He motions to me, and I join him in the office.

"Lizzie, this is big. Sit down."

Zed proceeds to tell me that, because of the shortened timeline, Everlast Wedding Planners is willing to pay more than we take in for all our other summer weddings combined. And that an event this large requires a level of systems thinking that Zed admits he maxed out on several years prior.

"If we can pull this off," Zed says, "You won't have to worry about being short on hours in the winter season."

If we fulfill this contract, my job is safe for at least the next year. I won't have to search for something new, to let go of this place I've already come to love. One piece of the stability I've craved for the last year is finally in my control. I can't stop the smile that spreads across my face, mirroring Zed's.

An event this high profile is also sure to bring in new business, probably setting us up for a lifetime of floral arrangement success. The way the Massachusetts crowd operates, once you've successfully held a tasteful event for one person in high society, you're suddenly overrun by them all. Where they come from, I'll never know. Mom once suggested there may be an endless supply of Kennedys hiding in a Cape Cod cave. I think she's onto something.

"Don't worry, I'll still be involved, kiddo. This order is what we've been waiting for, and we need to take advantage of the position it puts us in. I think this could be a perfectly, mutually-beneficial set up." I notice his shift from "I" to "Us." I must have missed something.

"I'm sorry, what?"

Our typical operations are smooth: Zed works out all the business details, goes to the meetings, figures out what the clients want, and then I make their vision a reality by putting together the arrangements.

"You'll do a great job launching and owning this department. You've always said you wanted something to be 'your thing,' right? Well, this can be the thing!"

I stare at Zed like he's grown palm fronds for arms. Maybe he's been working a little too closely with pesticides. It seems they've gone straight to his head.

"Wait a second, Zed. You want me to do this entire event *on my own?*"

Zed nods so hard, I'm sure I'll watch his head roll down the monstera aisle.

"This is fantastic!" He stops nodding and claps his hands together once, as if in prayer. "Great for the greenhouse, great for you. Something fun to try out. We're going to need to assess inventory," he mumbles to himself.

"Floristry by Lizzie has a lovely ring to it. Those classes couldn't have come at a better time. Obviously you'd get compensation, either a percentage of the department sales or equity in the company, that we can discuss…"

"Zed!" I put up a hand, a physical barrier from the deluge of thoughts. "Pump the metaphorical brakes, please. Just so I am clear, you now want me to manage this wedding and launch a new floristry department." My words come out slow, viscous with disbelief.

"Dream big, Lizzie! This," he gestures around, "has so much potential. And I know you can achieve it."

When did my hands get so clammy? I push aside the dirty apron and wipe them on my AC/DC t-shirt.

"Lizzie, I don't know if you realize this, but you are already capable of running this place with your eyes closed. You're hands-down the best employee I've had." He scratches his chin. "The only thing lacking is customer service."

"It's not my fault everyone's a shoddy conversationalist," I grumble, even as my heart plays jump rope in my chest.

I would much rather bury myself in loam than speak to a customer for more than five minutes. Which is why the one thing standing in the way of the offer Zed has made is the idea of being beholden to clients. And, to some degree, Zed. And, okay, maybe also myself. What if I screw this up?

"Zed, I can't let you do this."

Zed smiles, calmly. He sits and puts his hiking-booted feet up on the desk. He told me this morning that he's breaking them in for the next trip he and Chris are taking. Apparently, they're tackling New Hampshire's 4,000-footer challenge, which consists of some forty-eight peaks he has to summit. Sounds like torture to me (I like athleisure with a side of indoor bathroom and ending with a mimosa, please) but it fits Zed and Chris perfectly.

"I love this job, I truly do. It's just… a lot to process." I chew my lip.

His lips twitch with a smile. He knows he's luring me in. Could I be prepared for this? It feels like I haven't been able to succeed at anything lately. I imagine a charred patch of earth where the greenhouse stands, hit by lightning summoned by my bad luck streak.

Zed takes a sip of kombucha and stares at me thoughtfully. Of course, he's calm now that I'm the flustered mess. "Listen, Lizzie. I know what it's like to take on something you feel unprepared for. This whole hiking thing? Totally not my bag until Chris forced me into it. Now it's one of my favorite things in the world. It's one thing if this isn't what you want to do with your life. I'll get that. But it's another thing if you turn away from something you want to try because you're scared of how it'll turn out. That's all the wisdom I've got. Now, if you'll excuse me, I have to pee. I'll give you some time to think about it. Let's talk again at the end of the week."

Zed uncrosses his feet, plants them on the ground, and leaves me surging with anxious energy. I stand still for a second to get my bearings.

When I worked with investment portfolios, grinding

towards a promotion gave me heartburn. That lifestyle meant hours spent anticipating every mistake or pitfall. I had to be *on* every day if I wanted to grip the next rung on the corporate ladder. The only exciting piece of it all was the money, and after a while, even that stopped being a compelling enough incentive. It was doubly hard living with someone whose profession seemed embedded into their genetic makeup. Lionel was happiest when he was submersed in music.

I will my heart rate to slow and consider how the floral arrangement class released a pressure valve on the rest of my life. Creating beautiful things fills me with joy. Even as I tell myself this isn't a huge deal either way, this decision feels monumental in charting the next decade of my life.

I decide to take Zed's advice and table this internal dilemma until after work. I head off to fertilize the azaleas; even if I struggle in my own life, at least I'm great at helping others grow.

I manage to not overthink until I am settled in the kitchen, helping Mom prep dinner.

"This is quite the pickle. But a good pickle. Like a crunchy Dill," she offers while spiralizing a zucchini. I worry over the safety of her fingers. I am always waiting for disaster to strike where Mom is concerned.

"Can I do that?" I open my palm and wait for her to hand over the vegetable. She concedes and moves on to stirring the sauce. I grab the zucchini and start twisting it myself. I make a mental note to buy her one of those KitchenAid attachments for Christmas.

"All this is simple. What will make you *happy*?" Mom stops stirring and leans her hip against the counter. She looks so fragile standing like that. I want to hug her.

"You say that like I should know. It's not that easy," I sigh.

"Of course it is." Her new lease on life is annoyingly optimistic.

"If there's a possibility it will bring you joy, it's worth it. If it doesn't work out, you get to choose a new adventure," she says.

"I don't want to screw things up for Zed." The fear that I will muck up this decision leadens my tongue.

"Zed made his choice and invited you to make yours. He's a smart guy. Did I ever tell you he finished second in our high school class? He wouldn't have asked if he didn't have full faith in you."

I try to think of Zed as a teenager. That's what happens around here; people go to school together, then get married, have babies, buy houses, the whole nine yards. Mom once confided she had a crush on Zed when they were in middle school. That crush was crushed soon after when he started dating the school's tennis superstar, Bill, and she found out she wasn't Zed's type. Thankfully, they became friends instead.

I finish with the zucchini, pick up one of the matchstick carrots and swirl it in ranch. I don't want to talk about the greenhouse dilemma anymore, but it's the only thing on my mind. At least it's done a good job pushing out the Lionel drama.

"What would you do, Ma?" I ask, crunching on carrots.

"I would not take my mother's advice when she is clearly biased. I love having you nearby." The worried butterflies in my stomach flutter up to my heart. I walk around the island and wrap her in a hug. Even in the midst of treatments, when it seemed like a strong breeze might blow her away from me forever, it always felt like she was the one holding me. It still does now. I squeeze her strong arms and thank the universe that she's still here to hug me.

I never used to get choked up, but it feels like everything about me changed over the last couple years. The past year felt like walking on constantly shifting sand. It taught me to be prepared for everything to go wrong.

I do my best to force down the lump stuck in my throat.

Mom pulls out of the hug but continues to hold my hand. "Lizzie, I'll support you in any decision you make. You know that. But I can't help if you don't finish with that zucchini pasta. I'm starving." She squeezes once and then lets go.

My conversation with Zed continues to haunt me, even as I lay in bed watching *The Great British Baking Show*. I attempt to numb my mind with puff pastries and cakes that don't look like cakes (how does that look so much like a hamburger! I will never again trust my own eyes), but the bottom of my mind is soggy, too.

I pick up my phone to text Jessie, open our message thread, and then think better of it. I saw on her socials that they checked into their Italian villa—stop number two on their honeymoon. I thought about calling earlier, but I don't want to bother her with my indecision. Plus, she's got her life squared away; she doesn't need to figure mine out, too.

I lock my phone, then plug it in to charge and switch off the light.

When I lay in there in the stillness, I swear I can hear the heartbeat of the universe. I've never been afraid of the dark, even as a little kid. It always seemed like a friend, full of unlimited space and endless possibility.

It calms me, and I'm finally able to weigh this decision without panic. The pros: job security, a chance to build my floral resume, a cool creative project. If I take this on, I wouldn't have to rush out of this town onto the next thing. The biggest con: I've never taken on a project of this scale before, and I am shit-my-pants terrified.

The only reason to say no is the fear that everything will come crashing down, like the rest of my life. What if I truly want this thing, and I fail at it?

In the darkness, I make a vow to myself to stop being such a coward. I fall asleep, mind swirling with the prospect of a new adventure.

Zed is wheeling a cartful of arugula towards the back of the greenhouse when I break the news. I've let him beat me here so I could have a few extra minutes to summon my courage. I imagine my bone marrow turning into liquid strength. Then I blab, "Okay, I'll do it."

He stops the cart in its tracks and turns around. He doesn't seem shocked but yells, "Yippee!" and claps a few times, for good measure.

I hold up one hand. "On the condition that deciding whether or not I want equity is tabled until after the event."

"You've got a deal, Howie Mendel." Zed lets the cart go rolling away with his enthusiasm and thrusts out a hand.

"Let's shake on it! We'll talk details once I run through the numbers."

I shake my head as we shake hands. "I cannot believe you watch *Deal or No Deal.*"

"I like the thrill. Think of all the secrets held in those shiny little suitcases," he says, eyes aglow.

"There is way too much random chance involved in that game," I counter.

Zed waves that off, as if the stress of ending up with $1 instead of one million isn't terrifying. Taking chances without calculating risk is everything I've learned to avoid.

"But anyways, I knew you'd agree to it! This is going to be so great for all of us. Chris is the most supportive. He's been your biggest fan ever since you filled in for that Shakespeare reading with his family last Christmas. He's going to be so thrilled when I tell him we're free to hike. My heart is melting thinking of prime leaf peeping season." His eyes go glassy.

It takes a minute for my brain processes what he's just said. "Wait a second, I thought you said you were taking a step back. You won't be here?" I can hear my pitch go wild with panic. Zed said I was taking the lead. He never mentioned that he'd be trekking in the mountains without cell service.

"I told you, I haven't committed to officially joining management yet!" I backtrack.

He waves another passive hand. I can almost hear him saying details-schmeetails in his head.

"Don't fret. I'll make sure everything is set for you to go by then. Plus, I already called Nina in for an extra hand in July and August. They'll help you with the arrangements. I've got the rest of the usual part-time staff lined up to fill in at the greenhouse while you focus on the wedding."

"Nina. Okay."

My brain is sprinting to keep up. Zed is throwing me to the wolves. Sure, he's trying to hand me a dagger in the form of Nina. That doesn't make me feel less underprepared and overwhelmed.

"We'll discuss salary and percentages before we get everything in writing. If you'd rather, we can discuss contract work for this project."

I'm sure the shock that the normally unorganized Zed is following a very legitimate process is written on my face, because he proceeds to say, "I have run a business for thirty years, you know."

"I know, I just… Thank you, Zed," I say, and mean it. I can sense that this role is the right step forward somehow. Even if I am unsure of where it will lead long-term.

"You've always been a member, but this is your official welcome to the fam, kiddo." He pats my shoulder and walks towards his office, leaving me to soak in everything that's happened in the last day.

"Oh, by the way," Zed mentions off-handedly on his stroll back to the office, like it's a minute detail he pulled from the deep recesses of his hiking-focused mind.

"You are meeting with Lauren and the caterer on Monday at the Fairmont Copley Plaza in Boston. Apparently, Lauren's got an evening event at the hotel, and wanted to schedule something ASAP. You were already scheduled for that shift in the greenhouse so that timing should work, right?"

A meeting. Okay, I know how to do meetings.

"Okay, so you'll pitch the proposal and I'll bring some samples?" I ask.

I remember a book of edible flowers I saw the last time I was at Newbury Street, one of the Saturdays Jessie and I met for Boston brunch. I'll have to Google and see if it's available at my local bookstore.

"Actually, I was thinking *you'd* pitch the proposal. And bring the samples." He shrugs.

I'm so into compiling my mental to-do list, the shock of what Zed says next takes a minute to sink in. Zed might be a good boss overall, but I kind of hate him right now.

"You're not coming to the meeting either?" I don't love how squeaky I sound, but seriously, doesn't he know anything about easing people in?

"I have full faith in you, and I have tickets to travel to Martha's Vineyard this week. Chris' aunt is in some sort of play and the ferry's already booked. We can move the meeting if you need me there, but I told Lauren you'd be the lead on this anyway. Up to you, Lizzie."

"You're leaving me to fend for myself?" I try to tamp down the panic, but it builds anyway, pressure-cooker style.

"I would never leave you alone in this. I've already done some prep that we can run through today, and we can select the samples together. Lizzie, you've got this. I'd never trust you with my baby," he gestures at the surrounding greenhouse, "if I didn't think you were perfectly equipped."

Zed's belief in me sparks a little flame of confidence. He's right. I used to handle multi-million dollar portfolios. I can take on one meeting solo, can't I?

My mind skips tracks, back to when I had a solid career, a boyfriend, my own life. Then it fast forwards to a hospital room, staring at blue and white tiles while Mom went in for her chemo treatment.

I push the smell of disinfectant from my mind and breathe in the warm, damp air of the greenhouse. It smells more alive than any other place I've been. A couple of nose fulls and I feel grounded enough to agree—I can handle this.

"Okay," I say slowly. "I can do this one on my own. But next time you'll join if I want you there?"

"Sure thing, next time I will happily be your Robin, Batman. I do have a lovely new felt hat I've been meaning to wear." Satisfied, Zed turns his attention away from me and starts making little pst pst pst noises at Daisy, who dutifully follows him into the office to organize our orders for the week.

I don't have much time to think about being thrown into the fire. A couple customers walk in, chatting about which Harry Potter character would win in a dance off. It's a good reminder; if a bunch of teenagers stand a chance against Voldemort, then I can handle a teensy tiny wedding.

6

"Are you sure you don't want to come with me? What if they ask some hyper-specific question and I flop?" As we finish packing the samples for today's meeting, I can't help but confirm one last time that Zed expects me to lead this account.

"Lizzie, you know more about these flowers than I do. Didn't you spend the week studying them?"

I huff.

"I mean, yeah. But still! I don't think Lauren liked me."

In my usual fashion, I spent hours learning every detail of each plant I'd be bringing with me. I have notes on about fifteen others. There's nothing worse in the world than being caught unprepared.

"Well, win the caterer over and you'll be two against one. Then you can fight the forces of evil with a sidekick."

"I don't think she's evil. I think she's just hard. Like crusty bread. Like she'd break my tooth if I bit into her."

"If you're looking to soften her up, maybe keep that opinion to yourself. And no biting."

"Okay, fine. I will keep my opinions and my teeth to myself."

Zed helped me pick out our variety of edible flower samples. My instinct tells me to go in with samples, but to be open to pivoting. I couldn't find the name of the book I saw all those years ago, but I picked up a couple similar titles at the bookshop, so at least I've got resources even if I'm missing Zed's zesty energy.

"Good luck, kiddo." Zed closes the trunk of my Jeep (I'd

rather maneuver my own car through the city than our big greenhouse van) and gives me a thumbs up. I manage a weak smile. I've got this. I buckle up and pull onto the road, on my solo way armed with a company credit card and the suggestion that I take the caterer out to a working lunch.

Driving on I-93 on Monday feels like I've earned my own special place in hell. I loved Boston when I lived there. It's a beautiful city at this time of the year. You can walk to work without weaving through the throngs of college kids after they've emptied out for the summer. Exercising my brake pedal in stop-and-go traffic while listening to my air conditioner wheeze is a different story. I focus on the road and not my nerves while my favorite podcasters chatter happily to each other about fun facts in the background.

I try calling Jessie to tell her about my new gig and maybe get a pep talk. I've also been looking for the peanut butter cookie recipe we finally mastered last summer but can't find where I buried it in my notes app. The phone goes straight to voicemail.

She probably can't answer because she's drinking champagne in a hot tub on a balcony. Or maybe she and Clark are eating pasta out of each other's belly buttons. That's what I imagine honeymoons in Italy are like; endless carbs and endless orifices. Both intriguing and disturbing to picture.

Finally, the hotel appears. I'm hopped up on too much caffeine and desperately need to pee. I do my best not to spring out of the car like a jack-in-the-box, but fail spectacularly. The valet raises his eyebrows.

"Are you staying with us, miss?" If public shame is the price I pay for being out of my godforsaken car and one step closer to a restroom, smirk away.

"No, I have a meeting. A business meeting. With Everlast," I ramble as I open the trunk. When my pulse sprints, so do my words.

"Let me get Jason to help you with those." He summons a porter who starts loading up the small bouquets of flower samples I've clipped. Unfortunately, that leaves me standing there awkwardly, with nothing for my hands to do or my brain to focus on besides images of waterfalls and raindrops. I shift from foot to foot until the porter finishes and starts to wheel the cart inside. I follow dutifully and hope I look more confident than I feel.

The Fairmont Copley Plaza is in the heart of the city. It's gorgeous, with soft lighting that makes you feel like you're being bathed in gold. There is even a lobby dog, a black lab that sleeps in a bed next to the desk, at peace amidst all the bustle. He looks in my direction but doesn't lift his head. He's more relaxed in this hubbub than I've ever been in my life. I envy him.

They're setting up for Lauren's event that will happen later tonight in the Main Ballroom, but I'm placed at a table off to the side to await my companions.

"I'm going to run to the restroom," I manage to yell to the porter and he points the way down the hall. I settle into a half-jog, the gait that is exclusively reserved for bathroom emergencies and walking across a crosswalk while traffic stops for you.

Mercifully, I make it to the stall and avoid the disaster that would be peeing my favorite pair of dark blue slacks. I wash my hands, give myself a pep talk in the mirror, and go to meet Lauren.

In the ballroom, workers mill about, placing fresh linens on the tables and testing the up lighting. It's a lilac purple for tonight's event. The last time I was here was for a gala, a fundraiser for a children's hospital that my company supported. As event sponsors, they were given a whole table to fill. It had been a long weekend and everyone was heading out of town, so I'd snagged a pair of tickets for myself and Lionel with the thought that I'd be able to schmooze with some of the higher ups.

Dressing up isn't usually my forte, but Jessie lent me a long black gown with a sequined bodice (of course, everything she owned had to have some amount of sparkle and flair) and even convinced me to trap my sad little feet in too-tall heels. It was so out of my comfort zone that it felt like playing dress up. There's not as much pressure to be the top-notch version of yourself when you're cosplaying someone else.

The night was shaping up to be a blast. The hors d'oeuvres

were delicious, the signature cocktail was made with gin (my personal favorite), and I got a thousand compliments on Jessie's dress.

It would have been the perfect night, if I hadn't been so aware of how much Lionel hated it. He didn't say so explicitly, but I could tell by the way he kept fiddling with his bowtie and staring longingly at the doors. I sat next to one of the department VPs and chatted away, Lionel offering nothing beside me. After we left, he made me promise not to drag him to another one of "those boring hoity toity things." After that, we stuck mostly to dive bars and grungy music clubs.

I'm thinking about how cute the bowtie I'd bought him was, how it complemented my dress perfectly, when an out-of-place stranger strides in. He's dressed in a suit but his height and general build suggest he's a lumberjack in disguise. Even the way he moves gives me a suspicion that he came from chopping down a tree in the Public Garden. As he gets closer, I swear his eyes widen, but maybe I'm seeing things. It's not until I notice he's heading straight for me that I realize I'm staring. I remember my manners and stand.

"Hi!" *A little chipper, Lizzie.*

"Hello." He offers no introduction, but stands a few feet away front of me with a strange look on his face. It's hard to read, but it might be... distaste? But that can't be right. I haven't even done anything yet. I remember Zed telling me to work on my customer service, and I smile widely. I will win this man over, tree chopping be damned.

"I'm Lizzie. From Green With Ivy. Are you the groom?"

His eyes crinkle in the corners, one side of his mouth twitching upward. Well, at least he isn't glowering at me. Unfortunately, it's because he's laughing at me instead.

"Do I look like a groom?" I only glimpse his teeth while he talks, but they're perfectly straight with the slightest gap between them. I give him a tight-lipped smile instead of an outright frown and try to focus on anything other than his mouth.

"I'm supposed to meet with my new team. If you're here to meet with Lauren about the event tonight, perhaps you could wait over there," I say sweetly and gesture to a table in the other corner. Let it be known that I gave service with a smile a try, if Zed asks. Maybe it's the staring up at him that is making me light-headed, but I get déjà vu.

"Well you're in luck, because I'm part of your new team. I'm the caterer." The huff that comes out of me is involuntary.

"That's fine."

"Fine?"

"I mean, excellent. Wonderful. Jolly good." I would roll my eyes if they weren't so busy taking him in. "You look… familiar." A memory twitches inside my brain, a little flag planted in my hippocampus. I can't pin it down, but I'm supposed to know something about this guy. I researched the flowers and the venue, why didn't I research the caterer? What if I've seen him on *America's Most Wanted?*

"Maybe I've got one of those faces." The right side of his lip twitches again, like it's being pulled by an invisible string. Is this man going to spend the whole time laughing at me? I decide that I do not like his attitude, and therefore do not care what he thinks. I sit back down and he walks around the table to take the farthest seat away from me.

Jerk.

Like a savior in a pantsuit, in walks Lauren.

"Thank you both for coming." She's carrying a very big, very heavy-looking binder which she slams on the table, seemingly for dramatic effect.

The caterer stands and shakes her hand firmly, which makes me feel immediately inadequate. I stand too quickly and nearly lose my footing. I catch myself on the table in a way I hope looks casual as Lauren waits for me to regain my composure. Why did I wear heels to this meeting? I shake her hand and we both sit as I will my cheeks from tomato red back to their normal shade.

"I was on the phone with the bride. Miss Bernard will not be able to make the meeting today. She's promised to be at the next one." I make a mental note to search the hell out of anyone named Miss Bernard in the Greater Boston area when I get home.

"I assume you two have already met." She nods between us, and we nod back. I take a long, slow exhale to focus in.

"The bride insists this wedding be as sustainable as possible. It's a beach wedding at the bride's parent's estate. Vegetarian and seafood options, no meat, which we've already touched base on." She glances in the caterer's direction, and he nods once again, professional.

Meanwhile, I am still stuck on the word *estate*. I try to think if I've ever been to an estate and decide that the one time Jessie and I got invited to a lifeguards' party on his parents' private beach is probably the closest I've come. Even after working in that world for so long, I sometimes forget the amount of money that swirls around the coast.

"Ideally, everything used would be edible, biodegradable, and ethically sourced. Local is the name of the game. For theme inspiration think *Alice in Wonderland* meets *The Secret Garden* with a coastal twist." She flips open the binder to a section marked "theme" and turns it towards us. This wedding has actual storyboards and what appears to be a style guide, outlining fonts and colors.

There are lush lawns and boardwalks and dunes. The colors are sandy beige, and a deep purple of hydrangeas mixed with the muted orange that accompanies the last fingers of a sunset. There's a note that specifically says no capital letters are to be used, everything must be in lowercase, to appear *gentler*. And I thought Jessie's wedding planning was over the top.

"So, obviously, we need a lot of locally grown, fresh flowers. And the meals and drinks need to be light and airy while simultaneously feeling upscale. We're doing 'endless appy hour' and stations rather than full plated meals so as to reduce waste. So we're talking heavy hors d'oeuvres." She looks at Caterer Man to confirm that he understands what an appetizer is. He nods assent once more. Does this man speak, other than to tease me?

"It's the first time I've planned a wedding where a caterer and florist have to be this in sync," she admits. "But that's why we've chosen two companies who are located so close to one another and who are aligned in values. Small business, ethical systems, dedicated to sustainable practices. I am sure everything will go smoothly." She states this more like a threat than a supposition. As in *if everything doesn't go smoothly, we will be serving your heads on a platter at the next non-vegetarian wedding I plan.*

The caterer nods. He's totally zoned in. There's a subtle shift about him that I recognize as **business mode.** It's like throwing a car into sport—it's still the same vehicle, but operating with one set purpose.

"Miss Carver," she starts, turning towards me.

"Lizzie, please." I wonder if I should lean into the formality. It would fit this wedding bubble I'll be living in the next few months. But it feels too stuffy and besides, we're all going to see a lot of each other so we may as well treat each other as equals.

"Okay, Lizzie, then. Can you share some of your edible floral options with us?"

I think I black out, because the next thing I know, all the flower samples are on the table.

"I thought lavender might be a nice option, it'll be in season. And, in terms of scent, it may pair well with the food. The, um, hors d'oeuvres."

I show her the lavender I've brought, along with hibiscus, pansies, and calendula. I encourage her and Caterer Guy to smell everything, to imagine the impact of the florals and effect when the room is decorated and the scent perfumes each table.

"There are many more options, but I thought these might be some of the most easily incorporated." I nod, having explained all of the benefits of each flower. Good job, self. I've nailed it.

"Will any of these work for your dishes, Adam?"

Adam? The red flag in my brain waves frantically. I'm supposed to know this guy from somewhere, but I can't...

As Adam opens his mouth to respond, I freeze in horror. He's a bit fuzzier in my memories, with softer edges. But those are the same hands that reached out and offered me a hair tie as I prayed to the porcelain gods. I think I might implode right here in this seat. My insides certainly feel like a dying star.

"Will that work for you, Lizzie?" He asks.

Shit. I've been digging up the embarrassing snippets from my first encounter with him instead of paying attention to the conversation.

"Yes, definitely. Adam." I play along. I wish I knew what I was agreeing to, but I'm too mortified to care.

"Honestly, it doesn't matter to me what methods you use to get this done. I need the day to go off without a hitch. And your teamwork plays a huge role in that."

"Absolutely," Adam and I say in sync. He looks pointedly at me. I look pointedly down at the tablecloth.

We go through some dinner options, talk about number of guests, discuss day-of logistics, and then Lauren dismisses us.

"Thank you for coming, we'll meet in a month or so to see what you've come up with. I'll send you my calendar and we'll select a date." She stands, shakes both our hands again, and then she's gone. Damn, that woman walks fast.

Somehow, all of the people arranging tables have decided to break at the same time. It's only myself and Adam in the room, across the table from one another. We both stand and I wish this were a high top so he couldn't see me roll out my ankles to keep my feet from going numb.

He's staring at me with the start of an infuriating smile creeping across his face. He knows I know, and from the shit-eating-grin, this is the highlight of his day. Who needs TV when you can watch Lizzie self-destruct in real time?

I realize I'm going to have to speak first.

"So, Adam. Fancy seeing you here." I cough.

"I was wondering if you'd remember me. You look so… different. Must be the lighting." He smiles.

I am mortified. Oh dear lord, someone please save me. The crash of metal pots from the kitchen makes me jump but alas, no one brings out a knife to slice the tension. May as well own up to it.

"Not my shining moment. But to be fair, it was a rough night." I wish I could extract the defensiveness from my tone.

"It looked like you were having a grand old time. Until those fruit cocktails fought back."

"Yeah, well, I didn't ask you to save me."

He shrugs. "You didn't need saving. You just looked like you could use someone to take care of you. Besides, your friend was looking for you."

I want to be defensive again at his judgment (I am perfectly fine at taking care of myself, thank you SIR), but I'm disarmed by his friend comment.

"Jessie was asking for me?" It's a gentle warmth, the idea that she was looking out for me even at her own party.

"I think her name was Clara?" He snorts. "She's something. She told me you'd buy me a pair of Crocs as a thank you."

"Well, I don't think Crocs would go very well with that getup," I quip, looking up and down his perfectly tailored suit and then wishing I hadn't when he grins again.

"Getup, huh? How dare you insult my favorite suit," he jokes.

"Sorry, I didn't mean it like that. It's been a long day." I sigh. I need to temper my knee-jerk reaction to be mean to Adam in retaliation for embarrassing myself in front of him. Especially now that we have to spend the next three months in close contact.

"Life seems to be full of those lately."

I can only assume he's referring to having to spend time in this meeting with me. This man is grade-a annoying. It's worse that he's standing there like he's completely comfortable, and I want to take off these death trap shoes and sprint away as fast as possible. If anyone needs the aforementioned Crocs, it's me.

I can't wait to be out of his presence, I think, and then remembering my promise to Zed that I would take the caterer out to lunch. Shit.

I swallow my pride and clear my throat. "Would you like to grab a bite to eat?"

He looks down at his watch, then back up at me.

"Are you asking me on a date, Lizzie?"

"No, not like a date," I say too loudly. "Just like, two people who work together eating. Food. Together. I assume we will have to do that at some point in this collaboration." I may be yelling.

"What are we going to eat on this not-date?" He asks.

I brush a curl out of my face and try to look less flustered. I tried to pile my hair up with a clip but between my race to the bathroom and our table talk, half of it has fallen out.

"I don't know. Since you're the chef, I assume you have higher standards than I'm used to." I'm still being a jerk, but I can't seem to help it. Why does he get on my nerves like this?

"I'm sure your standards are very, very high. You pick, if you have a place in mind." He pauses and looks down at my feet. "Speaking of high, do you want to change those shoes before we go?"

I do. I really, really do. But I won't give him the satisfaction of knowing he's right.

"Nope."

Adam puts his hands up in mock defense. His eyes sparkle. Jerk.

"Okay then. Let's get lunch."

"Where are we going?" Adam walks beside me, my normally brisk pace slowed by the torture devices strapped to my feet.

We've ditched our cars at the venue to make life easier but in my haste to get outside and breathe fresh air, I forgot the torture of walking without my usual sneakers. What I wouldn't give for a pair of New Balance right now.

"A Thai place. Does that work for you?" I try to keep my voice professional, but damn if the annoyance doesn't leak out. Not being able to read Adam has set me on edge.

"I'm into Thai food. You just seem super familiar with this area. You didn't even look at a single Yelp review before deciding on a restaurant," he says.

"Yeah, well. I used to live around here, so I have a few favorites." I don't mention that I had planned to eat there whether or not Adam agreed to join.

"That's interesting. I don't get city vibes from you." Adam looks at me from my right side but I stare straight ahead through my sunglasses.

"What's that supposed to mean?" If he presumes to know everything about me after two measly interactions, I will happily set him straight. Even if I did tell Jessie almost the same thing after I moved out of Boston. That the pace of life once things settled down with my mom felt like releasing a breath I didn't realize I'd been holding.

Adam shrugs. "Nothing bad. It just seems like you'd enjoy a more peaceful setting, working with plants and all. City life is constant stimulation. But it seems like a cool place to live. Lots of amazing restaurants." He scratches his freshly shaved chin, as if he expects stubble there.

"Honestly, maybe I'm a little jealous," he continues. "Seems like you can always find a fresh start in a place with millions of people."

That's oddly cryptic. But I get what he means.

"It's true. But I guess, like everywhere else, you carve out a space for yourself," I offer. "I lived here for a while after college. My best friend and I tried new places, but we always came back to the same ones. Like the Thai place we're going." I omit mention of living with Lionel; there aren't enough noodles in the world to get me to talk about my ex on this business-lunch-definitely-not-date.

I watch him crack a smile, a dimple deepening his cheek. "I am honored," he says, "that you're about to share one of your favorite local haunts with me."

"Local haunts? I didn't realize I'd be recruited to host Diners, Drive-Ins, and Dives." I reach up and touch my hair. "I should have taken this opportunity to get frosted tips."

Adam lets out a booming laugh, so loud that people on the sidewalk across the street stare. I grin in spite of myself. We do have to work together, I reason, so I should at least *try* to like him. It has nothing to do with the fact that making him laugh on purpose feels like winning a prize.

It isn't until a jingling bell announces our presence in the tiny restaurant that I realize Zed probably wanted me to impress our new partner. Instead, I took him to a hole-in-the-wall with six tables, Christmas lights strung across the ceiling, and a chalkboard wall marked with a thousand handwritten scrawls.

"Sorry if this wasn't what you had in mind," I start to backpedal. "We can totally go to Legal Seafoods or something." I turn around to Adam's broad smile.

"This is perfect," he replies. "Plus, it's one of your favorites. I would never stand between you and your vetted restaurants."

With that settled, we slide into opposite sides of a booth. "In that case, are you ready for the best Green Papaya Salad of your life?" I fidget on the red vinyl, trying to get comfy, and sigh at the relief of being off my heeled feet.

"Absolutely," Adam says.

"How do you feel about spice?" I ask seriously. To my surprise, I don't feel nervous about ordering for us, even if Adam's job is food. I know this place absolutely rocks.

"More spice, more nice," he winks and his knee bumps my legs under the table. I'd forgotten how intimate this place is. Jessie and I used to love to gossip here, because the booths are so close to each other, you can lean forward and end up nose to nose. It's a great place for sharing secrets. I swallow and look down at the menu.

I remind myself to focus on the meal so I can more easily ignore the tingling feeling where our legs brush. "The larb is amazing. It's a spicy meat salad. Oh! And their green curry has literally saved my life after a night out." I look up to see Adam watching me intently.

"But get whatever you want. Those are my recommendations. I yield my time," I say. I try not to fidget again under his assessing gaze.

"What?" I finally ask.

"The way you talk about something you're excited about… it's hypnotic," he says, continuing to stare. I search for the joke in his words, but he's straight faced. If I didn't know better, I'd think he was hitting on me. But he's seen what a mess I am and now he has to work with me. I immediately let go of the idea.

Adam shakes his head, like he's breaking out of a trance. "I trust your recommendations. Let's share some stuff."

That's how I end up ordering more than two people could ever possibly consume in one sitting. It's worth it to watch Adam's react to all of my favorites. He appreciates food in a way that makes me appreciate it more, too. He regularly groans and focuses on the experience of eating rather than the ingredients.

As we are eating the papaya salad he says, "It's so bright. Really lifts you out of the seriousness of the meal. It put me right into a summer mindset." I nod, preoccupied with a mouthful. I understand exactly what he's describing.

The check comes in a little basket with two pieces of colorful chalk. I gesture to the wall. "You're supposed to write out a wish, dream, or something you want to focus on in your life. They do a nice ceremony where they wipe it down each equinox to give you a clean slate for the following half of the year."

"How many dreams have you written up there?"

I think for a second. Jessie and I must have scrawled our hopes for the future together dozens of times.

"Honestly? At least twenty."

"How many came true?"

"I'm not sure." I frown. I can't remember anything specific I scrawled, probably because I've been in a food coma after most late nights here. "But I've got a good feeling about this one." I grab a blue piece of chalk and find a tiny space between MORE PATIENCE and WIN A FREE YEAR OF TACO BELL.

What do I want? I write *FOR LIFE TO MAKE SENSE.* As I'm finishing the M, I notice Adam scribbling in purple to the far left of the wall. I finish my sentence and quickly walk away, so he can't tell which one is mine.

"What did you write?" I ask as we wave goodbye to our server and head out into the May humidity.

"I can't tell you or it won't come true. That's how wishes work," Adam says seriously.

"I think publicly written chalkboard wishes are exempt from that rule. That's only true for eyelashes and birthday cakes," I reply. Now I really want to know what he wrote.

"Still. Not going to risk it." Adam's smile slips as I stumble on a sidewalk crack, his arm lurching forward to steady me.

I recover quickly, but my pride does not. "Ah! These damn shoes," I huff.

"May I?" Adam removes his arm from my waist, where it caught me, and holds it out in a triangle, like a gentleman in a 1930s film.

"Don't worry about me, I always catch myself." My wounded ego won't allow me to willingly let Adam help, even as my body begs for the extra support.

"Please? I promise to never bring up lions again if you accept my chivalry," Adam smiles, refusing to move.

"If you were a gentleman, you'd never bring up Simba again without bribing me," I grumble.

"Well, I'd be *lion* if I said Nala wasn't kind of ho…"

"Ugh *fine!*" I concede and loop my arm through his. "Now, no more cartoon talk."

I lean some of my weight against his shoulder, trying to alleviate the pressure from the blisters that have formed on my pinky toes. Leaning on him is like being supported by a solid wall. Damn lumberjacks.

"Did you work with plants when you lived here?" Adam asks as he schleps me along.

"Nope. I was surrounded by finance bros while I managed a bunch of individual portfolios. My new leafy coworkers have *much* more personality," I joke. Not one of my coworkers was a part of my friend group when I lived here.

Being back in Boston is a strange mix of nostalgia and discomfort. I still love this neighborhood. It's in heart of the action, I had every kind of food at my disposal, and I could easily pay someone else to wash and fold my laundry. It almost felt like I had made it. Even my tiny basement apartment was a happy place, until it wasn't. Why did I leave my life here? What if my future was supposed to be in this city and not in my Mom's extra bedroom in the 'burbs?

Adam's follow up question snaps me out of it. "So, you'd rather be surrounded by plants than people, I take it?"

"Most days. I like people a lot, but it's hard for me to feign enthusiasm about things I don't give a shit about." After I've said it, I wonder if I've been too honest. And if I should stop oversharing and swearing around my now work colleague. Luckily, Adam laughs.

"I've noticed that about you. But it's different when you're into something, right? Like certain topics that I am no longer at liberty to mention but stem from a fictional talking-animals universe?" He asks with a smile.

"Hey, if you break the cartoon NDA, there will be consequences." I give his bicep squeeze with our connected arms. Instead of getting the leg up, I feel his muscles tense beneath my arm and find myself blushing. Great. I clear my throat. "Anyway, how did you end up in catering?"

"Now, that is a long story. But basically, cooking is in my

DNA. It's the one place where I feel fully myself. And although I don't like the craziness of the actual events, making people's nights memorable is worth it. That's why I only cater smaller events, so I can focus primarily on my role as a chef and then hire out a team to help execute. Being able to make a meal that leaves an impact is a powerful thing," he says.

"I do think good food has altered my brain chemistry before." I agree with him, that food and taste can stick with you. I try not to think of the hospital cafeteria, the way that every bite was tinged with the smell of iodine.

"Oh yeah? What's one time that you ate something super memorable?" Adam asks.

I think of all the disturbing inventions Mom and I have come up with for our pizza nights. Then I think about all the fancy events I've been to. But the one memory that floats to the surface tastes like sun-kissed skin and the freedom of summer.

"After my brother graduated high school, he took my friend and I to a Red Sox game. We were young, like twelve or something. He and I had never been close, but he was moving cross-country for college and I think he knew we wouldn't see each other much. He told us to get whatever we wanted. I remember getting a Fenway Frank and a lemonade. And I swear on Celine Dion's soul, that was the best hot dog I have ever tasted in my life," I say. "And now's the part where you make fun of me because my favorite memory of food is of hot dogs."

"Do you think I'm above hot dogs? I'm no snob."

"When's the last time you ate a hot dog?" I fire back. I'm expecting it to be some time back in the late 1900s, when I was still trying to swing high enough to loop around the top bar of my swingset.

"Let me think." He scratches his chin with his free hand. "Last year at my friend Pitt's barbecue. His dog stole most of the burgers straight off the grill. Apparently, his dog has finer tastes in meat than you or I do."

"Fancy dog. I like his style," I chuckle.

"But," Adam continues, "you get what I mean. Food that matches the experience can immortalize a memory. Like that baseball game. I bet sometimes when you're sipping a lemonade or eating a wiener" (he winks and I shake my head) "you flash back to that day. That feeling."

And I do get what he means. Even being back at the Thai restaurant made me think of Jessie, of a time when our lives were in flux. When neither of us had anything figured out, but it didn't matter because we were going through it together.

It isn't until Adam stops that I realize we're back at the hotel. When I unlace our arms to hand my ticket to the valet, the pressure returns to my sore feet. I didn't realize how much weight Adam had been taking off them. After he hands the valet his ticket as well, he looks down where our arms had been intertwined. I hope I didn't leave his shirt too sweaty.

I distract my nerves by digging in my purse for tip money.

"So, lunch was nice. Thanks for indulging my Thai food cravings." I shuffle in place, passing the burden from one foot to the other.

"You can still lean on me, if you want to." Adam steps closer, like he's thinking about wrapping a gigantic arm around me and holding me aloft. I lean away. I've already accepted too much help today.

"No thanks, I've got it." I stop fidgeting so he won't sense that I'd like to throw these shoes into oncoming traffic.

"Okay." Adam straightens as my car pulls up front.

"This is me." I am so close to sweet, sweet foot relief.

"Thanks again for lunch. I'll see you later this week."

"You will?" I gaze up, confused. A divot appears between his eyebrows, like I'm the one who's crazy.

"For the meeting that we agreed to?" When I continue to stare, he adds "When we were talking with Lauren? I'm going to come to the greenhouse to get a better sense of the plants and herbs and see which can be picked fresh that day for the dishes."

"Oh. Yeah." So that's what I missed while I panicked about working together. "Friday is good. I'm in after 8 a.m. Zed will be there too." I am embarrassed to seem out of control, again. I need to get my brain right so I can kick this project's ass.

"Well, I'll see you then!" My flustered self uses the rest of my pain tolerance to jog to my car. I throw the valet $5, slip into the driver's seat and wave as I drive away.

The last thing I see in my rearview mirror is Adam's grin as he lifts both hands, circle of life style, and mouths *bye Nala*.

8

Greenhouse life in May is hectic. Despite the flippant nature of a Massachusetts spring, people are excited to be outside, preparing flower boxes, mulching garden beds, or buying baby gnomes to adorn their walkways. The influx of gardeners and their constant questions make the week fly. I drink more caffeine than any sane person should, blink, and suddenly, my phone alarm signals that it's Friday morning.

"Urgh." I try to hit snooze but end up knocking my phone off the table. It ends up wedged perfectly between my mattress and bed frame. I grumble as I dig it out of the crevice, annoyed that I don't get my ten extra minutes of sleep. I am many things, but morning person is not one of them.

Normally, I toss my hair up into some semblance of a bun, throw on shorts and a t-shirt, and swipe deodorant haphazardly across my armpits, but today I've left myself time to shower. I promise myself it's not that I'm trying to impress Adam. It's just that deep craving for redemption from my first (okay, and maybe second) impression. I prep my cup of drip coffee and leave it to cool while I shower. I shave my ankles, in case we squat to look at plants on lower shelves. I am not a hairy person by nature, and I went through a stint of not shaving any part of my body in college. But something about my stubborn, wiry ankle hair drives me insane. I cut my knee in the midst of replaying the night I first met Adam for the millionth time.

I've thought about asking Clara to enlighten me with her memories, but toeing the line of self-loathing and embarrassment has prevented me from asking for details. I scowl at the watery blood swirling down the drain.

I need to keep my face from burning, I tell myself as I apply tinted Supergoop. I try not to think at all about why I've chosen today to up my lash game as I brush on a coat of charcoal black mascara.

I work mousse into my hair and pray the blood sacrifice from my knee placates the gods and they reward me with a humidity-free day. I *know* I'm being ridiculous. But, unfortunately, I am self-aware enough to realize that I am also *nervous*. I don't want to screw this up again.

As I'm reaching for my coffee, Mom pads into the kitchen, smiling like the early bird who's caught the worm. "Good morning!" She's decked out in the matching yoga set I got her for Christmas, ready to get bendy. Why anyone would voluntarily get up this early to exercise is beyond me.

"Morning," I grumble, needing caffeine before I can make conversation.

"What's on the docket for today? Oh!" She claps. "I forgot you have your big meeting."

"It's not really a big meeting. It's a collaborative conversation," I say while pouring a river's worth of coffee into my thermos.

I've tried to keep work talk to a minimum while giving her just enough detail to keep her satisfied. I very consciously did not mention that I previously met Adam. Or that she might have, as well.

"Oh, sure. No pressure then. This Aaron guy you're working with, is he cute?"

I sigh. This is exactly why I've only shared the basic details. "His name is Adam. I guess he's cute in a Thor, I could smash you with a hammer kind of way." I twist the lid too aggressively on my travel mug and it goes off the tracks. *Relax, Lizzie.* I breathe, then untwist and try again.

As she grabs her green smoothie from the fridge, she says casually, "Isn't 'smash' what the kids are saying these days when they want to get it on?"

"Ew, Mom! It's 6:30 a.m. Can we not? Also, he's my colleague. We have a very professional relationship. And he looks weird wearing a suit jacket." I do not add that he looks weird because if he were to flex, said jacket may rip in half.

"Sorry sweetie! Just trying to make pleasant conversation. I have to get going, I'm on carpool duty and Joan will be waiting." Even though we are close to the same height, she stands on tiptoe and kisses the top of my head.

On the way into work, I am distracted enough to drive through a yellow light just as it turns red. Blaring horns of impatient traffic fry the rest of my nerves, leaving me shaken. I try the breathing technique that helped when we were in the doctor's office, waiting for Mom's checkup results. Breathe in for four. Hold the breath for seven. Open my mouth and let it out for eight. I make it to the greenhouse unscathed.

Once inside, the plants absorb some of my tension. The air smells fresh, and I water all the flowers so I can breathe them in. The scent of wet earth rises to greet me. I inhale greedily. I find a fuzzy caterpillar on one plant and escort her carefully to the woods out back. I've learned that, if I pinpoint all my focus on small moments, it's harder to get lost in the spin of life. Focusing on the tiny things is like breathing into a paper bag for my brain.

I'm adding a stake to one of the monstera deliciosas when I spot Adam . He's fifteen minutes early. I tell myself that's the reason I feel unprepared. If he showed up at the designated time, I would be ready to tackle this meeting and move on with my day.

He spots me, smiles, and heads my way.

"Hey bananas," he says, his eyes locking with mine.

"Excuse me?" What's that supposed to mean?

He points at my chest, and my cheeks flush. "B-A-N-A-N-A-S. I like it."

I forgot I was wearing a Gwen Stefani shirt that I bought from some man standing outside the stadium. It has Gwen in a kick line, surrounded on either side by Bananas in Pajamas. It is, admittedly, awesome.

"Oh. Yeah. Hi. Thanks."

"So effusive this morning," he teases.

"I don't usually warm up for my set until the scheduled time.

Which happens to be in fifteen minutes," I jab back, busying my hands with the plant so I can take a break from his blue gaze.

"Sorry for being here ahead of time. I got an early start this morning. Thought my pit stop would take longer than it did. Go figure," he shrugs.

"Pit stop?"

"Heya, pal!" Suddenly Zed appears behind us. How did he creep over so silently?

Adam pivots and extends a hand. "Hi, I'm Adam. From Clásico Catering."

"Nice to meet ya, I'm Zed. I know you've already met our resident plant expert and project lead, Lizzie."

I give a thumbs, not trusting myself to speak.

"Let's meet in my office and we can talk through what else you need from us," Zed suggests.

"Sounds good. Let me run to the car quick. That should give Lizzie enough time to finish up the watering," Adam aims a smile at Zed and heads outside.

When his back is to me, I study him. It's weird to see him in shorts and a t-shirt. I guess I imagined him wearing a suit jacket to the supermarket. Somehow, I got it in my head that he walks around Clark-Kent style everywhere he goes. In a suit he's formidable, but this outfit is more worrisome because it makes him look approachable.

I half-ass the rest of the watering in an attempt to beat Adam to Zed's office. Of course, he walks in the moment before me.

"I brought some treats." He's balancing a box and a tray of coffees, presumably what he went to the car to retrieve.

"You brought donuts?" I can't hide my excitement. I love sugary treats but since Mom's health food focus, I only eat them outside of the house. I wonder if I should tone down the enthusiasm, but decide that as long as I'm being fed, I don't care. What kind of sociopath doesn't get excited for donuts?

Adam runs a hand through his hair and smiles. I watch Zed buy into the sweet boy-next-door demeanor from the doorway of his office.

"Yup. Got the good stuff. I'll let you two get first dibs,

70

although if you go after both blueberry glazed it means war," Adam says.

"No worries, I prefer to keep my donut and my fruit intake completely separate," I say.

He flips open the lid of the box and offers me first pick. I take a plain with chocolate frosting and sprinkles shaped like stars. One bite and star sprinkles are everywhere. Zed gives me a look that screams *ANTS*!

I carefully pull a napkin from the stack next to the donuts.

"Brought some beverages as well." Adam places the cups down and shrugs.

"I don't do coffee, but I appreciate the gesture." Zed is strongly anti-coffee since he read about the benefits of replacing it with mushroom water.

"Two of these are tea. I don't drink coffee myself." Adam is grinning from ear to ear now. Zed gives him googley eyes, like he's met Cher.

"Wowza. You've got all your bases covered! Lizzie, looks like you'll be having a two coffee kind of day!" The two of them laugh while I shove the rest of my donut in my mouth and try not to make my I-ate-a-Sour-Patch-kid face. I don't mention that this would be my third coffee of the morning.

Zed stirs his tea and Adam gestures to the coffee, which I won't take out of principle. How does this man so effortlessly win everyone over while I scatter crumbs and get stuck on tables? I chalk it up to his permanent five o'clock shadow being simultaneously charming and frat-broey. Maybe he spray paints it on in the morning, trying to strike the perfect balance between sexy and laid back. I chuckle thinking of Adam in front of a mirror, a spray paint can in hand.

"What's up?" Zed asks.

"Nothing, nothing. Just excited to get this party started," I say.

"Yes! Let's get down to business. Lizzie showed you some of the floral options, that's right?" Zed asks.

"The samples she brought were beautiful. She sold me on all of them, honestly. Made it tough to decide what to use. I thought, on our visit today, maybe we could talk through some common pairings and see what you think," Adam says.

"That sounds like a great idea! Let's take a stroll."

Because you want to spend more time basking in his charming, boyish glow, I think. I do not care to admit that I might be thinking the same thing.

We spend the next half hour walking around, looking at the flowers that might be viable options. Adam makes a point of asking about medicinal uses of the plants or any interesting fact that might inspire the dishes. We linger by the nasturtiums, which have come into bloom late in May. They're lovely shades of orange, and I can tell he sees how perfectly they match the wedding's vision.

"These are Nasturtiums. Every part of the plant is edible. The flowers are reminiscent of watercress, slightly peppery. From what I've read, they work well with salads and stir fry," I recite.

Adam nods his approval and jots down a note in the small Moleskin notebook he pulls from his back pocket. Something about the pen and paper notes softens me, just a bit. We walk through a few more flower options. He uses words like "zesty" and "radiant" to describe some of his past dishes. I would think he was pretentious if he hadn't told me how much he loves his job.

"A wedding so last-minute is a big ask, but I think the flower idea is brilliant. It will transform the dishes," Adam says as we walk towards the herbs. "I've never worked a wedding like this before," he adds.

"The way you talk about food sure makes me hungry. I'd love to taste test some of your dishes one day, to try them out myself," Zed says.

"If you're wondering if I'm any good, you could always ask Lizzie," he says playfully. The light of both their attention shines on me.

"Did I miss samples at the meeting?" Zed looks at me, envious.

"No, sir. Lizzie attended an event I was catering."

I don't know what to make of that goddamn devilish gleam in his eye and the one dimple that pops out. I thought we had an unspoken agreement not to relive that night.

Fine, two can play at this game.

"Lizzie! You didn't tell me that. What did you eat?"

"I ordered the chicken. It was excellent, second only to the incredible service I received. Clásico goes above and beyond to make sure guests are satisfied."

"Service with a smile! That's the way we operate," Adam says. "If I remember correctly, we pulled out the fine china for that event, too. Porcelain, even."

"I did hear that some guests got an upset stomach afterwards. But I'm sure that was all the dancing." I smile pointedly back.

"Ah, what I wouldn't give to be a guest at this wedding. It's going to be amazing." Zed, oblivious, sighs dreamily.

"Well, I always make sure to set extra plates aside for staff. We'll save some tropical drinks for post-event."

Cue glare from me, boring directly into the side of his head.

"It's a shame I won't be there."

My heart stops. "What? You're not coming? To the event?" Panic leeches into my words. How many times can Zed pull the rug out from under me?

"No can do, that's the weekend of Chris' Iron Man in Maine. Remember, I hired Nina to be your extra hands? They'll help you out so you'll be set to go."

"I thought you'd be away before the event. I didn't realize…" I shake my head, plaster on a smile. This is a deviation from the plan that I will deal with after my new colleague leaves.

"No problem. I'm sure Adam can pack you a to-go plate," I say, faking calm.

The phone rings in Zed's office.

"Aw, shoot. Can you show him the herb options, Lizzie? I think rosemary would be a great fit. Gotta grab that!"

Zed jogs away to his office before the phone goes to voicemail, leaving me and Adam alone. The greenhouse feels hotter than usual. A bead of sweat slides down my neck and the length of my spine. It gives me goosebumps.

"Yup, so, herbs."

"Sorry if I threw you off with the wedding talk." I look up

at him, thinking I'm going to see that dimple again. I'm thrown a little off-balance when I realize he's being serious.

"It's alright. Not my best showing." I shrug, feigning indifference.

"What was going on that night, anyway? I didn't get a chance to ask at lunch."

"What do you mean?" Another bead of sweat trickles down my back.

"You don't seem like the type of person to get plastered at her friend's wedding. No shade, it just seemed out of character. I figured something else must have been going on." He frowns.

"Glad you don't get 'fixes problems with alcohol' vibes from me." I know I am being defensive, but I feel rattled and overheated with him in my greenhouse, occupying space in this controlled slice of my world.

"I didn't mean it offensively. You seemed sad. Like all night."

He'd been watching me all night? My head is trying to decide which wins out; it being subtly sweet that he noticed me or mortifyingly embarrassing that he watched my slow progression to bent-over-toilet drunk.

I sigh. "I was sad."

"Was it about that handsy kid?"

"Who?"

"When I came and offered you another drink. That kid was like, feeling up his girlfriend in front of you. I get that it's a wedding, romance, that old song and dance. But it was gross."

Lionel. He's talking about Lionel. I had somehow forgotten that they directly interacted with each other.

"Oh I, um, didn't seem to notice." That is very clearly a lie, but Adam shrugs.

"I thought you played it pretty cool. Is he your friend?"

"He's my ex," I admit. Something flashes behind Adam's eyes and I expect him to get weird.

Instead, he says, "That makes sense. What a prick." We are standing directly across from the cacti section and because I have had too much caffeine and my life is a disaster, I grab on to the humor like it's a life raft. I snort. Loudly. And then the snort turns into a deep belly laugh that has me bent in half, scrambling to catch my breath in what seems like increasingly thin air.

Adam looks at me like maybe he's broken my brain, so I point.

"Prick… cacti. Good one."

My giggles unspool until they hook in Adam. Daisy raises her head from the nearby shelf at Adam's booming laugh.

I haven't laughed this hard since I was at Jessie's and sparkling wine fizzed out of her nose.

I put an arm out to steady myself against a nearby lime tree, but the laughter has tipped me off balance. My hand meets Adam's forearm instead, and a zing of electricity zaps up my spine. I yank my hand back, sure that my hair is standing on end.

"Oops." In my laughing fit, I dropped the orchid I was holding (not edible, but beautiful enough that we want to include them in the centerpieces).

We see it at the same time. Adam bends down to pick it up, then pretends to get down on one knee and holds it out it to me. There's a strange crackle inside my heart, like a bunch of Pop Rocks flying around. Maybe it's all the talk of my best friend, and my ex-boyfriend, and the wedding that we have to work together that's made me sentimental.

"Thank you." I hope my voice is polite and not at all melty.

"You're welcome." He brushes the dirt off his knees. I try not to watch his thigh muscles flex as he stands.

"So." He says.

"So?"

"Zed got me thinking."

"Oh boy, sounds dangerous."

His one-sided dimple accompanies his smile.

"What if we worked on some of these recipes together? I think, because you are so much more familiar with their historical uses, it could help shape some of the flavor profiles. If you have time, of course."

"Are you trying to make sure you don't accidentally poison someone?"

"Something like that."

Spending more time together is appealing. Which means it might be a very bad idea. I can't let anything get in the way of this event's success and I have too much ex-boyfriend energy floating around to deal with any more male-centered drama. I take a breath. I have to remember he's a professional. I shouldn't assume this is anything but teamwork. Maybe he does want my input.

"That sounds… interesting. I'm not sure how much cooking skill I can offer. But I am a very agreeable taste tester. Unless it involves broccoli." I make a face.

"You're what, twenty-five? And you still don't like broccoli."

"I'm twenty-nine. And no, I have no qualms declaring that broccoli is disgusting."

"Maybe you haven't had properly prepared broccoli. I agree that the steamed-bag broccoli is crap."

"Maybe I don't like broccoli."

"Maybe you haven't given broccoli a fair shot. Give me a chance to change your mind. I'll work it into our taste testing." His eyes gleam with the challenge, and I know I'll have to eat broccoli at least once before this event is over.

"Okay, I'll brocco-leave that up to you."

"You really said that." He sighs but doesn't look unhappy. "What's your Saturday look like?"

"Tomorrow?" He wants to hang that soon? That seems like a lot of Adam in one week if I'm trying to keep this all under control.

"I can't. Tomorrow is Pizza-zaz Night."

"Sorry, it's *what*?"

"Like pizza night, but pizza with pizzaz." I do jazz hands, for dramatic effect. "My mom and I try to out-weird each other with pizza recipes every Saturday."

My favorite so far has been a pickle and pear with a cream cheese sauce, while Mom swears her favorite is a Sriracha with flaming hot Cheetos (she's got the highest spice tolerance of anyone I've ever met). Pizza-zaz night is awesome and it's also the only time she'll happily eat artificial flavoring.

"I could see if we can switch to tonight. I bought all my

ingredients already," I admit. The truth is, I was going stir crazy at home worrying over this meeting. The grocery store was a good distraction.

"Right, okay. Well, if you can switch Pizza-zaz night, great. If not, no worries. Wouldn't want you to have a pizzaz-less weekend on my behalf," he says, giving jazz hands right back. Which makes me feel less silly and is, regrettably, quite endearing.

He takes out his phone, unlocks it with his face (I notice that he smiles when he looks at the screen, like it's going to take a picture; so cheesy), and hands it to me.

"Would you do me the honor of entering your cell?" He asks.

I nod, afraid that I'll start babbling if I speak. He's asking for my number strictly in a work context. We are professionals, after all. Professionals who do professional things, like put our personal cell numbers into each other's phones and plan to eat food together for a second time. *Taste* food together, my mind autocorrects. Wasn't that what I told him at our last meeting?

I type in the number and my fingers fumble, so I end up writing Lizzi E with a capital E.

"Oops, wait…" He scoops the phone back before I can fix it and smiles.

"I like it. Kind of rebellious of you, E, since capital letters are banned from the wedding." Adam's laughter is interlaced in each word. But the more time I spend talking to him, the more I think maybe he wants me to be in on the joke. I offer a tentative smile.

"I should get going. I have another appointment this afternoon. And of course, I'll make sure tomorrow works for Zed, too," Adam says.

My stomach dips but of course, this is strictly business. I feel a little zap of disappointment, but I tell myself that having Zed there is a net positive. Now things won't be awkward between us.

"Thank you for the plant tour. And for the spirit fingers," Adam says.

"It's the least I can do for donuts. Have a good meeting."

"Hopefully I'll see you tomorrow. Just you and Zed, no pricks allowed. Bye, E." Adam beams and I give another thumbs up. I guess thumbs up is my thing now.

"Sounds good, donut miss me too much," I toss over my shoulder as I head towards the mulch section. I don't have any work to do there, but it's far enough to escape Adam and gather my thoughts.

I hear him chuckle as I walk away.

9

I've always considered thunderstorms a good omen. There's something magical about how quickly the atmosphere changes, the charge of electricity in the air. When my friend's uncle (a notoriously bad golfer) got struck by lightning, survived, and went on to win the local golf tournament a week later, it solidified my belief that storms spark miracles.

The late spring storm that rolls in Friday night fills me with this same sense of possibility. The weather cancelled Mom's yoga in the park, so we're working our pizza dough. The only downside is that Pizza-zaz night has basically turned into barbecue night with how much Mom is grilling me about tomorrow's tasting with Adam and Zed.

"I wish you got a plus one! I'd just love to taste the creations you two are working on," Mom says while she opens a jar of peanut butter.

"We *three*. Zed's going to be there too, remember?" I keep bringing up Zed so she'll stop hinting that this might be anything more than a work gathering.

Zed didn't take much convincing. Free food and Adam's charming company? Count him in.

"You three, right." Mom waves a spatula covered in peanut butter like a fairy wand, probably trying to will Zed out of the equation. Thankfully, Mom's not the where-are-my-grandbabies type. But she did try to set me up twice, first with her organic produce vendor and then with a "nice man" who sells the essential oils for her diffusers.

She says she wants me to find "someone who makes you

happy." In reality, I think she wants me to date a yogi so she can drag him to a class in my stead, like a substitute kid.

"Anywho, I think it's *nice* that he invited you to hang out on a *weekend* and *eat together*," she says.

"Mom, you're saying *eat together* like he invited me to participate in an orgy." I preheat the oven while Mom continues to smear the goopy mess.

"Did he seem like the orgy type?"

"No! But now you're making me feel like I agreed to attend something explicit, like a peep show. Should I bail?"

"No!" She shrieks.

Tonight's pizza test is peanut butter and jelly pies—the idea is we'll make it into a big pocket using two pizza doughs, one on top and one on the bottom, with mozzarella cheese on the outside. Mom and I spent a lot of time debating whether this counts as a pizza or a calzone. We agreed that it falls in the pizza category, due to the outer cheese.

"You have to go! I want you to make more friends around here, Lizzie. I love hanging out with you but I'm sure at some point you'll get bored of me. I want you to find reasons of your own for being here." She doesn't look me in the eyes. This mix of her own guilt and pity stings.

"I have reasons to be here. I have you. I have Jessie close by. More recently, I have Clara," I say to assuage her guilt. It stings, that she thinks my current life is the result of being a victim of circumstance. Even if it's sort of true.

The truth is, my mom does have way more friends than I do. She grew up here and moved back after she and dad divorced. My hometown isn't very far away and neither is the city, but before my new job, Mom was the only thing tying me to this place.

Admittedly, I haven't been in the friendliest stage of my life. It doesn't help that most women in my age bracket don't have spare time to make new friends. It's hard when everyone around me is checking the house, marriage, kids boxes.

"Yeah, friends would be nice. Unfortunately, everyone my age either already has their own exclusive friend group or thinks going to Lamaze classes is a bonding activity. Did I miss the news that we are supposed to supply the next generation of baby boomers?" I put all my frustration into rolling out the top piece of dough.

"There have to some other fun singles around here!" Mom scoops out the jelly, shakes the spoon until it splats on the bottom dough, then starts smearing.

"Mom, please do not spend your time trying to find me a singles mixer. I think those went out of fashion in the eighties." I roll a tiny piece of dough into a ball and flick it at her. I snicker when it bounces off her nose.

"You're fresh!" She pretends to swat me with the spatula, so I pull a *Matrix*-style backbend. "Maybe you'll live here with me forever. Now doesn't that sound like a horror movie."

"If you make me drink those kale smoothies with you again, then yes. That is certifiable torture and I will be reporting you to the U.S. State Department." I tighten the lid on the jelly and we turn our focus back to our definitely-pizza-not-calzone masterpiece.

"Now let's get this monstrosity ready for the oven."

The next morning, I'm on the stationary bike Mom bought for "us" after I mentioned how I missed my Back Bay spin class. I'm crushing it; I've kept up with the RPMs and I've only taken a water break twice, a record low. Channeling all my nervous energy into the pedals seems to be working.

I slow to a halt when I see Zed's name pop up on the home screen three times in a row.

Zed: *So sry. I am sick as a 🐶.*

Zed: *Go on without me 🙏.*

Zed: *Send Adam my regards 👍*

I smile at Zed's overuse of emojis for half a second before my brain realizes what the message means.

Now, it'll be the two of us. Eating food together. In close proximity.

Which is totally fine, because he is your colleague, Lizzie.

Maybe Mom really did will this into being.

My heart hammers, thinking about the full of Adam's attention and the pressure of this event falling on me. I need to prove to Zed that he can count on me. I need to prove to myself that I can handle this. I text Adam.

Lizzie: *Zed's sick and not able to make it. He says sorry.*

I watch the dots appear as he types. Maybe he'll cancel or postpone. It makes sense that he'd want Zed there to opine. I leave the message window open and watch the bubbles dance.

Adam: *Hey, E. Bummer. Hope he feels better. Here's the address, see you at 6.*

He drops a pin.

I lean forward on my bike, rest my head on my sweaty arms, and groan. I unclip and drag myself off the bike to shower, a tried-and-true method to clear my head and slow down my nervous system.

I pick out the fluffiest towel (Mom's got an excellent towel selection) and turn the water up to the hottest I can stand. The Bluetooth speaker beeps and I queue up Metallica's *Master of Puppets* to hype myself up as steam fogs over the mirror. Jessie always jokes I could survive being thrown into a Yellowstone caldera based on my preferred water temp.

My muscles relax under the hot spray. I can handle this, just like I've handled everything else life has thrown at me. Things haven't exactly gone according to plan lately, but I'll be fine once I can wrangle my future back under control.

After I am properly steamed and moisturized, I flop onto the bed in my bathrobe. The air conditioning raises goosebumps on my damp skin as I open social media. Even though I stopped posting a long time ago, it's still useful for checking in on my friends. I open the app and am immediately met by Jessie's posts. Sliding through carousel photos of her and Clark on their honeymoon is like watching my best friend star in a movie.

Everything looks perfect; the food and wine and cerulean waters that come with a Eurotrip. That itchy feeling that I can't seem to scratch starts in my neck and burns its way down to my stomach. Jessie's life is so wildly different from mine in a way it's never been before. The terrifying thought that we'll never feel as close as we used to be hits me like a freight train. What if we just keep drifting apart? What if I can't connect to this phase of her life?

Jessie's life has always appeared picture-perfect, which never bothered me. But maybe that's because I used to be a part of it. I was *there*. I was the one holding the phone while she posed in front of a herd of rocking horses at Ponyhenge on our graduation New England roadtrip. We stood side-by-side as a stranger took our photo in front of Big Tex on my first trip to visit her in college. Although our lives weren't perfectly parallel, there were all these experiences we shared. Now, each curated post she puts out into world feels like a brick in the wall between us.

The sense that everything will be ripped away from me gnaws at my heart. Like there will be nothing I am allowed to keep, not when it comes to my relationships, my career, or my future plans.

My phone pings, so I close out the app and open a message from Clara.

Clara: *Hey there hot stuff* 💧 . *Wanted to let you know James' firm will def have an opening in the next month. Send me your resume if you're interested. P.S. see you for brunch tomorrow. Get ready to watch me go Joey Chestnut on a stack of pancakes.*

I consider her offer. The thought of being back in an office makes a part of my soul wilt. But this job could give me other types of freedom.

The headquarters are in the city. The pay would be better than the greenhouse. I'd be using my degree again. Maybe this job is what I need to feel like a grown up, to get back on track. Even as I think of accepting, my stomach sours.

Lizzie: *Can I think about it?*

Clara: *You know what, I'll have him email you so I don't have to be in the middle of this. Thinking about working with numbers makes me want to explode into confetti. Not in a fun way.*

Lizzie: *Great, see u tomorrow.*

Clara: *Can't wait to see you, you bad bitch.*

I think of what I wrote on that chalkboard after lunch with Adam. I want to build a life that feels right. Now that I'm outside of it, returning to an office job would dim the light in me. To placate my inner planner, I vow that I'll get my materials together and seriously consider it if the wedding fails. Even if it makes me wilt like a sunflower in July.

The first step of keeping me out of a cubical? Acing tonight's meeting.

10

Several hours of panic and four outfit changes later, I'm outside the address Adam sent me.

In all of the movement from our Friday meeting, I'd somehow forgotten to ask what kind of establishment I'd be visiting. I assumed we'd be in an industrial kitchen, a sterile place with exposed beams and sharp metal objects. It seems I misjudged.

I look down at my black t-shirt, reworked flannel, and stretchy jeans, underprepared to enter what is clearly Adam's home.

"It's fine," I say out loud, to myself and the otherwise empty car. "It's just a house. I have been in houses with men before. Many, many man houses." I wipe sweaty palms on my jeans as my brain triple jumps from one scenario to the next. I can maintain professionalism, even when we're in a comfortable space. I am a whole ass adult. I bite my lip, trying to set a boundary with myself. If Adam does that sexy toss move with a frying pan, I am leaving.

Only one more problem to solve before I head in… do I park in the driveway or on the street? Street means I have a longer walk to the door and the summer sky promises rain later this evening. But the driveway might say "I feel like I belong here," and I don't want to be too forward. Or maybe driveways are a metaphor for confidence? I shake my head. *Stop over thinking this.* I park in the driveway.

The steps to the front porch creak. It's a muggy night, and I wish I wore sandals now that my feet are sweating inside my shoes. Adam opens the door before I reach for the bell. He catches me staring down at my sweaty, Vans-clad toes. I look up.

"Hey." I can't tell if all those teeth, with their perfect sliver of a gap, are smiling or laughing at me. "Come on in."

"Hi. Thanks." He steps back, giving me plenty of room. There is a mat for shoes to the right of the door, so I step out of them and hope my socks at least look dry.

"Nice shoes." He nods at the Vans. Is he making fun of me again? I feel his eyes boring holes into my outfit. Or maybe I'm projecting, as I scan his tight gray t-shirt, jeans, and very comfy-looking slippers. I realize a second too late that I'm staring, and glance up to find him grinning.

"I wasn't sure if this would require close-toed shoes," I say a bit more aggressively than I planned.

"You thought I'd make you lift some heavy bags of flour or something?"

I shrug. "Well, how should I know you work from home."

He grins again. I'm starting to think Adam might be a very handsomely disguised Cheshire Cat. "Touché. It's a temporary setup," he says.

"And anyway," I add, "I hate walking around other people's homes barefoot." I look down to my socks. Why do I feel like I always need the last word with this guy?

He raises his eyebrow. "Interesting."

"It feels a little too intimate."

"Bare feet on a wooden floor is intimate?"

"And cold," I add.

"Intimate and cold. You don't usually hear those two words together." He chuckles.

I purse my lips and cross my arms, unwilling to say more lest I be taunted. He doesn't seem to notice.

"Wait here." Adam disappears down the hallway. When he returns, it's with a pair of slippers in hand. He places them by my feet.

"For you, m'lady. Wouldn't want you to get cold feet." The gesture is so unexpectedly nice, I smile. He watches as I step into his much-too-large shoes.

"Thank you."

When I look up, Adam's still staring. He clears his throat.

"No problem. Welcome to my home office. Please keep your socks on for the duration of the tour."

"Not to fear, all articles of clothing will remain on my person." I cringe after the words leave my mouth. It's not *Adam* making things awkward that I need to worry about. Clearly, I'm the one with an affinity for sabotaging professional relationships.

Adam looks back at me and laughs. It is deep and genuine, and it splits his normally unreadable face into a mask of pleasure. It makes my traitorous mouth smile. If I were interested in this man, I'd say the joy on his face looks like a glimpse of the far side of a rainbow.

"On that note, this is where the magic happens." We walk into one of the most beautiful kitchens I've ever seen.

"Are we in a Pottery Barn? Or did I hit my head on the way in and now I'm conjuring up something from the pages of a cooking magazine? This is beautiful," I say, marveling at the electric blue backsplash.

Adam glows at the praise. It's clear from the way he's gauging my reaction that that this kitchen is his safe space, the heart of his home.

The lighting is warm, and all the appliances gleam like they've been recently polished. My first thought is that he must care for them like I care for my plants. I'm pretty sure that's an industrial oven and stovetop with one of those fancy metal hoods. It smells heavenly and lightly sweet, like butternut squash soup. Like food that warms you from the inside out.

He motions towards the granite island.

"I got started a bit early. I figured you might be hungry." He strides over to the island and uncovers a bowl of steamed bao buns. They're not at all what I was expecting, but my stomach gurgles. I can't help it; their doughy little forms smell decadent.

He quirks his head at me, the lights playing across his face. "If we are being honest, I think I was getting a little hungry and I used you as an excuse."

"They look like perfect little pillows."

"Let's hope they taste that way, too." He's at the fridge now, pulling out all sorts of bowls.

There's a cabbage mixture and some pork that I can tell is tender just by looking at it. My stomach growls again. I didn't realize I was so hungry.

"I assumed you were not vegetarian, since you got chicken at that other event," he says.

"Your assumption was correct." I try not to blush at the fact that he remembered what meal I ordered. He probably does that will all the guests. Right?

"Perfect. Because I'd feel guilty eating pork this delicious in front of you. It is, for lack of a better term, the shit. The sauce is my dad's recipe." He starts uncovering the dishes and the smell makes my mouth water.

"Your dad is a chef too?"

"Yup, taught me everything I know. He's retired now but he mostly worked in barbecue restaurants, so meat was kind of his thing. I learned how to bake bread from my mom."

"Your dad is a chef and your mom is a baker?"

"In her free time, as a hobby. She was a teacher before she retired."

"Were your family dinners always five-star affairs? I'm picturing freshly baked rolls, a whole ham, and every type of casserole in existence. Like, Easter dinner all year long."

He chuckles while he grabs utensils from a drawer.

"Sit." He points a fork at the stools. "Please."

I do as I'm told, sitting across the island on a spinning chair. I brace my hands on the granite and twirl mindlessly from side to side. Maybe the motion will quell the rising curiosity I feel about the man standing across from me.

"Not quite," he continues. "My sister and I were picky eaters. We grew up on chicken nuggets and white bread, like the rest of 1990s America."

I wonder what Adam would do now if I tried to get him to eat a Cosmic Brownie. I imagine picking off the colorful dots and force feeding them to him, bite by bite. Picturing my hands being so close to his mouth makes my stomach drop. I shove the thought away, afraid he'll be able to read it on my face.

"Sounds familiar. My mom's been on a health kick. I shudder to think what meals would look like if I was five right now." I try to picture my five-year-old self eating a green goddess salad.

Adam places all the dishes in front of me, so I can assemble my sandwiches while seated. When he hands me a plate, I take it eagerly.

"Sorry, forgot to offer—would you like a glass of wine? I got this bottle of shiraz. If you like red, it's good."

"Sure, thanks." He turns to uncork the bottle and I watch his shoulders flex under his t-shirt as he works the cork out. Should I have some wine? Probably not, since being near him seems to have frazzled my entire nervous system. I accept the glass he hands me anyway.

"So you live with your mom?" He looks at me from across the counter. The smug smile seems to have dropped at the kitchen threshold. Which should be a relief, but his full, smirkless attention makes me squirmy. I uncross my legs and tuck one foot under my butt, then fiddle with the stem of my wineglass.

"Yup." I take a sip. It's full bodied and delicious. I savor the wine and hope the conversation about my mother ends here.

I should have never brought Mom up. I hate talking about her illness. I've watched people flinch at the word cancer and listened to enough people say sorry to last a lifetime. I've also fixated on the possibility of a relapse enough for all of us.

"Wow, that's good," I say, hoping we can shift the conversation back towards food and drink.

"Thanks, it comes from the finest aisles of Trader Joe's."

"Good man, good man. To Joe." I raise my glass in salute and cheers him. The glasses make a pleasant noise when they clink together.

"So, why Windstone?" He asks.

There's never any getting away from that question. I sigh internally and try to keep it short.

"My Mom got sick, I quit my job, went through a breakup. I guess all the chips kind of fell and I ended up here. That's why I live with her right now."

"Wow, you did all that to be with your mom? That's really

kind," he says. He's looking at me like he discovered a new piece of a puzzle.

"I mean, I guess a little. Not fully. I was supposed to travel around Europe with my boyfriend at the time." I take another sip of wine so I can power through the rest of it. "His band was big there, they got signed for a tour. I was already set to go. I guess I got pulled in this direction instead of his. So, yeah."

"Wait." Adam puts down his wine glass. "*That's* the douchey ex from the wedding?"

"Mhm. That's Lionel."

"Your mom was sick, and he *left* you? You were going to follow him and he left and went to Europe without you?" Instead of going wide with shock, Adam's eyes turn a steely gray. It reminds me of the ocean before a storm tears apart sky and sea.

"Sure did." I gulp my wine and ignore the spark of justice I feel at his reaction. Now that he's laid it out like that, it is an undeniably shitty thing to do.

"Fuck." He shakes his head, disgusted, like he's seen a cockroach. For the first time, I see how Lionel does come off cockroach-esque in this situation. For some reason, my chest warms at Adam's curse. Yeah, fuck is right.

Adam takes a swig of wine in solidarity. I like that he's not pretentious about food and drink, like I'd assumed when we first met. If I was wrong about that, maybe I'm wrong about other first impressions.

"That's shitty. I'm sorry," he says. "But happy you made it here." He smiles, but the storm in his eyes doesn't let up. If Lionel were here, I think he'd be getting an earful. I get the sense that Adam is not someone you want to piss off.

"Me too. To sending shitty exes to live out the remainder of their days in grimy Berlin music halls." I can't help but sound a touch bitter, but it fades completely as Adam raises his glass to mine in a salute.

"Okay, eat and then let's get cooking," he says.

I do just that.

The evening's game plan is to decide which flowers and herbs we can incorporate into the hors d'oeuvres without the floral taste becoming overpowering. Throughout the night I move closer to watch Adam's process and listen to his stories.

He tells me about the time his tooth got knocked out walking past a kids' baseball game when he was five, and he wore a mouthguard any time he went out to play for months afterwards. How he ate a spoonful of wasabi on a dare in high school and then ran to the nearest gas station and chugged a half gallon of chocolate milk. How he'll try any new hobby at least one time (juggling, axe-throwing, salsa dancing, you name it).

After several embarrassing stories on my end, I find myself leaning against the island on the side closest to the counter. Adam, I learn, is excellent at pairing completely unexpected ingredients to create unique flavor. I laugh when he wraps a walnut in basil.

"Taste it."

I give my most skeptical stare. "We're going to feed them a nut and a leaf? I know they want simplicity, Adam, but are they on a paleo diet?" The wine, the food, and the company is combining to make me giggly.

He just keeps smiling, all quiet confidence. "Try it. You'll like it." He offers it to me and then faces me to watch, leaning his palms back on the counter.

I pluck the tiny taste test from his fingers and pop it into my mouth. It's yummy. And certainly interesting.

"Okay, I see your point. Not terrible," I admit mid-bite.

He laughs deeply. "I guess I will accept 'not terrible' as high praise."

"I don't understand how you do it. How do you come up with combinations in your head? Without any recipe?" I look at all the seemingly random foods he has laid out. There are grapes and cheeses, nuts and vegetables, and fruits and herbs I've never tried before.

"I don't know, honestly." He leans back, resting his forearms on the counter so his body forms a triangle. He's different in his home, I realize. Still composed, but more comfortable to be around. Easier to read. Maybe it's the slippers.

"It's always been fun for me, guessing at what to mix and match. I always say I'll try anything once. I live for that aha moment when two unlike things pair surprisingly well."

I nod, trying to understand. "I can't imagine pulling ideas like that out of thin air. I like to have my instructions and ingredient list ready so I know exactly what I'm getting into."

He raises an eyebrow. "But see, that's the thing," he says. "You never *really* know what you're getting into, even with a recipe. The quality of ingredients could be different. You could be at a different altitude than the chef who wrote it. Maybe you don't like cilantro, so the end product tastes soapy to you. There's always got to be room for the unexpected. That's the beauty of cooking." His eyes sparkle and his voice dips lower. He pushes each word towards me with a pressing desire for me to understand. Even his body leans towards mine, like he's letting me in on a secret, just between the two of us. I haven't seen him like this before and the zip of heat it sends up my spine makes me stand up straighter.

"There can be beauty in the unknown. Like things could all go to hell, or they could end up better than you imagined."

I lift my eyes to meet his and energy fizzles through all parts of me. Adam looks hungry, in a way that no amount of food is going to remedy. And, from the way my body leans almost imperceptibly towards him, I guess that I am too. My brain dings uh-oh while all the rest of my body says *more please.*

The few feet between us begs to be closed, and I picture Adam stepping forward, pushing the plates the aside and lifting me up onto the granite island.

For the sake of my job, I need to reel this in.

I clear my throat. "Where's your bathroom?"

My words break the tension. Adam straightens. The kitchen cools down a few degrees.

"Guess I forgot to show you, sorry. It's over here." He walks around the island and points to a door past the staircase.

"Thanks, be right back."

In the bathroom, I stare at myself in the mirror while I wash my hands. What is happening here? I almost laugh—of course the first person I've been attracted to since my breakup is my colleague on a job I absolutely can't afford to jeopardize. I place a cold hand on my wine-warmed cheek. *You can do this, Lizzie. It doesn't have to get out of hand. You're in control.* The pep talk almost convinces me. Almost.

When I come back out, Adam's fiddling around the kitchen, assembling appetizers that are a bit more sophisticated than the herb-and-nut combo for us to try.

I slide back into my former seat and try to look calm.

"Awaiting further instruction, sir."

"I've almost got our next samples queued up," he says without looking back.

I pick up my wine glass, more to avoid picking at my own fingers than anything else. Mom says I've always needed something to do with my hands while my brain is working, even when I was a little girl. She calls it the fidgets.

"Sorry I don't understand much about cooking."

"It's no problem." He's placing what looks like mint on the top of a slice of banana.

"Thanks for being cool with the collaboration thing. I know I can be difficult to work with. *Rigid*, I mean." That word was a Lionel special, when I disagreed with some part of his very specific worldview. It was drilled into my head early on and he brought up so much, I came to accept it.

Adam stops what he's doing and turns around. He leans back against the counter and crosses his arms. He shakes his head, dark hair tousling.

"I wouldn't ever say that. I think you're a pleasure to work with." He looks at me straight on, so it's clear he means each word. I get the impression he doesn't throw words around to fill space, like I find myself doing lately.

"I like how whatever you're into—plants, restaurants, Bananas in Pajamas—you're fully invested. Makes talking to you fun. I think you're extremely cool, E." He shrugs, but I can see his cheeks glow a little. So much for the calm, cool, and collected exterior. Bathroom Lizzie is disappointed by how his words echo through me, warming me to my core.

Maybe this moment is too delicious to let it pass by, or maybe I'm worried about how much his words disarm my defense mechanisms. Regardless, I call him out so that our score is a bit more even.

"Are you blushing?" I give him a wide-eyed surprised face, eyebrows lifting into my hairline.

He shakes his head side to side slowly, staring at me. He bites his bottom lip, an involuntary tic.

"Me? Blush? Never. Must be a trick of the light."

He turns back to the food but motions above his head with a knife, then begins to chop up jicama. "They warned me about that side effect when I bought these Edison bulbs."

"The classic blush bulb. I'd almost forgotten about that lighting trickery. You have to be careful what IKEA aisles you walk down, or people might get the wrong idea," I tease.

He smiles, even as his focus is on the food in front of him. I watch him move over the appetizers, his huge hands making the tiny morsels look even smaller. If cooking fails, I still think he could have a fruitful career wielding an ax.

"What do you think about this?" He places a bite-sized slice of what I thought was banana but I now realize is fried plantain in front of me. On top is a piece cheese and a tiny sprig of mint.

I take a bite. It's still hot from the oil and the salt is the first thing I taste. Then the creamy cheese on top (brie? Camembert?) and a refreshing hint of the mint. I basically moan.

"Thesh are sho gewd," I drool. It is extremely unattractive, but this tastes too amazing to care. Mom and I have never been much of cooks—Pizza-zaz night is the closest we come to creative food.

Adam is grinning ear to ear, like a proud dad. His little plantain babies passed the test.

We spend the rest of the night in that slippery tension, caught between chemistry and genuinely enjoying each other's company. Adam creates more interesting combos, testing out scallops with all kinds of herbs and promising that he's making a broccoli dish next time. I get a burst of energy thinking of doing this all over again.

I look up at the clock and notice how late it's gotten. How is it already eleven?

"Shoot, I should get going." We've tag-teamed the cleanup, and Adam packed a to-go box of samples to give Zed if he's feeling better tomorrow. He's made me promise to eat them if not— apparently, food is only as good as it is fresh. Tell that to the year-old granola bars in my glove box.

"Wait." He steps towards me, licks the pad of his thumb, and reaches for me. My body tenses at the contact. I know I should be turned off by the fact that his saliva is now on my face, but holy hell, this is hot. He strokes my cheek, above the freckle on the right-side of my lip. Before I can stop the thought, I wonder how it would feel for him to stroke other parts of me.

His hands smell like the forest, whether from cologne or dish soap, I can't tell. I try not to melt with the warmth of his fingers on my skin in the air-conditioned room.

"Soy sauce," he says. I would be embarrassed, except that he smiles and lets his thumb hover on me for a second longer than necessary.

As if on cue, an army of raindrops pounds at the windows. We break eye contact to watch lightening rip open the sky. Nature mutes the rest of the world in the way only a New England rainstorm can.

"Oh, shit." It's then that I remember I've left my windows cracked, anticipating leaving before the heat of the day had worn off and trying to save myself a stifling ride.

I groan. "All of my windows are down."

"Give me your keys," Adam demands.

"I can do it…"

"That's silly. I'm the one in my own house, full of extra clothes. I'll do it." He leaves no room for argument. He puts out his hand and I dig through my purse and reluctantly hand him the keys.

"You don't have to do this, honestly…"

"Don't worry, I move fast." He grins at me and winks. Now the bulbs are making *me* blush. Before I can retort, he sprints out of the house and practically dives into my car. I watch the windows roll up when he starts the Jeep, but only one of my headlights shines through the rain.

The car turns off and Adam's back in the house in a minute.

"Well, it's certainly wet in there." Adam is absolutely drenched, the gray t-shirt clinging to him for dear life as he stands on the welcome mat. I try not to objectify his very noticeable pecs under his shirt.

"I'll grab you a towel, so you don't get the floor wet. Where are they?"

"Bathroom, in the closet. Thanks."

I go where instructed and find a neatly rolled pile of fluffy towels. If the towels are any indication, his good taste clearly extends beyond the kitchen.

I rush back to the front door, where Adam has pulled off his shirt and stands with his back to me, looking out at the rain.

"Here you go." I hand him the towel and watch his back muscles tense as he turns to grab it. I imagine my fingernails digging into his golden skin, tanned from late spring sun. I swallow, wondering if I'm the only one experiencing the tension winding tighter in me every second.

"Your headlight is out." He doesn't look at me, just peers out the slim window beside the door and frowns at the pelting rain. Guess that tense feeling is just me, then.

"It must have just happened. Thanks for noticing, I'll get it fixed tomorrow." I grab my purse. "Anyways, I should get going. Thanks for tonight."

I move towards the door and accidentally brush his skin. It's dotted with goosebumps, the vent above us bathing him in a shower of cold air. He's still wet, he must be freezing.

"Let me drive you," he says. It sounds more like a command than an ask which flares an ember of anger in me. What the hell, does he not think I'm capable of driving in the rain?

"I'm fine. It's not too far, barely twenty minutes."

"Please," he says. This time, the words are pleading. "Your car is soaked; it'll probably fog up all the inside windows. And your headlight is out. This rain is a nightmare. It's dangerous." Panic laces his voice.

Something about his anxiety resonates. I've felt that way before—wanted to do anything to try and keep someone safe from harm. It's less savior complex and more disaster prevention.

"Okay," I relent. "You can drive me home."

Adam changes into a dry pair of clothes while I sit in the kitchen and wonder what prompted that driving freak out. Then we load into the truck parked in his garage.

"Thanks again for doing this," I say to break the silence.

"I insist. There's no need to thank me. Making sure you get home safe will help me sleep better."

As he reverses out of the garage and past my car, rain beats the roof like a drum. We stay silent for a few minutes, enjoying the sound of spring turning to summer.

He drives like my grandpa used to, the speedometer maxing out at 35. After a few minutes, he turns on the radio, which is connected to his phone's Bluetooth.

I gape. "Adele, Adam?" Another surprise.

"She's an artist of our generation." He says this without a hint of embarrassment, which I love.

"Oh, I know it. I am queen of sad girl singers. I did not expect you to be their king." The rain outside makes this conversation intimate, like we are alone in the world. No other cars pass us, and the drizzle on the windshield blurs the streetlights. I have a near irresistible urge to touch him.

"I like sad girl songs because of their specificity. Sometimes small words can make you feel big things," he responds. I am too stunned to play it cool. It's like he's crawled into my head and extracted that thought from my brain.

"I agree," I say. "If the devil's in the details, then so is salvation." He nods, his focus never leaving the road. "Adele has a way of making you feel a thousand heartbreaks in just a few words," I add. He nods again.

We sing to Adele softly, empowered by the strength and volume of the storm.

When we reach my house, I slip down from the pickup truck's tall seat and land gracelessly on wet pavement. The rain has slowed to a drizzle, and before I know what I'm doing I've paused to I smile up at him.

"Goodnight, Sad Girl King. Thank you for the ride. I'll swing by tomorrow to grab my car."

"Goodnight, Sad Girl Queen. Get some rest." Adam's smile is soft as he waits for me to make it inside.

I close the door. The house is quiet, but Mom left the kitchen sink light, like she's done since I was a teenager. Maybe it's the Adele, or the red wine, or the soft caress of the summer wind on my cheeks, but I can't stop smiling.

11

A tongue leaden by sulfates greets me when I wake, an immediate reminder of last night and the inappropriate thoughts I will never speak aloud to Adam. Bless the wine spirits, at least I don't have a headache.

Adam is trouble. He's nice. He's an excellent cook, sneaky funny, and smells like the forest before a storm. Like pine and spice, an outdoorsman turned chef. The way that I'm trying to remember his scent is damning evidence.

I'm distracted from images of towering trees by a very real craving for water. I open my bedroom door slowly, turning the handle and pulling the door up a bit so it doesn't creak on the hinges. Then I try my hardest to soften my usually heavy footsteps as I tiptoe down the hallway. It's early and I'm hoping my mother has finally out-slept me.

I turn the corner into the kitchen and am met with Mom's chipper, smiling face. Alas, no such luck.

"Good morning, sweetie!"

"Morning. Need water," I croak.

Mom grabs a glass from the cabinet and fills it.

"Your car wasn't in the driveway, I thought maybe you stayed over your man friend's house." She hands over the cup. It washes down my throat like a salve. Once I chug half the glass, I come up for air.

"Mom... I told you... he's a *colleague*." That's the problem with living with your parents; they bear witness to everything.

"Okay, well how did the evening with your *colleague* go then?"

"It was fine. Nice. He makes delicious food." I tell her about all the bite-sized delicacies I got to try.

"Mom, you're smirking."

"I am not! I'm happy you had a good time, that's all."

"Mhm." I polish off the rest of the water and go for a refill. "Anyway, can you drop me off to get my car?"

Mom checks her watch. "I have a yoga class at eight. After?"

"Sure. Crap! I told Clara I'd brunch." The realization zaps me awake. It's been so long since I've had Sunday plans that I forgot, despite yesterday's reminder.

"That'll be nice, honey. It's good to get out and about early. Make the most of a beautiful day!" She finishes filling her own water and puts the pitcher back in the fridge.

I glance at the window, where puffy gray clouds hang low, threatening rain showers.

"Cheers to you for making the most of everything. I'll see what Clara's up to and we can get my car later when I get back?"

"Sounds good sweetheart." She gives me a quick hug, then grabs her key out of the basket on the counter and raincoat off the hook before humming her way out of the house. Mom loves rain, just because there's a chance she might glimpse a rainbow between the drops.

I pour myself an iced coffee and slink back to my room. My phone is abandoned on the bedside table, where I left it charging. I flop onto the bed and open my text thread with Clara.

Lizzie: *Hey! Left my car at hair tie man's last night. Long story. Might be tough to get to brunch.*

I pick at my thumbnail. I hope Clara doesn't think I'm bailing. I knew I had plans this morning, I should never have agreed to leave my car. I chastise myself for poor planning.

Clara's typing bubble's pop up almost instantly.

Clara: *!!!!*

Clara: *No prob, I'll pick you up then bring you to get it after. Be ready by 10?*

Lizzie: *Are you sure? I don't want to be a hassle.*

Clara: *Don't be silly. I can't wait to get out of this house. James is smoking meats outside and the smell is making me want to vom.*

Lizzie: *Prego sensitivities?*
Clara: *Yes. I need carbs and sugar, not smoky flesh*
Lizzie: *Ewwww flesh. There are pancakes with your name written all over them in whipped cream.*
Clara: *I hope we are doing sweatsuits. All of my maternity clothes have holes in them. They must have gotten in a fight with the dryer.*
Lizzie: *I'm down for sweatpant chic if you are*
Clara: *K gonna shower, pickup's at 10* 🌀

Clara wasn't kidding about the desire to put every carbohydrate in her mouth. Our table is laden with every kind of breakfast pastry in existence. We have a stack of strawberry pancakes, a cheesecake Danish, toast with marmalade, and a chocolate croissant in a to-go bag ("for when I get hungry on the drive home"). I also ordered a breakfast sandwich which I suggested we share, but she says eggs are on the Do Not Eat list.

"Ask me a week ago and I would have eaten twelve hard-boiled eggs in a row. Now? They remind me of feet."

"Pregnancy sounds like a roulette wheel of things you can't do and things you suddenly don't like."

At first, I worried my pregnancy skepticism might bother Clara, but she may be more skeptical than I am. I peel one of my legs from the vinyl booth and tuck it under me. Clara butters the toast before she globs on some jelly.

"Pregnancy is a bitch."

"Sounds like it. It's crazy how I always thought of pregnant people as angelic. Like, they stop swearing and have to stop drinking and basically try and do everything perfectly, so their baby comes into this world sweet and untainted," I say. Clara does not match up with this vision. I love her for it.

"Honestly, I've started swearing more *during* my pregnancy. These hormones hit different." She sips decaf coffee. "And did you know that you can lose all of your teeth? This little monster is sucking the calcium from my bones as we speak."

"That sounds like it's straight out of a sci-fi movie. Or *Twilight*. Is this baby going to break out of you and have a taste for human blood?"

"Very possible. Okay, anyways. Enough about me growing

a human and wanting to puke. Tell me about Adam."

I'd delayed this conversation, dodging it in the car and promising further details once food was in front of me. But even in the presence of over-buttered pancakes, I don't want to talk about it. It makes me jittery in a way I'm not ready to unpack.

"He's cool. He's fun to work with."

"And?" Clara waves a hand in the air.

"And he makes great food. We had a nice time."

"Lizzie."

"What!"

"You left your car there! This can't be all that you give me. I am living a boring life." Clara pretends to gag. "I need to live the wild, adventurous side of me that is currently on hold vicariously through you."

"I don't think you'll get much wild adventure from me. Jessie's more your girl for that."

"Jessie's been boring ever since she got serious with Clark. It's always Clark this, Clark that, let me tell you a funny joke Clark told me. Clark is nice, and a good accountant, but that guy is the farthest thing from funny. The last joke he told me was about a baby buffalo." Clara chugs her chocolate milk.

"Oh, the one where he leaves and says 'bison'?"

"Yes. That one." Clara's sour face makes me laugh.

"I like Clark." I do like Clark, but I also feel like it's my duty to defend Jessie. I assumed Clara and Jessie would be super close now that they're launching into new stages of their life simultaneously.

"Clark is fine, but Clark is tapioca. Don't get me wrong, some people love the blank slate that is tapioca and whoop-de-fucking-doo for them. But it's never going to shock and awe the masses. There's a reason Marie Antoinette said 'let them eat cake.'"

"Okay, agree. But he's stable. It's good for Jessie," I counter.

"If you say so. But I don't give a flying fart about Clark. I want to hear about if you boned this man or not."

"Clara!" I look around the restaurant, making sure Adam isn't secretly hiding at the next table over. "Oh my god, no. I didn't sleep with him! He's my coworker," I hiss.

"As if no one has ever slept with a coworker before." Clara rolls her eyes.

I hunch up my shoulders and shrug, because of course she's right. It was a running joke at my old job, how many employees married each other. It's easy to date someone who works the same insane hours and dedicates their life to the same company. Makes for solid default conversation. At least I dodged that bullet.

I sip my second cup of coffee of the day to buy time.

If we are going to be real friends, I don't want Clara to think I'm keeping secrets—I'm not. It's just that I can't pinpoint what it is that draws me to Adam. I wish I didn't feel this magnetism that pulls me unyieldingly closer every time we're together, since anything between us could blow up my chance at staying out of a cubicle for the foreseeable future.

"We spent most of the night talking and eating. Drank some wine, it started raining hard, and he drove me home."

"Wine. I remember wine." Clara smiles whimsically, a woman on a no-alcohol, minimal caffeine diet daydreaming.

"Why'd he drive you home?"

"Long story but it involves rain, sunroofs, and my fear of going to the mechanic," I say. "I think we are maybe making our way into buddy territory? He said we're friends." I try to act natural as my heart sinks all over again.

Clara nods. I think she's accepted my answer until (in a regular volume voice) she follows up with, "It's fine if he's your friend. Great, even. I'm just saying, I don't usually want to sit on my *friends'* faces."

I choke on a bite of Danish and have to spit half of it into a napkin.

"Jesus, Clara!"

"What!" She grabs her heart like I've wounded a gentle animal.

She continues, "The way you describe this man it's like he's carved out of marble. And yet he somehow still manages to have a personality. I only met him for thirty seconds while my feet were on fire and I still remember wanting to watch him wield a hefty fire hose to put those puppies out. And yes, that's an innuendo."

I take another long swig of coffee. "I didn't realize pregnant people could be such pervs."

"You do know how people get pregnant to begin with, right?" She wiggles in the booth and holds up one finger excitedly. "I have an idea!"

"Oh boy, I'm scared. What is it?" I ask.

"You should bring him to my baby shower."

"But I'm going with Jessie." I frown. Designing our couples costume is the only plan Jessie and I have when she gets back from Europe. We haven't *created* our SpongeBob and Sexy Patrick costumes yet, but I've got most of the accessories we need saved in my Amazon cart.

Clara's face twists, confused. "Didn't she tell you? Clark finagled his way out of that conference. They RSVPed that he'll be there, too."

My heart sprints. I don't know anyone going besides Jessie, and Clara's baby shower was supposed to be our return to normalcy. It was going to be the perfect opportunity to get back in our old groove. I'd already bought a mini pineapple purse for me and a mini rock purse for her as a surprise. Why wouldn't she tell me Clark was going?

Clara's eyebrows pinch. She looks pretty pissed on my behalf, a lopsided frown deepening the longer she looks at me. I can tell she's trying to gauge if I'm okay. I plaster on a smile.

"Oh! Well then. That's nice." I've never been a great actress and Clara doesn't buy it.

"Sorry, Lizzie. She told me last week. I'm sure she's still planning on you going, too. You can be an outfit threesome." She grimaces at her phrasing. "Maybe trio would have been a better way to phrase that."

Then Clara stretches her hand across the table and squeezes mine. Her palms are warm and soft. A few seconds pass, but she doesn't let go. Cursing or not, she's going to be a great mom.

"It's okay," I say, even though it's not. Clara's baby shower was the one thing Jessie and I had planned for this summer that felt like the old us. Something that we could scheme and craft and be ridiculous about together.

"But please tell me you're still coming? And please bring your hair tie hero! You know what, not please. You're bringing him, I demand it as my shower gift. For the love of god, tell him it's shirt optional. Like, he could use body paint or something. We'll all need the distraction from the annoying games my mom insists we play."

"Clara, I've literally hung out alone with this guy *once*. In a work-related setting. I can't ask him to be my date to my friend's baby shower."

"Sure you can." Then she reaches for my cup. "Just one tiny sip. I don't condone lying to your life partner, but save me from his excessive WebMDing and don't tell James." She takes a swig of cold brew coffee, then lets out a moan. "Holy hell, that shit is good. Anyways, didn't you and Adam do lunch together, too?"

"I mean yeah, but the waiter was there."

Clara rolls her eyes. "Would you not count dinner as a date if the waiter was there? I went on a date with a girl in college who tried to finger-bang me under the table. It doesn't matter if someone else was present."

"It wasn't a date! And no one got close to finger banged." My chest heats and a blush crawls up my neck at the memory of Adam's fingers wiping soy sauce off me.

"Well, at least think about it. If he'll drive you home in the rain, he's interested enough to dress up and eat cake with your friends."

"Maybe," I answer noncommittally. I say the thing I know Clara wants to hear, despite feeling that I'll regret it later. "I promise to be there either way, even if it's solo."

I don't want to go to Clara's party alone. But I want to show up for her.

"No problem. It's a buffet, outdoors, and open seating so you do what you gotta do, girl. Lucky for you I gave up planning this before I even started, so we're going with the lowest maintenance set up possible. With that said, I expect to be kept up-to-date on your sexual exploits." She lowers her eyes at me, as if I'm guarding a deep well of untapped secrets.

"I promise. You will be my hair tie guy confidante."

"Normally I'd require a blood pact, but a handshake will

work." Clara smiles toothily before sticking her hand out. I do the same. We shake once.

"Alright, now let's get to work on these hotcakes." Clara pushes the plate towards the middle of the table and smothers them in syrup.

"Hotcakes? Are you a Midwestern grandmother?"

"I'm on my way there. You better get in on these before there's none left." She cuts straight through the stack like it's a pie and forks a slice that's three pancakes deep.

My stomach is churning too much to enjoy food. I guess Jessie and I must be farther apart than I thought.

"Earth to Lizzie."

I swallow and snap back to reality. "Sorry, what?"

"You're upset about Jessie." Clara looks at me sympathetically as she shoves the largest forkful of pancake I've ever seen into her mouth.

"No, I'm fine." I force a smile.

"Liar. Luckily, I am too distracted by food to dredge up deep emotions." She takes another gigantic bite. "How's your mom?"

"She's good. She joined an aerial yoga troupe or something."

"Oh my god, how's your mom so much cooler than us? Even before this, I was a loser compared to her."

I laugh at the unexpectedly absurdity of that statement. "Clara you're not a loser because you're pregnant."

"I'm pregnant because I'm a loser. That's how that *Mean Girl's* quote goes, right?" Despite her claims of hating pregnancy, Clara rubs her belly like it's the most important thing on this earth.

"I can't imagine the work it takes growing a human. Or modifying your life to do it. It all seems so out of control." I admit.

"It's not that different from modifying your life to help anyone else you love though, is it? Physically it's more of a bitch, but at least there's a reward at the end.

"When my dad went into hospice, we changed so much. We moved to be closer to him, I rearranged my work schedule so I could visit on Fridays. It's kind of the same situation except it's changing me from the inside out." Clara shrugs. For all her split-second wit and wild stories I've heard, Clara's thinks things through.

"Hey Lizzie, can I say something before I shove my mouth full again?"

"Yeah, of course."

"Why don't you call Jessie and ask her about the party? Or about the Lionel stuff?"

I want to tell Clara that I can't do that. First, because I've shared nothing about my recent life with Jessie that could possibly upset her. I never wanted to be the downward trajectory, sob-story friend. And second, how would Jessie understand my mess of a life, anyway? Her life is panning out the way we always knew it would.

All I say is, "I'll think about it."

"Okay, I'm turning my pedestal into the pancake-eating contest stage now." Clara arms herself with her fork once more and spears another cake. She makes it through the rest of the stack on her own. I sit there in awe, knowing that Clara can do anything she sets her mind or stomach to. Joey Chestnut wouldn't stand a chance.

If I could summon a sprinkle of that chutzpah, I'd invite Adam to the shower. But I love my new job, and I'm trying to build a life here. Adam threatens to make my life messy, complicated, unpredictable. None of which I need more of.

Clara hums happily. I stab at my cold eggs, wondering when every relationship in my life got this complicated.

12

Every event needs an X factor, a specific hook that sticks with guests long after the party is over. My daily text brainstorms with Adam about new plant findings and his suggested pairings have yielded some solid ideas, but I have this bone-deep sense there's an element missing. We need something cohesive, something that ties flowers and food together.

I'm watering the daffodils and watching a bee swirl amidst the flowers when an idea pops into my head. I open my phone, scrolling past notifications of clips Clara has shared (how many videos of shirtless men making softcore cooking porn could possibly exist on this app?) to text Adam.

I type one word:

Lizzie: *Honey.*

His typing bubbles pop up almost immediately.

Adam: *That's a little forward, no?*

Lizzie: *No, goof. Honey, like from bees. Not a pet name.*

Adam: *Sweet, sweetie*

I know he's teasing. But even if he doesn't mean it, I still feel a little gooey.

Lizzie: *We could pair honey from local bees with local flowers. The sustainability people will eat that up. Literally.*

Adam: *I like it! I'll make some calls but believe it or not, I already have a local honey hookup. Free tomorrow if she can meet up?*

A honey hookup… like he's sleeping with the beekeeper? My stomach drops to the cement floor. Maybe that word choice was intentional. It somehow never occurred to me that Adam might be dating.

Either way, it shouldn't matter. We are colleagues first and foremost. I try to slow my heart rate with a few deep breaths. At least I know where I stand if that's the case.

Lizzie: *Sounds like a plan. I'm off at 2 tomorrow.*

I thank the messaging gods that I can maintain the illusion of calm over text.

Adam: *I'll meet you at the greenhouse, we'll go from there.*

Lizzie: 🤏

Adam: *Have a nice day, busy bee* 🐝

I smile stupidly at my phone.

"Lizzie!" I look up to find Nina standing a foot away, their fingers separated in the middle to make an alien "V".

Nina, the part-timer helping with the floral arrangements, is here to get the run-down of the event. They were in Zed's office, doing inventory of flowers to ensure we have enough available for all the bouquets and centerpieces. Now, they're watching me daydream.

"I come in peace," Nina says. We've worked on projects together before and make a great pair. Probably because we are both the same brand of weird, and I'm type A while Nina is fully fly-by-the-seat-of-their-pants creative brain.

"Sorry, was texting the event's caterer. I had an idea," I say.

"Oh, do tell."

"Pairing up local honey with some of the dishes. It ties together the whole locally sourced, nature theme."

"I like! I've never seen someone smile like that over honey before." Nina smirks as I blush.

I may have told Nina about Adam and accidentally mentioned that he is charming and knows how to handle a spatula. But in my defense, it was Zed that jumped in and told them about our food pairings night and fan-girled endlessly over the "very fit, very interesting chef" (his words, not mine). I remained quiet, which must have made Nina even more suspicious because they've been on my case about it all day.

"I need to see this dude myself and decide if he's worth the hype. From both you *and* Zed," Nina says earnestly.

"You'll probably love him. That seems to be the norm," I reply with a sigh. It's true. I'm shocked all the plants don't turn towards him when he walks in. Adam just has that it-factor. People want to laugh at his jokes, make him smile, and feel the warm glow of his attention. Or maybe that's just me. Maybe *I'm* people.

"The guy cooks? Already a ten in my book." They sigh and run a hand through their thick brown hair, causing it to stand on end. "Derrick's cooking skills only extend to boxed or frozen food." Nina's partner is a wonderful person, but that tracks. The three times we've gone out for lunch together, he reliably orders some version of chicken tenders and fries.

"Anyway, let's talk shop." Nina gestures to the print-outs they've got of the available flowers.

I shake away thoughts of Adam bent over a stove, stirring something delectable. Clara's videos must be rotting my brain.

"Right. Let's do it."

Adam and I wave to Zed as we leave the greenhouse the following day. Zed didn't seem surprised to see the truck roll in. I shared my honey idea, but I may have neglected to tell him Adam was involved in this errand.

"I trust you two will get job done! I'll hold down the fort here," he says with a smile when Adam comes inside to say hello. A few people mill about the greenhouse, one talking in baby voice to Daisy who is asleep beneath the hydrangeas.

It's a sunny day but the wind comes in gusts, blowing my hair across my eyes as we step outside. I rake the brown strands back and throw them up into a big curly bun on top of my head. Adam's lips tug up at the corners.

"This crazy hair day is not my fault." I shout over the wind as I grab a handle and swing myself up and into Adam's truck. I land ungraciously in the passenger seat.

"I like it. Wild hair suits you."

Despite the gusts, I feel warm all over. I clear my throat.

"So, you've got connections to local honey makers, huh? Beekeepers? I guess technically bees are the ones making the honey." I'm rambling, but this is the easiest path for my anxious energy to escape.

"This thing has to be shit on gas mileage," I continue,

eyebrows raised.

"I wasn't born a truck guy. I mean, I now own a truck. But it's mostly so I can move things."

"How many things are you moving?"

"I don't know if you've heard, but I do own a catering company." Now *he* raises an eyebrow.

"Yeah, yeah. I guess that makes sense."

"Unfortunately, being the truck guy also means every person you know asks for help moving."

"I get that. When I moved from Boston, my mom asked Zed for a favor. He let me borrow one of our delivery trucks. I don't think the Jeep could have made it. How many moves are we talking?"

"Well, all my sister's friends for starters. When she finished college, I basically had to move out an entire dorm," he says.

"Although my own sibling wasn't around for my college years, I assume that's what big brothers are for. Lifting heavy objects. Does your sister live close by?"

Adam freezes, then taps the steering wheel. It takes me a second to realize where I've seen that kind of discomfort before. It's the *I don't want to talk about this because it'll make us both uncomfortable* kind of tick. I get like that when people ask about my mom's treatment.

"No. Megan died a few years back." Adam's words are steady, but his back's rigid.

"Shit. Sorry. We don't have to talk about it." I try to ease back from the conversation to give him a way out.

He glances at me, surprised, then relieved.

"Thanks for that. Everyone always asks what happened."

"I get it. Sometimes you're not in the mood to talk about the worst things you've lived through." I wish people had given me a way out of the never-ending cancer conversations. I look out the window, eyes suddenly stinging. I mean it, too. I don't want to force anyone into accepting sympathy—particularly when they're not in the mood for it.

"So, the honey," he redirects.

"Hm?"

"The first farm is relatively new. It's a retired guy who got super into beekeeping. You've probably seen his stuff at farmers markets around here; he has a solid social following and sells a lot online. The second lady was my third-grade teacher, but she's legit."

"Woah, woah, wait." I hold up a dramatic hand. "You're bringing me to meet someone who knew THE baby Adam?"

"I wouldn't say I was a baby in third grade," he teases.

"Okay, sorry, THE child Adam. Bowl cut Adam. Adam who probably wore a baby watch on his tiny baby wrist before he even learned how to properly tell time."

"That's where you're wrong, E. I was born knowing how to tell time." He chuckles. "It would be great if you refrain from embarrassing me, since we may be partnering with her."

"Oh sure, sure." I flip a hand haphazardly, a wild grin unfurling across my face.

"Just sending these to you so I don't forget to ask your teacher," I say as I text *Did baby Adam try to get all other kids to eat mud pies at recess?* to Adam's phone.

My text flashes across the car display that's connected to his phone, the message coming from **E** ✿. The fact that he updated my contact makes my stomach flutter. I hope he can't sense my relief at the fact that honey hookup is a platonic personal connection.

"I don't trust you. Or that face you're making right now." Adam pretends to frown, but my face must reflect pure glee, judging by how my cheeks hurt. He cracks, a smile leaking out.

"Alright, fine. Dig into my metaphorical and physical childhood dirt. I'd ask you to limit the embarrassing questions, but we both know you won't."

"Like I am sure you would do if roles were reversed, right?" I stick my tongue out at him, then realize what I'm doing and quickly regain my composure. It's too easy to have fun together. I vow to rein in the fun and turn on the business charm.

We reach stop number one, a split ranch on a big piece of land. The mailbox says "Bob's Sunny Farm" and has bees painted all over it. I am immediately endeared to Bob before ever meeting him.

"Let's see what all the buzz is about, eh?" I lean all the way over the cab to elbow Adam in the ribs. He shakes his head. "Lizzie, why do I ever doubt your ability to out-nerd me?"

Bob comes around the corner of the house in his beekeeper's suit, a gloved hand waving us over. He's built like a linebacker, tall and wide-shouldered with a mustache I can spot through the black mesh of the face mask.

"Hi. Bob. Nice to meet ya." He nods in our direction.

"Nice to meet you, Bob. I'm Lizzie." He gives me the most authoritative handshake I've ever received. Adam introduces himself and is subjected to the same.

"Come on this way." Bob motions us forward, to the backyard.

"Did I mention I'm terrified of bees?" Adam hisses as we walk around the side of the house. I raise my eyebrows—he does look a little on-edge. I'm not the biggest fan of bees either, but you grow to appreciate them when you're around plants all the time. They're the tiny superheroes of the plant world.

"That might have been a good bone to throw me beforehand," I whisper. "Don't worry, I'll protect you."

As we step closer to the hives, his posture betrays him. He radiates fear. The buzzing I thought was in my head surrounds us.

"Those over there are the hives, we got about six frames in each one." Bob points to three large, white boxes in the middle of the field.

"How many bees is that?" Adam asks. His cheery tone can't hide the tension in his voice; he's focusing on details rather than the swarm of insects buzzing around his head. I watch a bead of sweat roll down his neck and have the strange urge to lick it off. *Gross, Lizzie.*

"Hm, gotta be about 70,000 at this rate." Bob smiles proudly.

"Wow. I've never been this close to 70,000 bees," I say, trying to sound impressed and not horrified. I know bees are good for the environment, but that's too many pointy ends for my liking.

"Yup, they're good 'uns too. Each box'll make, hm, about thirty five pounds of liquid gold."

"Wow, that's a lot." Adam pales.

"It was my retirement dream and hey, I'm living it. No more selling farm equipment to bigwigs for me."

Bob gives us the rest of the tour. I'm impressed by how well Adam holds it together, despite being pale as buttermilk. "Now, how about I get you some of the fresh stuff to try?" Bob says once he's schooled us in the logistics of beekeeping. He gestures to the side of the house, farther from the hives. It's not until we are seated in the shade that Adam slumps against the white vinyl siding.

"Are you alright?" I ask once Bob heads back to the bee boxes.

"Not really. I also should have told you I have an EpiPen in my pocket. Just in case," he says with eyes closed.

"Wait, what?" I feel my heart leap up my throat. "You're *allergic* to bees and you thought coming out to a bee farm was a good idea?"

"You asked."

"Well, you could have disclosed that you couldn't go because you'd be putting your life in danger!" Worry raises my voice an octave.

"You were excited about it. I wanted to come." He lifts a shoulder to his ear, but his back stays against the wall, like his body yearns to be as far from the hives as possible.

"That's very nice," I admit. My heart beats a stupid, sporadic pattern at his admission. "But also ridiculous. I could have come on my own if I knew I was dragging you closer to imminent death!"

He breathes deeply, as I process the horror of him standing a few feet from potential anaphylactic shock.

"It'll take more than a couple bees to do me in. But hey, if I get stung, seriously, stab me with this." He puts the EpiPen in my hand. I gawk.

"You're insane."

"So I've been told." He runs a hand through his hair.

"Can I help?"

He cracks open his eyes and looks at me.

Were his eyes this gray before? I am being pulled into the

ocean, fighting a current I'm not prepared for. I look away, worried I'll be swept off solid ground.

He stretches his fingers and places his hand gently over mine. Electricity, as real as a bee sting, zips up my spine. It spreads behind my shoulder blades, sunshine lighting me up from the inside. Somehow his hands are cool in the summer heat. He stares at me for an extra second, daring me to move, then closes his eyes and rests his head against the wall again.

Our hands stay stacked on the bench as I turn my attention to Bob, who is smoking out the bees. He uses a brush to gently remove them from one of the frames. "Ironically, honey is one of my favorite foods." Adam's eyes stay closed as he says this, and I watch his chest move as he takes slow breaths. I am praying the bees stay far away. I'm not in the mood to stab anyone in the leg today.

"I don't think you are legally required to watch the honey be made to consume it. We could have done the normal thing; picked up samples and had an offsite tasting where your life wasn't in peril."

"Probably right. Per usual. Shocking how you can be so effortlessly beautiful *and* smart."

"You're just saying that so I'll make sure to stab you if necessary."

Adam squeezes my hand without opening his eyes. "I'm not." That Pop Rocks feeling returns to my chest.

Bob finishes up with the bees and walks towards us. I slide my hand quickly out from under Adam's. I don't want Bob to believe we're anything other than platonic business partners on a mission to purchase a large batch of honey. Luckily, Bob's too into his bees to notice us at all. He ignores Adam's pale, clammy skin and insists we try the honey right off the comb.

I break off a small piece and suck the honey out of it, as Bob instructs. It's gooey and waxy and I think I can taste a hint of the lavender that grows all around, if that's possible.

"Ya've never tasted anything quite like it." He beams, a proud father to thousands of bees.

"Is it possible to taste flowers in the honey?" My question is rewarded with an enthusiastic nod.

"You've sure got a good palate. Honey flavors can be subtly influenced by all the plants around. You know, different types of nectar and all that. Not everyone notices that, but you're good."

"Lizzie's got great taste."

Adam's perked up but he's still pale. I try not to worry about him and fail.

"Could I have a glass of water, please?" I ask Bob.

He nods and motions towards the house, as I'd hoped. "Come on inside. We can discuss facts and figures in the aircon."

I take polite sips of the water Bob hands me, even though I polished off my water bottle in the car. We go over tentative amounts, pricing, and timeline. We leave Bob with the promise that we'll give him a call by end of week.

"Let me know either way. I 'ppreciate you thinking local," Bob says as we walk towards Adam's truck.

"Of course. Thank you for meeting with us on such a short timeline," Adam says.

I have no idea how to properly compliment a beekeeper so all I can think to say is "Your bees were lovely." I cringe internally but don't let my smile falter.

Bob's face lights up. Laugh lines crinkle the sides of his eyes when he smiles, and I decide he is definitely a softie, despite his harsh exterior.

"They are, aren't they? Being around them makes me pretty darn happy, you know?"

I steal a glance at Adam, to find him looking at me.

Unfortunately, I do understand that sentiment.

13

Once we're inside the truck and free of potential beestings, I watch the color come back into Adam's face. I let out a breath I didn't realize I was holding.

I've just pressed "Start" on the Google Maps route to our next meeting when we stop at a red light. Adam turns towards me.

"Thank you for that."

"For what?" I ask. My cheeks heat at the way he is staring at me. Like he wants to hug me. Or touch me, or something. It's the *or something* that makes my cheeks bloom.

"For talking me through the bee thing. And then asking for water to move us inside. I appreciate it."

"No problem. Hydration is important."

"You chugged an entire Nalgene before we got there. So please accept my thanks."

Adam's attention to detail, especially where it concerns me, makes my stomach flutter.

"Fine. You would have done the same if I was in the presence of a wolf or something."

"Wolves and bees are different."

"Yes, but my body doesn't have an all-systems-failure when I touch a wolf."

"How about if a wolf touches you?" He raises a rakish eyebrow, so cheesy it's cute.

"Most of the wolves I've been approached by turn out to be dogs," I quip.

"Good one, E." His lips quirk up in a smile, and I have to

force myself to look out the window to avoid staring at him for the rest of the drive.

From the second you step into her presence, it's clear Mrs. Carol is an elementary school teacher. It's not just that she comes out of the house to greet us with a pencil poking out of her gray bun. It's the way she looks at you, like you're still full of infinite potential. If I had to read her aura (which is more Jessie's thing than mine) it would be sunshine yellow.

"Now, that can't be Adam Weaver."

I watch Adam flush and then give Mrs. Carol a hug. It might be the cutest thing I've ever seen.

She turns to me with a sweet smile. "He always was a star pupil. And you must be the lovely fiancé?" She looks to me, and I choke on my words. Thankfully, Adam steps in.

"No fiancé here. This is my colleague, Lizzie. We're working together on the wedding I messaged you about."

Mrs. Carol covers her mouth with one hand.

"Oh dear. My apologies. I thought you were sampling for *your* wedding."

I finally find my voice. "No problem at all, Mrs. Carol. It's super great to meet you."

"You too, sweetie. Gosh, I'm so sorry about that. You two do make such a beautiful pair though." Then she claps her hands, and we're on to the next subject. "About the honey, then. Please don't mind my manners, come. Come inside!"

A delicate porcelain tea set that I'm afraid to touch sits next to a small platter of cheese and three jars of honey, each with its own honey dipper. I'm relieved to find this will be a much less hands-on experience than Bob's house.

"Sit, sit!" She ushers us inside where the air conditioner whirs. Stepping in from the heat makes my arms tinge with goosebumps. I take a seat at the breakfast nook while Adam hovers.

"May I use the restroom, Mrs. Carol?"

"Adam, we've been through this. Call me Nella, please," she tsks. "Down the hall to the left dear."

Once he's gone, Nella grabs some cloth napkins from a

118

drawer and sits in the chair on the other side of the bench.

"So, Lizzie! What got you into the wedding business?" She sits quietly, hands folded, the perfect image of a riveted listener.

"It's a long story. The short version is, I started doing some floral arrangements for fun. Then my boss realized it would be a good opportunity to expand the business, and the next thing you know," I raise my shoulders.

"That sounds lovely, I'm sure you're a perfect talent. Is this your first time working with Adam, then?"

"Yup. He's a good partner. Really thoughtful, funny. In work, I mean," I ramble. "Much more detail-oriented than I initially pinned him for."

"That sounds like Adam. The year Mateo died, Adam was such a saint. There was so much to do after Carlos' passing, I got lost in the weeds and forgot all about snow removal until our first big snowstorm hit. Adam had been checking in on me every couple weeks, and before I could even call anyone, he was out there with that snow blower, making sure my little car could scoot out. He's a lifesaver."

"I'm so sorry for your loss."

"It was a while ago now, not that it makes it any easier. But somehow you get by in the day-to-day." She smiles sadly and touches her wedding band.

I try not to fidget. It's not the talking about death that makes me uncomfortable, it's sensing that unfillable hole that losing someone leaves in your life. Grief isn't always a big, looming monster you can hide from. Sometimes it's cached in the small moments that will never be the same.

"It's lovely that you and Adam stayed in touch. He's been a pleasure to work with so far." I blush and vow to never again say Adam and pleasure in the same sentence. If this keeps up, Pantone will have my cheeks to thank for a wide array of new pinks and reds.

"After his sister's car accident, I felt terrible. I had been Megan's teacher too, she was such a spunky, silly girl. He was so shut down, would barely speak to anyone. His parents flew in, of course, but they were devastated. I think it was too painful for them to come back here after that. And Adam just carried on, grieving on his own. I had this sense that he needed more people in his life, so I invite him over for dinners every now and again. But he never talks about his personal life. That why I made that assumption about you two. I apologize." She shakes her head, smiling sadly. "Usually, I have to find something new that needs fixing just to get him to come over. I sense that he feels like a burden."

The pieces of the puzzle slide into place. *A car accident. That's why he insisted on driving me home that night.* My chest tightens, remembering his panic. Oh, Adam.

"When he called to set this up, he mentioned a wedding and by the way he was describing you… well, it just sounded like he was absolutely enamored. You must be amazing at your job." Nella smiles, not realizing what that comment does to my heart. I wish she'd tell me, word for word, all the things Adam said. Instead, she continues, "Anyway, Adam's yard work is surpassed only by his cooking."

On cue, Adam returns from the bathroom. Nella looks at him like the sun revolves around him. And it sort of appears that way, as he ducks below the light bulbs in her low-ceilinged home.

"Oh, there you are."

"What did I miss?"

"Just singing your praises! Now sit down. I think you're going to like the honey, it's a great batch this year."

Nella bustles into the kitchen as the tea kettle boils, right on cue.

"What were you two chatting about?" Adam asks. Now doesn't seem like the time to revisit the subject of his sister, so I tell a half-truth. "We were talking about what a sweet baby angel you used to be."

"I highly doubt *that* is true. I was a pretty cute kid though."

"I wonder what happened," I say.

Adam grins wickedly.

Nella pours the hot water into the teapot. "That needs to steep for at least eight minutes. I'll forget all about it if I don't set this." She sets a kitchen timer shaped like an egg. I love it.

"Now, kids," she claps her hands, "let's talk honey."

120

An hour later, we load into the truck with full bellies and a decision on our hands. Choosing between Bob or Nella as our honey supplier is not going to be easy, since I have a soft spot for them both. I stick my hand out the window and let the breeze zip through my fingers.

"Wow. Okay, Mrs. Carol is officially the cutest human being in this solar system. She's like if Miss Frizzle came to life but didn't ask you to adventure on a bus into people's intestines," I say.

One side of Adam's lips ticks up into his version of an amused smile.

"I knew you'd like her." He glances sideways and adds, "She was very clearly a fan of you, too. I can't believe she gave you her banana cream cupcake recipe. I've been asking for that for years."

"It's a secret I'll take to the grave."

Adam's smile dips back down to neutral. "I don't know how we're going to pick between them. Mrs. Carol's honey is amazing. So smooth, and it tastes golden. But Bob's has more depth to it. You caught that with the subtly of the flavors, too."

I frown, thinking about letting buttoned up Bob or yellow-aura Nella down. I swear, the clouds part and the sun shines through as I yell, "I've got it!"

Adam jumps. "Did you get stung by a bee? Was one hanging out in here while we were inside?" He starts to roll down the windows.

"No, no, this isn't about bees." I wave a hand, swatting away his worries. "I have an idea. What if we use Nella's honey in the recipes, and pitch Bob's honey as the wedding favors? Lauren just told us they were having trouble finding so many last-minute local products. And Bob mentioned wanting to expand into retail markets."

"That's a great idea, E. Maybe we could even print a signature recipe to use with the honey on the little vials or something. I'll give Lauren a call tomorrow and pitch it, unless you want to?'"

Enthusiasm bolsters me, rising like a hot air balloon about to take flight. This excitement is what I was missing all those years clacking away at a computer.

"No, no we have a better chance of success if you do it. She likes you better anyway. She'll probably keep you as her exclusive fancy caterer from here on out."

Adam laughs. "Not sure how many more last-minute weddings I can fit in before I leave, but I'll make sure you're our exclusive florist partner if a contract comes through."

What does he mean, leave?

"Leave?" I voice aloud.

"We talked about this… haven't we?" Adam glances my way, and I must look as confused as I feel because he says, "Shit, I thought I had told you but maybe that was in my head."

"What?" I ask. I have the very distinct feeling that whatever he tells me next is going to taint an otherwise lovely day.

He drums his hands on the steering wheel, clearly uncomfortable. "I'm hoping that this wedding will launch my career. Exactly like you are at the greenhouse." I don't remember specifically telling him that, but I'm not surprised he's picked up on it; Adam is most certainly observant.

"Right before your friend's wedding, I met the owner of a growing catering company in New York. He asked me for a portfolio of my work, my cooking style. I built Jessie and Clark's whole menu knowing that their wedding would be my test. Like, an audition."

"And you knocked it out of the park, obviously." Despite the blurry parts, I remember everyone raving about Adam's food. I try not to let my voice betray the anchor weighing me down, the sinking feeling in my gut.

"I worked my ass off, had to fill in for missing staff. But I guess I impressed him. Between the samples of the menu and your friend's review, he asked me to come join his team." He goes on, "I'm not big on the city scene, but it would be a fresh start. And the money from this wedding would make a huge difference, moving to a more expensive zip code."

My heart plummets into the deepest part of my stomach. Either I do a bad job of hiding it, or he sees through me, because he continues, "It's not that I don't love it here. It's just, I can't live here anymore." His words are pleading. "Around all these people who knew my sister, who ask how I'm doing and get that heavy look in their eyes when they see me. Taking the same roads where I taught her to drive. Missing her, thinking of her… it never goes away. All my memories here are colored by her death. Most days, it's too much." Adam shakes his head, like he wishes every single part of it wasn't true.

"Of course. That totally makes sense." I nod like this isn't causing me inexplicable panic. Like my mind isn't spiraling trying to process the fact that, once again, someone I'm growing close to is leaving. I take a breath and chastise myself. I want Adam to be happy, and this has nothing to do with me. I should be better at handling change by now.

I put on my brightest smile and hope it doesn't look like a grimace. "Well, we'll have to make this a charts-topping wedding. Like, if this were a song, we'd make Casey Kasem proud."

Adam frowns and touches my hand. "I'm sorry I didn't tell you earlier." We're finally pulling into the greenhouse parking lot. He cuts the engine and stares like he sees the deepest part of me, the place where that little flame, that illogical hope that something will happen between us, sputters out.

"No worries! I'll forgive and forget if you slip me a few more samples," I say, trying to keep things light. I slide out of the car.

"Lizzie…"

"I have to jet—Zed wanted to go over our fertilizer order today. Let me know how the Lauren honey pitch goes. Thanks for the ride!"

I shut the door and manage a wave as I retreat into the greenhouse. Water from the misters drips down the glass, blurring Adam in the parking lot. I hide between the ferns until he drives away.

14

I've always believed I'm above bread and circus. Surely my solutions-oriented self could have survived the horrors of Ancient Rome without turning to food and drink and cheering on hunky gladiators.

But, as I sit at the counter eating brownie batter with a spoon while Adam dons oven mitts, my faith is shaken. Turns out, I *am* easily distracted from real-life problems by delicious treats and a weapon (if that weapon is a wooden spoon yielded by strong, tan forearms).

Adam invited me over under the guise of testing out desserts, but I'm pretty sure he's using my sweet tooth to apologize. After all, we aren't even responsible for desserts. It only took one day of stewing about Adam's imminent move before I agreed to be wooed with baked goods.

Which is how I find myself quite literally drooling as Adam pulls a batch of brownies out of the oven. It doesn't help that he's wearing an apron and has rolled his sleeves to his elbows. I didn't realize I had a thing for domestic men, but it turns out I really, really do.

"Get 'em while they're hot." He places a steaming square in front of me and fine, I will definitively admit that a hot Roman gladiator baking me treats would absolutely distract me from my impending doom. Then he turns to the sink to clean up.

"Thoughts?"

"They're incredible," I sigh. They truly are the best brownies I've ever tasted. "I thought chefs weren't supposed to know how to bake. Aren't those two separate skill sets?"

He smiles, wrist-deep in suds. "Not for me. Mom would have been mortified if I couldn't nail at least a few of her recipes. But not going to lie, those brownies are the best of my baking skills. I wanted to make something you'd like."

"Is there anything you can't do?" I take another bite. The top is crispy, but the inside is gooey and warm. I, too, am gooey inside both from the deliciousness and this gesture of apology.

"I am a terrible poker player. I've got no game face. I also suck at vacuuming."

"How does one suck at vacuuming?" I snort. "You just plug it in and push it around."

"I usually zone out and forget to go in straight lines. Some patches end up super clean, others remain unvacuumed. Bad habit to have when you're constantly dropping food."

"Maybe you need a dog. You know, to eat up all the dropped food. And for company." I imagine Adam living alone in this quiet house and remember Nella's words. A wave of sadness rolls over me.

"Yeah, maybe you're right." He faces out the window while scrubbing a mixing bowl. "Megan used to live here with me when she graduated. It was my parents' house to start, but when they moved to Florida, I bought it. I used to get so annoyed at her for leaving her stuff everywhere. And there was always background noise, some music playing or a TV on. Now I kind of miss the sound and mess."

I don't want Adam to leave, but I understand why he wants to go. I can't imagine the grief of living in a space where he's surrounded by reminders of the sister he lost.

"Sometimes it feels like pieces of me, who I used to be, disappeared. I'm trying, but I'm not sure I can find them here."

I think my initial impression of Adam, his words wrapped up in humor that was hard to parse. I guess it's difficult to figure someone out when they're rediscovering themself.

"I get that. I get why you want a fresh start." *But I already know I'll miss you*, I don't add.

Adam finished with the dishes and turns around. "Sorry again that I didn't tell you sooner. I guess I alluded to it, but I was too chicken to tell you straight up. I know brownies can't buy forgiveness, but they're the best way I know how to show you that I mean it. That I would never intentionally hurt you, E."

"Don't worry about it. Plus, now there's way less pressure if we screw this up." I meant the wedding, but it suddenly sounds like I mean *us*. I wonder if that's exactly what my subconscious was going for.

We're both quiet for a minute, until Adam moves.

"I'm done with cleanup. Let's hang in the living room. The oven's made it hot in here." He unties his apron and hangs it on a wall hook, then sheds his flannel so he's just wearing a blue t-shirt. *As if it's just the kitchen that's hot*, I think. His being so creative while simultaneously organized and meticulous is unexpectedly sexy.

"Leave the brownies?" I fake pout. Adam laughs. Then he wanders over to where I'm sitting on the stool and gets *very* close to my face. He reaches out a freshly washed hand that smells of mint soap. My stomach flutters. I am so afraid he'll touch me. I'm also terrified he won't.

Adam says nothing, but his thumb brushes across my cheek and then drags across my lip, so slowly. I hold my breath as he lingers, eyes on my mouth.

"Crumbs," he says in a low voice that has me feeling like I'm made of melting chocolate. I blink and try to clear the haze. This is the second time he's touched my face like this. I hope it's not the last. Goosebumps erupt down my arms.

"Go sit in the living room. I'll bring you another brownie," Adam demands.

"Oh, yeah. Okay." I make my way to the living room and curl up against the arm of the couch. Adam's living room is cozy, with a cheerfully faded woven rug and green sofas that sink with your weight. It feels lived in, like time and love shaped the space.

"Here you go." He places a plate with *two* more brownies and a glass of milk next to me.

"Is this real, from-the-cow milk? Did you know or just guess that I'm a failure to milk-substitute Millennials everywhere?"

"I read the sticker on your Dunkin' order," Adam says, as if that's the most normal thing in the world. "I saw you take whole

126

milk in your coffee. If you don't want an entire glass of it, I can put it back."

"No, I… thank you." Out of all the things he's done, this one brings me the closest to tears. "Do you think the cows hate me? Because I haven't started milking almonds instead?"

"I'll let you in on a secret," Adam says, before plopping down in the middle of the couch, close enough to touch. He leans over to whisper in my ear, "I like whole milk too."

The warmth of his breath on my neck makes my scalp prickle.

"I feel so much better knowing we are both terrible representatives of our generation." I can't stop ogling his t-shirt and gray joggers. I turn towards the brownies to distract myself.

"So, what should we watch?" Adam grabs the remote from the living room table, as if the whole point of tonight was to watch a movie. Maybe this is some sort of team bonding?

I can't convince myself this isn't every bit as intimate as it feels.

"Superhero movie?" He flips through options on the giant flatscreen TV. The rug may be old, but this HD behemoth looks fresh out of the box.

"Nope, not my jam," I say with a wrinkle of my nose. "What about something spooky?"

"Hard no. I hate scary movies. I won't be able to go to the bathroom alone."

"What about reality TV? Now that I think of it, you *do* have a Jeff Probst dimples." I regret the words as soon as they fly out of my mouth. He smiles, bemused.

"Is that so? Please fill me in; who is Jeff Probst?"

"Oh my god! You don't know Jeff Probst?" I pretend to faint, draping myself over the couch arm. "He's only the best TV reality host of all time. Haven't you ever watched *Survivor*?" I avoid mentioning that Jeff Probst was my childhood crush.

"Nope, never."

I crane my neck to look at him from my draped position. "Did you even have a childhood? Do you know what *Survivor* is?"

"No, I only played with knives and hand grenades as a kid.

Of course I know what *Survivor* is, E." He rolls his eyes.

"You scared me for a second there. If you don't know a sex icon like J.P., what else has been kept hidden from you," I scoff.

"You think I look like a sex icon?" That stupid (amazing) dimpled grin transforms his face. *Oops.* The damn those joggers and Adam's proximity make it hard to form coherent thoughts.

I sit up, trying and failing to regain control of this conversation. "Well, I said *half* of a sex icon. You can pick which half."

"I'm too sexy for my shirt, too sexy for my shirt, so sexy it hurts." Adam shakes his shoulders, like a model on a runway. He looks so hilarious trying to be dainty, I laugh.

"Are you laughing at my swag?"

"No, I'm laughing at you being short one dimple."

I don't know why I do it, but I reach out and stick my finger in that beautiful indent.

He holds my hand to his face and grins. His voice dips dangerously low as he says, "Watch where you put your hands, Lizzie. Get too close, and I might not be able to resist taking a bite." Then he reaches around and tickles my ribcage. I snort *very* loudly, and then he's the one laughing.

"Okay… I admit it… your one dimple… is enough…" My head is fuzzy. Adam's leg is jammed against mine. I summon all my strength to retaliate. I move my hand that's touching the dimple to under his armpit and he lets out the most high-pitched squeal I've ever heard.

"You're in for it now." Adam puts one knee on the couch and aims for the armpits I've glued to my sides. He tries to protect his left flank but loses balance and, in a blink, Adam's on top of me. He catches himself on the couch back with one hand, the other resting next to my head so his full weight doesn't crush me. Each breath pushes my chest against his. The contact sends a shock through every part of me.

His laughter brushes against my lips and suddenly a thousand ideas have replaced tickling in my head.

"Oops." He says. But it doesn't sound like an oops, and he doesn't move. Adam hangs there, only an inch away. I prepare myself to feel the press of his body against mine. Instead, he forces himself upright, like he's doing a pushup, and returns to seated. He laughs and smooths his shirt. If I had my doubts before, I now know for sure that manifesting is bullcrap.

"I think I won that round." I say, breathless.

"I am not too proud to admit defeat in a tickle fight."

"So it's true what they say, chivalry is not dead." I push the fly aways from my face, trying to make myself look in control even if I don't feel it.

"It's a lot easier to concede when I have that sex icon comment to use against you for the rest of time."

"Ughhhh." I shove my red face in my hands. The central air kicks on. The vent is right above me, and despite my overheated body, I shiver.

"Is it okay if I sit closer?" He asks. He's my work colleague. He's leaving. And I know the closer we get, the more this will hurt me. But I am so tired of being responsible, calculated, pre-planned. I want to prove to myself I'm kind of person who can have fun. The kind of person who can live in the now.

While these thoughts tip imaginary scales in my head, Adam takes my silence as a refusal. "No pressure, you just looked chilly. I can grab a blanket instead."

"Wait. Yes. If you promise a truce." I stick out my hand. He smiles and we shake, then he moves so our legs and upper arms are touching. His body sags the couch cushion, keeping me glued to him. I let myself sink.

I sneak a look at his face to decode any message I'm missing but Adam flips slowly through the options, like it's normal that parts of us are touching. Maybe this is how he acts with his friends. I try to imagine him and his buddies cuddled up after a tickle fight and grin.

"Are you making that face because I lingered too long on *Lés Miserables?*"

"Are you kidding? If you picked *Les Mis*, I'd be doing a jig. I love musicals."

"Me too."

"*Really?*" I never would have pinned Adam for a musical man.

"Don't look so surprised. I may not be able to sing but who

can resist a musical number? I've got good taste."

"If that's a chef pun, I'm proud of you." I beam and pat his leg. His lips tug upward and a bolt of heat flashes across his eyes. It takes a beat before I realize my hand's settled on top of his thigh.

"Oh, sorry, I…" I go to remove it, but he gently places a hand over mine.

"It's okay. It doesn't bother me." Adam looks down at our hands, then back up at me. His eyes are gray tonight and full of questions that I am too afraid to answer. "Does it bother you?" He asks.

"No," I whisper. It should; the potential for disaster should bother me a lot. But all I can think about is Adam sneaking glances at my coffee order and singing my praises to Nella and braving bees to spend time with me. I've never been someone who can ignore consequences. But with Adam, it is so frighteningly easy for my mind to say *fuck it*. I already know I am going to lose him, so why not enjoy my time with him while he's here? The scale tips decidedly in his favor, and just like that I am in this, whatever *this* is.

"Good." Adam resumes the movie search and we decide on *Chicago,* something we've both seen a boatload of times.

Adam leaves to make a bowl of popcorn. When he comes back, he splays his fingers across my bare thigh and squeezes once. I lean into him, absorbing his warmth while the central air skitters across my skin.

"Relax, Lizzie." He turns just slightly and lightly rests his chin on my head until I let my neck fall onto his shoulder.

"You smell nice," he mumbles into my hair. Then he rests the side of his head against mine. And Adam may be leaving but *oh*, this moment is too comfortable, too perfect to give up.

I'm no chef, but I know this is a recipe for disaster.

15

Mom is famous for attributing all good things to "the winds of change." The winds of change get credit for the old crotchety neighbors moving away to Arizona, for the tourists going back to the city in the fall, and for ushering in the spring flowers. I wouldn't be surprised if Mom told me the winds of change whispered the winning Keno numbers in her ear.

If the winds are to be believed, then today promises to be extra lucky. It's a gusty Cape Cod day, the sun covering me in sweat before the breeze sweeps in to gives me chills. I watch the trees outside the greenhouse shake while drafting a list of flowers I'll need for the wedding. After we see the venue for the first time next week, I'll finalize my list.

I peel hair off my sticky face when my phone buzzes with a text from Adam. My heart plays hopscotch.

Adam: Hey, see you tomorrow for game night?

Lizzie: Sounds good. I hope you managed to get that kernel out of your molar.

After resting my head on Adam's shoulder, it only took forty minutes of *Chicago* to lull me asleep. I woke in the wee hours to the Netflix homepage, curled even deeper into Adam's side. Which would have been embarrassing had he not also been sound asleep. I feel slightly guilty about sneaking out, although I did make sure to text that I made it safely.

Adam: Sure did. Did you know you snore like a faerie?

Lizzie: A. I do not. B. Do faeries snore?

Adam: They must.

Adam: It's like you're expelling a little whoosh of air

with each breath. Kind of dramatic. Kind of hot.

I turn scarlet. I imagine what Jessie would say. She'd probably tell me my role as the solitary single friend is to have fun, carefree hookups. Maybe I can't be carefree, but I can enjoy a good thing while it's right in front of me, can't I? Even as I think it, my eyelid twitches.

Zed wanders over to interrupt my revelry, and I do a double take. Which confirms that he is indeed wearing sweatpants-looking overalls paired with rainbow Crocs.

"Morning', star shine," he says.

"Zed, what are those things?"

"Oh, this little number?" He sticks a leg out to model the outfit. Did I mention that the overalls are shorts? "These are my new OverSwolls."

My blank look must indicate that I know not what Overswoll means, because he continues.

"Overall-sweatpants. They're awesome. Comfort and function, all in one!"

"They sure are… something."

"They were a Kickstarter. I got in early!"

I've got to admit, they look extremely comfortable.

"Wowza, these came out great." Zed beams down at the arrangements I'm putting together. I like to make full samples of each bouquet, so I know exactly how many flowers are required. Each one is bursting with summer color and looks a thousand times better than when I first started practicing. I smile at Zed, who glows back at me.

"You've really improved, kid." He puts a hand on my back like I've hit the T-ball team's winning run. "I'm proud of you. If this wedding takes off, you'll have brides and grooms lining up to tap into your floristry prowess. Maybe we can discuss building out the back area so you have more room to work."

I flush, a warm fullness settling in my chest. It sounds like a small thing, but this greenhouse is Zed's baby. Modifying any inch of this place is like pulling teeth. For him to suggest we carve out a piece that's mine feels like sun breaking through endless winter.

"I'd like that. If this wedding goes well, of course."

"It will. I have no doubt. Maybe you could even figure out a longer term arrangement with that food fella," Zed winks. Like the floor below me has fallen a few inches, my stomach drops. *Adam's leaving* plays on repeat in my head.

"I don't think that'll be possible. This wedding will be a big deal for him, too. It's his ticket out of here and onto bigger things."

"Oh is that so? I was starting to like that donut delivery. Anywho, I'll be in the office if you need me." I chide myself for my stinging eyes. Adam isn't my boyfriend. He isn't *my* anything. I pluck out a couple flowers and shuffle them around just to have something to do.

Zed's kind of the best at giving people space. He pats my shoulder once, then heads towards his office, leaving me sitting in the middle of my flower arrangements, my brain flitting between two thoughts; 1. how to convince Adam I am totally chill stepping out of the friend zone followed directly by 2. why that is a terrible idea.

To escape this loop, I switch modes and focus on my biggest task of the day; the flower baskets we need to assemble for a one-year-old's birthday party (for the record, I don't believe the one year old will be impressed, but Zed says its for the parents to celebrate keeping a child alive for a whole year).

As my shift is wrapping up, I turn to find Clara testing a Venus flytrap with a piece of her own hair. She's wearing platform sandals and a spectacularly bright pink bodysuit, her belly displayed proudly like a spandex beach ball. I'd forgotten we'd picked today to buy favors for her baby shower. Despite Clara's non-traditional theme, her mom's insisted everyone take something "nice and appropriate" home on her dime.

"Hi!"

Clara stops trying to make the trap close and turns to me. She looks so vibrant. I take my own hair out of the elastic and re-do my crooked bun so it's closer to the middle of my head.

"Hi. These things are cool! Are you prepared for a torturous day?"

"I see you have a very positive outlook going into this," I tease.

"As a product of non-traditional conception, I think I should be exempt from the traditional baby path myself," she grumbles.

Clara's mother decided to have a baby on her own when she was thirty-four, which seems pretty badass.

"Who's to say what traditional conception looks like?"

Clara gestures to her stomach. "Well, I can draw you some diagrams of how this happened that match up pretty neatly with health class..."

"Okay, point taken," I raise a hand. "Regardless, your mom wants to do something nice for you," I add. "I'm sure it's exciting for her too, having her first grandbaby."

"Yeah, yeah." Clara waves a hand, brushing the idea away and almost grazes one of the carnivorous plants in the process.

"Careful!"

"What if we give out these vicious plants as favors instead?" Her eyes sparkle.

"Call me crazy, but I think the guests will prefer the original plan. Homemade soaps perform better with grandmas than killer plants."

I'm rewarded with a sigh.

"If my mother tries to measure my stomach with a string, she's dead. And she better still dress up. This is *my* costume party to derail. Come on, let's do this."

By the time we reach Scentsational, it has become apparent that the way people look at you while you're pregnant is my actual nightmare. Clara shares horror stories of strangers touching her stomach that make me want to scream "hands off" every time someone approaches.

"It's wild how people think they have a right to your body, doing things they'd think were totally inappropriate to do to people who *aren't* pregnant. When is the last time someone reached out and put a hand on your belly? In public, no less. It's disgusting." Clara scrunches her nose.

"That is so disturbing."

"Being pregnant has turned me into a member of society everyone thinks they have access to. All these people who had a baby thirty years ago can't stop word-vomiting advice to me.

Some lady on the street stopped me to tell me how my baby will have weak teeth if I don't breast feed. It's nuts."

The bell above the shop doors announces our entrance, and we're surrounded by the clean, soft scent of soap and candles. Because everything's made from natural products and soy, the effect is more garden than perfume.

The woman at the front desk, Ginny, introduces herself as the owner.

"What brings you in today?"

Clara, who is still grumpy about the shower and all the belly touching (who can blame her?) points to her stomach. Ginny is very clearly confused, so I take it as a cue to step in and explain.

"Hi! We'd love to buy some products as favors for a baby shower. Preferably something floral to match the theme. Maybe lavender? We're open to options!"

"Gotchya, let me show you a few of our samples and give you my spiel."

Ginny proceeds to tell us about her 100% organic, cruelty-free products. Every candle, bar and liquid soap, and hand cream is made with local ingredients.

"My grandmother taught me how to make soap when I was a little girl. Of course, I didn't get into it until my classmates and I took a trip to Plymouth Village. Once all the other kids thought churning butter and making soap was cool, I was all in. I've never seen Nan so excited as when she realized my disillusioned teenage self *cared* about her old-school hobbies."

"Anyway, she taught me to make candles when I was a teenager and I sold them in college. Everyone in my family has some high-powered job, but after my Nan died all I could think about was sharing something I loved so other people might love it, too. And that's how this all came to be." She lifts her arms, showcasing the store around her.

"That's amazing."

"It is, right? It was hard to go the non-traditional route. But somehow easy at the same time. None of my family understands, but I know Nan would have loved this place." Ginny's soft smile makes it clear this where she belongs. She's living the soft-scented, entrepreneurial dream.

"This place looks incredible, like you've put your whole soul into it."

Her personal style is evident in the curated displays, the bright pink area rugs and the variety of framed rainbow art that covers an entire wall.

Ginny smiles and nods. "I want to love what I do. A big part of that for me is making sure what's happening outside of my brain matches up with my internal dreams."

"It must have been hard without a background in business. I think that's so badass. I heard about you from a friend. Don't worry, you totally live up to the hype." Clara smiles, her mood turned around after rubbing her hands with a year's worth of buttery, lightly scented creams.

"I want people to take home something that has a piece of me in it.

"It was hard. But there's so much support out there. I met a small business group on Reddit and the community of entrepreneurs have been more supportive than I've ever imagined. It's the 'rising tide raises all ships' mentality. Everyone wants to help each other. But enough about me, I'm sure you have plenty to do today. Let me show you our packaging options." Ginny leads Clara to the front to look at the gift wrapping options for the lemon verbena candles she's selected while I whirl the spinning rack of cards made by local artists. The idea of going solo scares the ever-loving shit out of me, but there's an electrical thrum lighting up my veins when I think of embarking on this type of adventure. The planning and checklists and time and determination that all ends with a physical manifestation of your dream. How you'd have to fully rely on yourself to make decisions and your community to support you. I respect Ginny being able to block out the doubts and I am also superbly envious.

"Lizzie, you good?" Clara saunters over, looking ready to star in an 80s workout video.

"All good here. I love this place."

"Yeah, this place fucking rocks." Clara makes a rock and roll hand gesture.

"You are so perfectly weird," I laugh.

"Hey, consider yourself lucky I didn't flip the bird or flash the shocker."

I shake my head, but it's nice to see her excited.

"Okay ladies! You're all set." Ginny materializes behind us, brandishing business cards. "If you need anything in the meantime, let me know!"

"Thanks. We'll see you then!"

Clara chirps brightly about hand soap on our stroll back to the car.

"Isn't Ginny awesome?"

That sense of longing I've felt since meeting Adam bubbles up, threatening to spill out. I guess it extends beyond my relationship with him.

"Yes, she really is. She's built something incredible." I wish I could do the same.

16

I wait outside of Adam's front door, sweating more than the fruit salad I'm holding. When Adam originally invited me over for game night, Clara and I were too busy giggling in her car for me to pay attention. She demanded I reply yes immediately, or she'd pull over (her exact words being "if you don't tell that big boy that you're down to play *any time*, I will make you walk home"), so I replied **okay** before his second text came through. That text explained that game night is a weekly tradition that rotates between his friend's homes, and I should be prepared for a level of competition that makes Wimbledon look tame.

I glance down at the perspiring watermelon, strawberries, and pineapple and take a deep breath. I tell myself it won't matter once Adam's gone, but the truth is, I want his friends to like me.

Muffled laughter filters through the wooden door. When it swings open, there is a very built, tattooed man standing in front of me. He smiles at me and the corners of his eyes crinkle.

"You must be Lizzie," the large man says in a deep rumble. "We were just giving Adam shit. Thought you might not exist. But here you are in the flesh!"

"Yup, that's me. At your service."

He grins and opens the door wider to let me pass. "Name's Brett. Nice to meet you."

"Nice to meet you, too. You own a barbershop, right?" I remember Adam mentioning Brett the last time he got his hair cut.

Brett smiles wide enough to crack his face. "That I do, that

I do. Pride and joy of my life."

"Nice! Adam says he will trust no one else with his hair. It's an honor to meet the prince of shears." I feign a bow.

"Got to keep him looking fresh for his new company." Brett winks, and I try not to blush. Does he know that Adam's new haircut made me want to crawl into his lap and pet his head? Among other things.

"Have you ever played Catan before?" He asks as I take off my shoes.

"A few times. My friends aren't game people. Well, I guess we are but my best friend doesn't care about winning while I have a hard time controlling my… enthusiasm."

Brett nods, "Competitive will fit right in around here."

"So I've heard."

We walk down the hall, towards sounds of light arguing and more laughs. "Game nights are sacred. Adam must really like you." Brett's words make my stomach dip. "Maybe you're the chosen one who can finally kick his ass."

"I will try my absolute best," I promise as we make our way to the dining room.

"I heard that!" Adam shouts down the hall. In the kitchen, Tame Impala plays on the speakers. A petite redhead mills about the island munching on bites of a charcuterie board and what look to be homemade appetizers. Adam is sitting at the table, finishing the board game set up. He gets up to greet me, but before he can, the short woman springs into action.

"Lizzie, hi!" She places her cracker on a napkin and turns to give me a big smile and an even bigger hug. "I'm Geraldine. It's so nice to meet you! I've heard so much about you. Wow, your hair smells nice. I'm so glad you're finally here!" She gives me a squeeze and lets go. I feel like I've just been caught up in a small tornado and am immediately endeared to Geraldine.

"I'm happy to be here, and to meet you. I hope I can hold my own at game night." I want to stop smiling, but I'm finding it hard not to be swept up by her enthusiasm.

Geraldine nods aggressively and pushes some plates around to make space for my fruit bowl on the counter.

"I told the boys we should do something that doesn't

involve god complexes and destroying each other's egos, but they never listen. We'll just have to crush them." She takes the bowl from me and pops the last bite of cracker in her mouth.

"Who are we crushing?" Brett wanders over to load up a plate of snacks.

"You. Adam. Pitt, if he ever gets here. Lizzie, do you like sesame? It's not usually my thing but ohmygod you have to try these crackers, they are my absolute favorite with this peach jelly."

"Sounds delightful." Geraldine proceeds to slather a cracker with jam.

Before she can hand it to me, I feel a light squeeze of my elbow. "Hey, thanks for coming. I see you've met some of your competition." I turn my head to find Adam beaming down at me, my skin tingling where he continues to hold onto me. I wonder if he even realizes he's doing it, or if the magnetism that makes me want him as close as physically possible affects him, too.

"Wouldn't miss it." If only I could stop blushing. Hopefully Geraldine and Brett won't notice.

Adam leans forward and bends towards my ear, and for one breathless second, I think he's going to kiss my face. I am flustered and disappointed when he sets a wooden spoon next to the fruit bowl instead.

"Grab some food and we'll go through a refresher of the rules before Pitt gets here," he says.

"But we didn't even get to chat!" Geraldine frowns.

"I promise to make this first game quick and decently painless, so there'll be plenty of time to chat after." The fire of competition sparks in Adam's eyes and it's clear he intends to destroy us all.

Geraldine sticks out her tongue. "Good luck with that, after last week's sheep port disaster." She laughs at Adam's frown and hands me a plate I didn't notice she was filling, laden with a bit of everything.

"Aw, thanks. You didn't have to do that."

"Consider it fuel for the battle ahead. Study up, because this one," she jerks her thumb at Adam, "needs a big slice of humble pie. You serving it to him would be the cherry on top."

I nod eagerly; I want to claim victory just as much as everyone else. "So, you've played Catan before, I hear?" Adam asks as we walk to the table.

He looks me up and down, sizing up his competition. Adam's usually one-hundred percent supportive, which makes him a great colleague. But I find this competitive side of him kind of... hot. I like how it draws out my own thirst for victory, a part of me I feel the need to suppress when I play games with my friends or Mom.

"Yes, just a few times. I've never played... oceans? Or whatever this version is." I gesture down at the blue tiles around and between the land hexes. He leans his elbows on the table, so his face is close to the game. I saddle up to his side and do the same. If I turn to the right, we'll be nose to nose. But I ignore the urge to pop the bubble between us and turn to the game.

"This is the expansion. If you already know the game, then there are only a few additional things to learn. Don't worry, I'm a good teacher." He turns towards me, gray-blue eyes and five o'clock shadow inches from my face, and smiles. When he gently bumps my right hip with his left, I remind myself that there are other people around; daydreaming about him throwing me onto this table may be frowned upon.

"What's this thing?" I rip my eyes away, picking up a piece at random just so my fingers won't get any ideas about grabbing him.

"That's the pirate." He plucks a gray piece from the desert hex on the board and holds it up. "You know what the robber is?"

I nod.

"This is basically the equivalent on the water. You can move this instead of the robber and steal from a hex next to it. And it blocks ships from being built."

"Ships?" Adam pauses and reaches towards my face. His callused fingers tuck a strand of hair that's flown free back behind my ear, then stroke down my neck. His stare slides down to my collarbones and lower, towards my racing heart. Maybe he isn't just sizing up his competition, after all. Adam clears his throat, then turns back to the game.

"You can build them to access other islands. They count towards your longest road. "Now, let's talk conquest." His face splits into a wicked grin.

Sometime during Adam's game explanation, Pitt shows up and the rest of the group chooses seats. Once I've got a grasp on the unfamiliar components, we get started.

"Don't let Adam sweet talk you into any crazy trades," Geraldine warns.

"Geraldine, if anyone knows how to leverage a sheep at this table, it's you."

Pitt sighs. "She had a sheep monopoly last game. Took me for all the ore in my hand at one point. One day I'll win, I swear."

"Not with the shit position of your starting settlements." Brett grins, and places his second settlement. "Let the games begin."

We play two games. I lose the first by one point. Adam wins and is so gloatingly gleeful that everyone sabotages his second game, all but refusing to trade. Even with the embargo he's a relatively good sport.

I find my own competitive nature ignite, a muscle that hasn't been flexed in too long. Although I'm upset I don't win, it's awesome to watch Geraldine scream "suck it, boys!" when she builds the longest road to clinch victory in game two.

We finally wrap up around ten o'clock, when everyone starts to yawn. Pitt leaves first, citing an early wakeup.

"He's always the first of us to jet. I think he misses his dogs when he's away from them. He'd never admit to that, though." Geraldine rolls her eyes. "Brett, you ready to roll?"

Brett hands her a Tupperware of leftovers and keeps one for himself. "Yup, let's get going. It was awesome to meet you, Lizzie. Text me about that class."

Turns out Brett's running a marketing course for small businesses. I think about how great it would be to have more know-how to advertise my floral services. I mean, *Zed's* floral services.

This wedding is the key to our mutual success, and I so badly want to crush this for both of us. But the more people I meet who are passionate about their businesses, brands, livelihoods… it's hard not to envy that drive, the joy that entrepreneurialism seems to give them. I put a pin in the unease, deciding to focus on what I've got in front of me and worry about the rest later. That seems to be applicable in many areas of my life lately.

"Sure thing. It sounds great."

Brett gives me a brisk hug before Geraldine elbows him out and wraps me up. "Can't wait for next time at our place. I promise you'll be more impressed with my performance if we play a word game. They never want to play Scrabble."

"Last time we played Scrabble, Pitt tried to play the word "chub" and argued it was the full version of a half chub," Adam laughs.

Brett snorts. "To be fair, the dictionary confirmed that chub *is* a word. It's apparently a 'thick-bodied' fish. But should he get points without knowing the actual meaning of the word? I lean no."

"Okay, the chub argument is our cue. Bye!" Geraldine waves. Adam and I wave back from the doorway as the pair walks to the car, still arguing about the validity of playing a Scrabble word without knowing its meaning.

Adam latches the door and turns to face me. He leans against the frame and I lean against the opposite wall, facing off across the hallway. "So. Those are my friends."

"They're super nice. And easy to be yourself around," I offer.

"They're ridiculous," Adam says but I watch my approval soften him.

"That's why I like them. It's fun to watch them tease you. It helps me understand you better."

"It does?"

"Yeah, when we first met you were always joking. I thought you were teasing me, but I now know that's the highest form of flattery." I try to act like his teasing didn't affect me. That it didn't matter what he thought of me. But he must see through it, because his gaze intensifies before he continues. "I'm sorry if I made you uncomfortable. I wanted you to be my friend from the second I met you."

"Hm, is that so?" The word *friend* flashes like a neon sign. I guess that's what we are. Friends come over for game night. Friends cook homemade apology brownies. Friends text every day. Right?

"Not entirely." Adam shrugs, then pushes off the door and steps towards me. He closes the space between us, stopping a foot away. My heart gallops, every atom in me screaming to lean forward, to touch him. Instead, I arch my neck to keep eye contact. He blocks the overhead light, casting me in shadow and looks at me like I'm something he's planning to devour.

"What I really wanted," Adam says in little more than a whisper, "was to ask you out. Make you dinner."

"Too bad we ended up being work colleagues instead." I shrug, like I'm not affected when, in reality, every second we spend this close threatens to unravel me.

"Yeah. Too bad. Now I have to spend all this time with the most beautiful woman I've ever met. I have to watch her drool over the food I make." He closes the final step so that he's flush against me. His hands slide down my ribs, then settle on my hips. My skin turns molten under his touch.

"I don't drool," I whisper, even though I might currently be drooling on the carpet.

"Mm, I think you do. I think I make you very hungry." His voice is low, a caress and a promise. He brushes his nose against mine.

"I'm starving for you, Lizzie." His lips hover just above mine, as his hands snake around to grab my ass. He stays just like that, breathing quickly. I am a live wire, tingling from toes to fingertips with want. His hands are warm and firm on me, and I'm wrapped up in the fresh scent and essence of him.

I am not a risk taker, never have been. But a girl's only got so much control before she snaps. I push up on my tiptoes and wrap my hands around the back of his neck.

When our lips meet, nothing else exists. I thought our first kiss would spur panic, send me running. But all I want is to be *closer.* The first few seconds of kissing are polite, like we're both giving each other time to pull away. But after a breath, there is nothing chaste about the way I open for him. I let his tongue explore me in a way that turns my body pliant and willing.

He breaks away to nip at my bottom lip and trace wet, hot kisses along my jaw. He grabs me tighter, squeezing my ass as he picks me up and presses me against the wall.

"Lizzie, you are so fucking hot," he says, pushing between my legs so his hips have me pinned before his mouth is back on me. I sigh as he kisses my collarbone and bites my shoulder. I pull at his hair and listen to the indecent noises he draws out of me.

I know with complete certainty that I can never go back to being just friends, or whatever we were pretending to be before this.

When I tell him "I want you," it sounds like a plea.

Adam pulls back, hands still cradling me. The vent above us turns on and a shower of cold air washes over my flushed self. He rubs my arm then nuzzles my cheek, a contrast to every hard inch of him pressed up against me.

"Want to stargaze? I have an amazing hammock." His voice is honey, sweet and dripping with desire. I'm coated in it.

"Who can say no to that?" I sound as breathless as I feel.

"Not sure, I've never asked anyone before," he teases.

"Well in that case, I'll happily be your first." Without thinking about it, I bite his nose. He lets out a gruff breath, shakes his head and then rests his forehead against mine.

"Sometimes it's hard to believe you exist, E. You are so mind-blowingly perfect."

His confession mends some part of me that I hadn't realized was broken.

"Come on." Instead of putting me down, he lifts me up higher, so I'm above his hips.

"What are you doing?"

"If you think I'm letting go of you, you're out of your mind." He proceeds to carry me down the hall, then he hesitates. He stops in the kitchen and perches me on the island, suddenly serious. The cold countertop replaces his hands. "Unless you want this to stop here. I understand if this isn't what you want." He looks down at me, hands on either side of my thighs. He's giving me the choice, and I know we are equal partners in this decision. His eyes are dark beneath full lashes from this angle.

"Adam. The only feeling that could rival beating you at Catan is *this*. And since I didn't get to experience a board game victory tonight, I will accept a consolation prize."

His grin is wicked when he picks me up, but he carries me like I'm the most precious thing he's ever laid hands on. When we get to the sliding glass door, I open it with my foot.

"Nice work. Have I ever told you how talented you are?" He kisses my head as he carries me outside, and I lean into his warmth. Adam places me gently in the hammock, then climbs in himself. His weight pulls me in, and I let myself fall into him as the night sky sparkles above us.

17

I blink my eyes open, expecting panic but finding only peace. The fan oscillates, mimicking the soft night breeze. It reminds me of Adam's fingers weaving through my hair. I half expected to fall asleep outside, until a distant clap of thunder and smell of petrichor sent us scrambling inside.

I've never spent the night with anyone I work with, which is not so much a rule as the result of working with finance bros who I found impossible to communicate, never mind flirt, with.

I roll away from the sunlight filtering through the fan-tousled curtains, and turn to face Adam. He's still sleeping, mouth open a smidge. His breath is soft, a tiny engine whistle. It is utterly adorable and the fact that my first instinct is to kiss his nose does make me just a tinge nervous.

Is kissing each other okay now?

I expect to feel worried that I've botched this whole working relationship. But I just feel relieved, like a storm has broken.

As if he hears the intensity of my thoughts, Adam blinks open sleepy eyes. His mouth shifts into a lazy smile.

"Good morning," he mumbles, reaching. He grabs me and pulls until I'm tucked under his chin, hands pressed up against his bare chest. His body is warm against my fingertips and I flush with an ethereal desire to hold onto this, to him.

"Morning. Don't let this go to your head, but you're kind of an adorable sleeper." I whisper softly into his skin. I'm afraid to move too quickly or speak too loudly, afraid to break whatever is between us that feels delicate as glass.

"Oh, E." He nuzzles into my hair. "I'm always adorable. More sleep and then pancakes." My hair muffles his voice.

"You're going to promise me pancakes and then fall back asleep? That is cruel and unusual punishment."

"The chef makes the hours." He closes his eyes and continues to hold me. I could wiggle away, could get out of bed and slip on my jeans and make a *see you at the office* joke. I know that's probably the sane thing to do, since this absolutely cannot become *a thing*. Adam is *leaving*, I remind myself. But I don't move—I'm etching this scene into a corner of my mind where it will stay safe. Even if everything comes crashing down, I'll have a memory of golden sunlight, a whirring fan, warm skin, and this blooming hope in my chest. I don't need forever, as long as I have right now.

Lured by the calm, I must doze off again, because when I wake up, the house is filled with the smell of butter. The bed next to me is empty and I hear Adam singing along to the Blues in the kitchen. It reminds me of Saturday mornings with my mom and brother when I was a kid (although Mom's pancakes come out burnt half the time). It's like the current moment is already becoming nostalgia, the future refusing to slow down. I try not to think about anything that will happen beyond stuffing my face with sweet, delicious carbs.

The stairs don't creak on the way down, so I'm able to stealth-sneak into the kitchen. Adam's at the stove, in his element. He's mumbling along to the music and flipping bacon that's sizzling in a pan. His black t-shirt's accidentally inside out. My heart gives a little squeeze.

"Morning," I say, voice drowsy. When Adam turns around, he's already smiling. "Why, hello there sunshine. I've made your pancakes, as promised." He gestures with the spatula. "Now sit down and eat."

"But you're still cooking?"

He blushes a bit. "Sorry, I ate one already. Wasn't sure when you'd be up. Plus, you've got to try them while they're hot."

He slides a pancake from pan to plate and plops another slab of butter on top. Apparently, butter is supposed to be 50% of a pancake's total weight.

I smother it in grade-A amber maple syrup and take a bite. "How'd I do?"

"How is it possible that the edges are so crispy but the inside is fluffy?" I proceed to fork three pieces and cram them all into my mouth at the same time. It takes willpower not to moan. The batter's made from scratch (of course). I would have opted for the good old add-one-egg boxed stuff, but the real deal is impossibly better.

Adam watches me scarf down several bites while he tries to keep his pancake production on par with my insatiable hunger. I guess I did forget to eat last night.

"It's like eating a toasty butter cloud," I say, mouth jam-packed with pancake. I lick some syrup off my lips.

Adam flips three more cakes then comes to join me. I grab my stomach.

"Ugh I think I'm going to go into a food coma." I groan. "But please, do not let that discourage you from making me pancakes on any and every occasion. Like, for my birthday, you could just wrap a short stack in a box and let me go to town."

Adam stabs at a piece on his own plate and laughs. "You know," he says while syrup drips off the golden morsel and lands dangerously close to the edge of his plate, "there can be other pancake mornings." He offers this up gently, like a baby bird in the palm of his hand. My heart bangs around my chest.

"Is that so?"

"Mhm."

I fiddle with my cuticles and take a deep breath. "Question for you."

"If this is a marry, bang, kill situation I promise I am underprepared, no matter who the options are."

"First of all, let's be adults about it. The game is called 'fuck, marry, kill.'" I take a swig of water. It feels like the heat got turned up a few degrees. I wonder idly if I'm having a premature hot flash. "And no, it's a much simpler question than that. Although now that I know you fear the game, I'm going to draw up some truly diabolical scenarios."

"I am shaking in my boots." He pretends to quiver in his slippers.

"No, I was going to ask if you'd like to be my date to Clara's baby shower. It's not your typical baby shower it's like… a party. And since she met you and knows we're… friends… she's made me promise to invite you. It's the week after the wedding." I don't add that Clara asked that Adam show up shirtless as part of her baby shower present.

"I totally understand if you already have plans. I know it's soon, I didn't know if you were even interested, and I didn't want to put you in a weird situation…" I ramble.

Adam lays down his fork and spins his barstool towards me so that my body is in between his legs. He reaches for my hands and I let him. He holds them between us. The air conditioner absolutely *has* to be broken because I am on the verge of overheating.

"I would love to." He looks straight into my eyes and smiles, then kisses one of my palms, which makes my insides feel a lot like pancake batter.

"Promise? Not in an obligatory way?"

"Promise. Spending time with you has never been an obligation. I do have a favor to ask in return, though."

"If you are asking me to cook any meal for you, I would rather bury myself alive in the loam pile. I once burned a can of beans."

"How is it possible to burn pre-cooked food in a can?"

"I was camping. I got distracted by ladder ball and may or may not have left the beans over the fire for approximately seventy minutes," I say. "When I came back, they were more like the essence of bean."

He smirks. "Well, did you at least win at ladder ball?"

"Of course I did. Everyone was doubly pissed that we didn't have beans for burritos *and* Jessie and I maintained our lifelong winning streak."

Lionel hadn't come on that trip. He'd been too busy recording a demo. He never wanted to go out of town with my friends.

"The favor I am asking does not include beans. It's much more in your wheelhouse. I mow Nella's lawn and I noticed she wasn't planting her window boxes or the garden in her yard. I know she's having a hard time with her arthritis and… I thought maybe she could use some of your help. If you're willing"

"To be clear, you're trading in a favor for someone else. Even if it means you have to wear a costume and attend an organized event on your day off?"

"Guess I am. If you're lucky, maybe I'll even dig up a pair of suspenders and go full nerd," he says.

"Suspend her? I barely know her."

He groans.

"I swear that slipped out involuntarily. But honestly, if you've seen me naked, you have to deal with my puns," I say. Flashes of Adam's hand sliding up my thigh, his mouth on me, hearing him swear as I bit his neck flit through my mind… I put a stop to that train of thought before I become too flustered to function.

"That sounds like more than a fair trade." He shrugs. "Anyway, I like your puns." He tries to grab my plate, but I hop up before he gets a hand on it.

"I'm on dish duty!" If I have to watch this beautiful man cook *and* clean for me, I may implode. I don't know how much more romance I can take before I am fully, irrevocably fucked.

"You sure?"

"Lack of cooking prowess notwithstanding, I am excellent at loading a dishwasher." I snatch our plates and start cleaning up, happy to give my hands something to do while my mind races.

Adam cleans up the counter, putting the maple syrup back in the fridge. I swoon at how methodically he moves, how, when I glance over, I can see that every item has a place in his perfectly organized kitchen.

"So, anyone I know coming to the baby shindig?" He asks.

It makes it a lot easier to talk about Jessie when I'm facing the bright windows instead of the warm glow of his face.

"Yeah, my friend Jessie."

"Oh yeah, she and Clark seem great. They were super fun to hang with at the tasting."

"Mhm, they're great," I say, trying to muster enthusiasm I don't feel.

It dawns on me that I'll have to tell Jessie about Adam before Clara's shower. Even worse, I'll need to explain my recent estrangement from my best friend to Adam. Maybe inviting Adam to a real-life event outside of work was a mistake.

I rinse out the sink and turn off the water. The spiraling in my mind only stops when warm hands slip around my waist.

"Just so you know, I am a *very* good dancer," Adam says. He spins me around to face him. He bends to land a sweet kiss to my temple. His hands stay on my hips and I lean back into the sink, pulled out of the labyrinth of my thoughts.

"I don't doubt that. I've seen you balance a tray of crostini topped with cherry tomatoes while being bumped around by a hoard of hungry drunk people."

"Ah, so you do have a few slight memories of that wedding," he dimple-smiles and looks down at me. Sometimes I forget how tall he is.

"That was before the fruity drinks took me down. Maybe if you'd force-fed me crostini, they wouldn't have."

"When I saw you talking to your ex and his new girlfriend, I didn't have a tray of crostini to interrupt with. I had to improvise."

I cock my head to the side, not following. "What do you mean?"

I look into Adam's eyes and he runs a hand through his hair. "I just… you looked so uncomfortable when your friend with the big blonde hair ditched you with the couple." My brain flashes back to Camilla leaving me to face Lionel and Fayette solo. "And I wanted to help. To interrupt, give you some space to breathe. So I grabbed a tray and pretended to be a server."

Adam shrugs. "Anyway, I'm happy to know I made an impression before I turned into 'the hair tie guy.'"

"How did you know I called you that?" I swallow, my throat thick with words I want to say but won't. The fact that Adam cared about me before he even knew me does strange, fuzzy things to my heart.

"Right before you left with Clara you shouted at me. I believe your exact words were 'see you on the by and by, hair tie guy!' Impressive rhyming, honestly."

"What can I say, I'm a regular wordsmith."

"That's only one of the many things that drew me to you."

"Is that so?" I raise my eyebrows.

"Yes. You looked like you were determined to make the best of a difficult night. And then talking to you was… this is kind of embarrassing, but it was infectious." He glances at me, sheepish.

"Every girl dreams of being called infectious," I joke, even as his words spread warmth through me.

"You know what I mean. Talking to you feels like being pulled into a separate plane, one where only we exist. I'd gladly be trapped in that dimension with your puns forever."

I hold in a sigh. I am being thoroughly wooed, and my fragile heart soaks it in like rain in the desert. Alarm bells go off in my head; *Adam is leaving. This can't last.* The panic I expected to feel upon waking finally rears its head, causing words to fly from my silly, overprotective brain straight out of my mouth.

"Well, my puns and I will have to pay you a visit wherever you end up," I blurt, and watch him wince.

Maybe I've ruined the magic, but it had to be done now. Before things slip from the realm of "I like you and we slept together" into something deeper. Even if it makes my heart hurt.

Adam coughs. "Yes, I'd like that. Here, let me help you."

We both busy ourselves with the dishwasher. Even though I haven't dropped a plate, I can't help feeling like I've shattered something delicate.

18

We are making solid progress on the wedding, and our presentation is prepped for final approval by the bride. We've decided on layout, bouquet suggestions, and the majority of the menu. Lauren seems genuinely pleased when I speak to her on the phone, especially about using jars of honeys as favors.

"Adam passed me Bob's contact information and we are coming to an agreement. I appreciate the suggestion," she says. I'm still not sure thank you is in her vocabulary, but I'll take what I can get.

"The bride will sign off on everything when we meet Wednesday. She's been happy not being overly involved in the process, but I've learned that it's better to get bride's approval than have to deal with the repercussions later on." I hear the clack of heels in the background and imagine Lauren power-walking down some marble hallway.

Meanwhile, I perch the phone between my ear and shoulder while I pick a caterpillar off a bougainvillea. "I completely understand. I have the sample bouquets, altar flowers, and two ideas for centerpieces she can choose from. I'll touch base with Adam about giving her a mock-aup of the menu." That'll be easy, since he and I have been talking nonstop since that night at his house.

"Great. See you at the venue on Wednesday at eleven a.m."

"See you then."

Even with Lauren's mild enthusiasm, it's hard not to feel like things are looking up.

Several shipments come in during the week, and Wednesday

arrives in a flash. For the first time going into a meeting for this event, I feel confident. It helps that Adam suggests we carpool. I insist on driving, and we spend the morning drinking iced lattes and commenting on our mutual disdain of hot coffee.

"This is one New England stereotype I am willing to fully own. I wouldn't call myself a Masshole, but I do require my coffee iced in all seasons."

Adam snorts. "I think the other people on the road might disagree."

"What?"

"With the fact that you're not a Masshole. You literally cut like six people off during the first ten minutes," he says.

"It's not my fault they weren't merging correctly! Hasn't anyone head of the zipper merge?" I throw my hands up in the air in exasperation.

"E, it's okay. You are a very good driver. Much better than me." Adam pats my leg and lets his hand stay there. The weight of his large palm presses me into the seat and my stomach swirls.

We have agreed that under no circumstances are we going to reveal our newfound whatever-this-is to Lauren. In fact, I haven't mentioned our situationship to anyone besides Clara. I tell myself it's because I don't know how to talk about something temporary. And that's definitely part of it. But it also feels like if I talk about how happy Adam makes me out loud, it will come crashing down.

"GPS says we should be right around the corner." Adam pinches in on the little blue dot.

Perfectly manicured hedges line the right-hand side of the road for at least a couple of miles. The ocean must be hiding somewhere behind them. To the left is a McMansion with an unnecessarily long driveway.

"There could be giraffes hiding back there. The bushes are so tall we'd never even see them. Holy shit, do you think they have giraffes back there?!" I do an excited little wiggle in the seat. Adam seems to be as gob smacked by these houses as I am.

"Is this Taylor Swift's house? Are we secretly working for Taylor Swift?" He gapes.

"TSwift's house is in Rhode Island, duh."

He shrugs. "The Cape, Rhode Island. Same difference."

"I'm impressed by the fact that you even know she has a beach house. I didn't pin you for a pop culture buff but this makes me *very* excited for future trivia nights."

"Woah, woah, woah, I never agreed to trivia. I don't live under a rock. I have Instagram for my company." He shakes his head.

"Everyone loves bar trivia," I insist.

"It turns out that everyone," he points to himself, "does not."

"What! It's the best chance to dunk on the locals with your worldly knowledge."

"Yeah, but everyone expects me to answer sports questions. Because I'm a guy." He frowns slightly. His pouting makes me want to crawl onto his lap and kiss him. This no-touching, no over-smiling meeting is going to be torture.

"Ah, so you hate the sexist implications of trivia. That makes so much more sense," I say.

"Take a right here." Adam doesn't get a chance to refute my trivia jab because we pull up to a wrought iron gate that seems to have grown out of the hedges. It's straight out of a fairytale.

I pull up to a call box and press the button. The fisheye camera stares at us as we wait. The way it's trained on me makes me self-conscious. I play with a strand of hair loosened by the wind, tucking it behind my ear.

"Hello?" A male voice answers

"Hi! We're here with Clásico Catering and Green With Ivy Floral to meet with Everlast Weddings."

"One moment." The voice clicks away before returning. "Miss Bernard will meet you in the guesthouse."

The gates open with a slight clanging and whirring. I drive through and crunch up a driveway of white seashells.

"Jeez, talk about texture. I hope these don't mess up my tires."

"They're seashells E, not shards of glass." Adam chuckles. I laugh, too, releasing some of the excited energy wound tight in my chest.

A huge, freshly painted clapboard house rises to meet us. It is beautiful, but what gets me is the landscaping. The grass is the brightest shade of green. There are approximately a million hydrangea bushes and a serene fountain trickling in front of the main entrance, tucked into the middle of the circle. Alongside the seashell road that has me flustered, flowers burst through mulch.

Off to the right, I notice what was called the guesthouse, a building that is larger than the home I grew up in.

"Where's the carriage house, am-I-right?" I joke.

I meant it to be funny, but Adam points left. Tucked along the hedges is a building with open garage doors. Oh snap, there *is* a carriage house. The hoods of a Corvette and a car that looks like it came straight from the 1920s peek out. I finally understand why Lauren called this place an estate.

We pull up to the guest house and park out front. What I presume to be Lauren's car (a pristine, white BMW) is already there, but the rest of the driveway looks empty.

"Here we go." I take a deep breath to lower my heart rate. Maybe I shouldn't have had that second latte after all.

"Hey!" Adam taps my shoulder, capturing my attention before we leave the car. "You're a badass, E." He smiles and flashes me his dimple. He squeezes my shoulder, but it's not until I nod and say "okay," that he pulls the handle and leaves the car. I breathe a little easier.

Lauren greets us inside the door. She looks perfectly poised, as always, in her starchy dress pants and a white shirt.

"Miss Bernard is grabbing swatches from the bridesmaids' dresses, she'll be right down." We make small talk while I admire the living room, whose back wall is all windows. The decor is tasteful and sharp but also looks comfortable. Every window faces an expanse of ocean that borders the edge of the property, sparkling in the early morning sunlight. I want to sink into the couch cushions and spend the day starting out at the waves.

"Isn't that right, Lizzie?" Adam looks at me, reeling my attention back in.

"Yes! That's right." I need to do a better job of focusing, but the more I lean into the conversation the more I realize how crisp Lauren looks and how tall and imposing Adam is. I try not to think of what kind of first impression I'll give, standing alongside these two.

"Ah! There we are, Miss Bernard." Lauren turns before I do.

"Lauren, please no more of that Miss talk," the bride says as she enters the room.

Suddenly, I wish I was on one of the ships that spot the horizon like dots, sailing away from here. Or even fighting for my life in the cold New England waters. Because it's Fayette who's walking down the spiral staircase, looking every bit as glowing and radiant as when I first saw her sitting next to Lionel.

Her eyes pinch with confusion, until recognition dawns. Her cheeks bloom pink, but it's subtle enough that I doubt if Lauren or Adam even notice. I, on the other hand, feel all the blood in my body rush to my head.

Luckily, Fayette recovers for us both.

"Lizzie! What a pleasure! I didn't realize we'd have you on the team." She steps forward and kisses me on the cheek without hesitation. I try not to go rigor mortis under her touch. She smells nice, because of course she does.

"I didn't know your last name," I say stupidly, as if that's enough of an explanation for the situation we are in.

"Oui! Bernard."

"Although not for much longer!" Lauren chimes in overly chipper, clearly confused and alarmed. She's trying to salvage the conversation, and I wish her the best of luck, because the snowstorm of thoughts is drowning out my capacity for speech.

Adam is staring at me, head cocked to the side. The worry radiating off him tells me I look as awful as I feel.

"Could I use the restroom? Long drive." I try to make these words sound natural, but they come out like I'm pressing too hard on typewriter keys.

"Of course. It's down the hall." I give what I hope is a smile and walk away.

"Have you worked with Lizzie before?" Lauren asks.

Graciously, Faye responds, "Yes, I have." It's the last thing I hear before I lock the door and sink to the bathroom floor.

My mind leap-frogs. When Faye told me about her family

vacationing in the States, I assumed it was a week-long Airbnb rental. Or maybe a fancy hotel stay. Not an entire Kennedy-esque complex. I fight off hysterical laughter as panic sweeps in.

I am going to attend Lionel and Faye's fucking wedding. I'm going to watch my ex-boyfriend get married to someone else and, as a bonus, I have to help make this a *very special day* for the person who broke me in a thousand ways, many of which I only recently started to understand. Fuck, fuckity, fuck. I will not cry in this bathroom.

I hear a gentle patter on the door.

"E?" Adam asks softly.

"One minute."

"You don't have to rush. I just wanted to check on you. Are you okay?"

I pretend to flush the toilet and wash my hands, in case the rest of them are loitering. Then I open the door.

Adam stands stick straight, staring down at me. His eyes flash concern, with no ounce of judgment or worry about how this will affect his job. I know if I told him I had to leave now, he wouldn't even question it. He'd tell them we had to reschedule and probably take the fall for me, blaming it on a kitchen fire.

"Never better. Let's get back to it." I try to fake it and move past him. Adam moves aside, but gently holds my arm to stop me when I try to walk by. "They're outside. We can talk about it."

I feign indifference, assuming the attitude that never failed me in my previous job when someone doubted my abilities. This unaffected air was my armor in a male-dominated field, but I never thought I'd need it around Adam. "No. Let's go." I shake off his arm and his face falls. But he doesn't understand; I have to forge on. If I let myself feel the upset, I will crumple.

Lauren and Faye are on the patio. I didn't realize sliding glass doors were built into the endless windows. There's a table that's set with coffee mugs and a plate of pastries to munch on after we finish our tour of the grounds. I wonder if this is where Faye and Lionel eat breakfast together every morning. It occurs to me that I don't know what she does for work. Or if she works.

Or if Lionel works any more. I take a seat and smile my unaffected smile. Inside, the tide of overwhelm is rising and threatening to get drag me under.

Adam steps onto the patio.

"Alright, now that we've got everyone, let's cover the layout." Lauren gestures for us to follow her through the grass.

I've memorized the layout from the renderings Lauren provided. Every foot of the landscape is stunning. The tent will take up a majority of the back yard, on the grass. The ceremony will take place on the sand, with a full pathway of flowers leading down the wooden stairs and boardwalk to the archway on the beach.

I zone out for most of the tour, on autopilot but still managing to comment when appropriate. I keep as far away from Adam as possible. If he shows any concern about me, the small fissures in my composure will deepen, crack, and split me down the middle.

Adam gives the majority of our joint presentation, and I only speak to add information about herbs or flowers. I display the sample bouquets I've prepared, and Faye's gentle gasp tells me I've chosen well. Even Lauren looks impressed.

They taste the samples Adam brought. He watches their reactions intently, writing notes on their feedback and beaming when they tell praise his choices.

"This, it is perfect." Fayette smiles brightly at him after tasting a goat cheese, honey, and fig crostini. I know they're delicious, because I tried them myself when Adam prepped all the samples.

Somehow, I survive the encounter. After food, flowers, and polite conversation, we say our goodbyes and head back to the car.

"Damn, I forgot the sample book," Adam exclaims once we reach the vehicle.

"No worries, I'll grab it," I volunteer. I've been a zombie for most of the day, letting him handle questions and scheduling. Plus, I feel like I've put him in a terrible situation just by existing. Running to get a book is the least I can do. He makes to argue, but I hop out of the car before he gets a word in.

I walk around to the back patio rather than go through the house, doing my best to avoid Faye and Lauren. They'll probably see me through the gigantic windows, but at least I can fake a smile and a wave and peace the hell out of here. I grab the book and return to the hedges on the side of the house, on my way back to the car, when their voices carry to me on the wind. They must have just stepped back outside.

"You're sure there's no one else?" Faye's soft voice sounds heavy with concern.

"The wedding is a month away. I understand your concern, but I assure you, there won't be any unpleasantries." There is a slight tinge of panic in Lauren's usually unbreakable voice. It's merited, since I can't fathom where she'd find a new florist a month before the wedding.

"I just don't want it to be *awkward.*" Faye sounds worried, and I can't blame her. I wouldn't want my future husband's ex in charge of our wedding.

"What if she cannot handle it? She was acting kind of strange today." Her French accent makes the word *strange* sound even more offensive. I can picture it, everything I worked for crumbling down around me because I'm labeled the crazy ex. Maybe I'm powerless to stop my past from bleeding into my present and derailing my future. My throat constricts.

"If it is make or break, I can ask that she not attend the night of the event," Lauren concedes. She sounds exhausted, like she's reconsidering if the wedding industry is the right career path. I'm thinking the same thing myself.

"Oh, I don't know. Let me think about it." I can't see Faye, but I hear her frown. I shuffle back to the car as quickly as I can manage without running.

My hands shake. Adam is on his phone, distracted as he fires off some emails.

"Did you find it?" When he looks up, his brows knit. Like a reflex, he reaches for me. When I get close enough, he touches my left arm and searches my face. "Lizzie, what's wrong?"

If I can just make it into the car, I think, *everything will be alright.* "Nothing. Let's go." I hate how my voice wobbles.

"Okay, but can I please drive? You seem shaken up and…"

"Yeah, of course." I hand him the keys.

I hop in my Jeep's passenger's seat before he can ask any follow up questions.

Once we've rolled far enough away, I finally let myself cry. I don't want to show this weakness, but there's a wave that threatens to drown me if I don't let some of it out. Tears burn their way down my cheeks, hot even in the sun-baked air of the car.

Adam reaches for my hand. I pull away, place my hands in my lap and shake my head. This whole situation is so messed up, the last thing I want to do is drag Adam into it. Especially when his job could be at risk.

"Please, tell me what happened." Adam's voice is gentle, verging on pleading. He wants to be let in on whatever is happening.

"I don't want to make this your problem. I don't want to be your problem." I dig in my bag for a tissue and blow my nose.

"You're not a problem, E. You're my…" Adam pauses to figure out the best word to describe us. "My friend."

Another piece of my heart bruises; we are friends. I know that's all we can be, even if I yearn for more. I don't want to pull everyone around me backwards, to keep their lives from moving on. If Adam loses business because of this, I'll never forgive myself.

"I have to work the wedding of my ex-boyfriend, who I was still in love with less than a year ago." I sob into my hands. "I'm not going to let you go down with the ship." I can barely see him look at me sideways; the tears blur everything.

"You're not a sinking ship, Lizzie. This is just a super shitty situation you've been put in. You don't have to do this alone." Adam's voice is so gentle. He doesn't understand. I've dealt with my own feelings on my own for so long, I'm not sure how to let someone help.

"Signing up to work this wedding is the worst thing that possibly could have happened to me. I should have stayed in Boston. What am I even doing here? I live with my mom. I don't even use my degree. All of my friends are doing shit with their lives, and I'm just floating here."

I let my head sink into my hands. I wish Adam wasn't witnessing my breakdown. I wish I wasn't living in a big, dark ballpit of sadness. I wish I was far away from everyone right now, somewhere I could wallow in peace.

"Hey." He rests a hand on my shoulder. It is warm and kind. I don't want it. I want to dissipate into the clouds.

"Can I make you dinner? I can make soup. We can watch a movie." The pleading in his voice begs me to let him fix the sadness. And I want to say yes. I want to let him hold me and feed me and mend my broken self. But I can't do it. Adam's life is full of potential and I would only hold him back.

"I think I need to be alone for a while." My voice comes out flat, deflated, empty. Like the void that I feel inside myself.

"Lizzie, please let me help," he begs.

Even though I know I shouldn't, despite knowing I should shut up, I rip off the scab that my mind's been picking for the last few weeks. It's the only way I'll get him to leave me alone. The only way I can make sure my life is just my problem, not his.

"Don't worry, this isn't your problem to fix, Adam. You're leaving. I get it, you're moving on. And I want that for you, I really do. This was always temporary, I've known that from the beginning. I'm sorry we started pretending it was anything more."

His hand drops from my shoulder and lands in his lap. He clears his throat.

My head pounds. The oozy, gross feeling of shame leaks through me like oil.

"I'm sorry." I say half-heartedly. I am so, so tired. I feel so much that I feel nothing.

We drive in silence, even after my tears subside. Thankfully, we don't hit any traffic since it's midday. Adam pulls up to my mom's house where he met me this morning.

"Goodnight, Lizzie. I hope you feel better. I'll text you tomorrow." He hands me my keys, and then climbs into his own car. He watches me all the way to the house, making sure I make it in before he leaves.

As soon as I'm inside, I collapse in a heap on the couch. It's not fair. It's not fair that Lionel is an asshole and still gets a dream life. It's not fair that I was the one who wanted to build a future with a partner, and now he's the one doing it.

The acidic ocean of anger in me swells, toxic foam leaking into my mind. I know I'm supposed to move on and be happy for my ex and his future wife, but I don't want to be. I want to be bitter. I want to stay mad. I want to be all the things I couldn't let myself be for the last year, to let out all that I buried so I wouldn't seem needy or selfish about my breakup while other people in my life were going through bigger things like chemo, and engagements, and pregnancy.

The emotion crashes out of me like waves, and I fall into a restless sleep in the slanting afternoon sunlight.

19

I wake in a fog, convinced that someone has taken a saltshaker directly to my eyeballs. The bright side of wanting to detach my retinas is that the pain distracts me from the aching in my chest.

If I don't hydrate soon, my eyes may fall out of my head. I blink my way to the fridge.

"Hi sweetie, how did you spend this beautiful day…" Mom freezes in the door frame. "Honey, what's wrong?" Her concern melts me into a gooey puddle, my brain's defensive setting of going emotionally numb having finally been turned off. It's a burden and a relief to have my feelings back in full force.

"It's Lionel's wedding," I manage to eek out.

"What is?" It takes her a minute and then, my mother (who never cursed through rounds of chemo) says, "Oh, shit."

I nod. "Yeah." Somehow, there are more tears left in me. They well in the corners of my red eyes and slide cinematically to my chin. Mom plucks a box of tissues from the end table in the living room and drops them on the kitchen island. I blow my nose aggressively and sob harder when she rubs my back.

"Let me get you a cup of tea, honey." She pushes me down into a chair. Mom is a fiddler by nature. I get my inability to sit still from her, the constant moving soothing something in our restless souls. She messes around with the teakettle, lays out a lemon ginger teabag, and lets her hands flutter to cover mine.

By the time the water boils, this round of tears has dried up and the relentless, throbbing sadness has returned. My head already hurts, my sinuses pulse behind my eyes. I know Mom will insist I wear her cooling eye mask to bed.

"Want to talk about it?" She sits next to me, trying her hardest to stay still. I've sat in that seat so many times, blocking out the sadness to focus on the solution. Trying to make a cancer diagnosis more manageable for the closest person in my life. I've sewed in the devastation leaking out of me, pulling my seams tighter until I was close to bursting. Now I'm being given permission to fall apart, but I'm not sure how to do it.

"No." I sniffle. "Maybe. I don't know. I just want everything to be different."

"Are you sad because it's Lionel?

I consider this. Maybe. But the hurt goes deeper.

"I'm not sad that I don't have Lionel. I'm happy I don't have Faye's life with him. It's just, life's moving on for everyone else. Like, they're moving at warp speed while my feet are cemented to one spot. Jessie's married and she has a house. Clara's about to have a baby. Zed's greenhouse business is booming. And Adam… Adam's leaving." Mom knows that I've spent a lot of time with Adam, but I've withheld this last piece of information. I didn't want her to worry.

My sniffles turn into hiccups.

"I'm just in some embarrassing holding pattern while everyone around takes the next steps into adulthood. I feel like I deserve to be sat at the kids' table."

"That's tough, sweetheart." I don't want platitudes, but my mother is my everything. When she talks, I listen. "Lizzie, everything happens for people at a different pace. And to make things happen, to change where you're standing, you have to be ready to move."

"I'm scared, Mom. What if everything goes to shit? What if I lose what I have and find nothing else?" *What if I'm faced with losing everyone I love again* are the words I can't vocalize.

I've never lost the sense that, one by one, everyone I love will be ripped away from me. My Mom, then Lionel, now Jessie. I can't come to terms with the fact that if I truly let Adam in, he'll leave. Even if it has nothing to do with me, I can't stand to watch more people walk away.

"Oh honey." She strokes my hair as I cry another round of ugly, hot tears. She's always been able to pick apart the tangled

166

yarn of my feelings.

"That's life. You have to take risks if you want a chance at the reward." She rakes a hand through my hair, her fingernails brushing my scalp. It reminds me of ballet classes, when she'd gather all my hair into a ponytail. She taught me to do it myself but sometimes I'd mess up on purpose, just so we could have a quiet minute together before I was dropped off in a room full of pink slippers and loud voices. It wasn't until I met Jessie that I felt comfortable in that class.

"If there's one thing I learned from the hell of cancer, it's that you can hope nothing ever happens to you, but life continues on regardless. I don't want to sit twiddling my thumbs, waiting for something bad to happen. If I'm ever going to be caught off guard again, it will be while I'm finally nailing a yoga headstand or laughing at a table in the sunshine with my friends. Or concocting a crazy pizza with my perfect daughter." She's picked up the thread so seamlessly, I sniffle again.

I say the words I haven't spoken since her diagnosis, since her recovery. The ones I tucked behind the wall of steel will and forced smiles and silent pleas to the universe. The ones I've avoided in order to block out the fear.

"I was so afraid I'd lose you. I think I still am," I whisper. The elephant walks off of my chest and stands in the middle of the room. It's the first time we're both looking him straight in the eye, together. He reminds me of how life tried to tear away the most important person I have. But I'm still here, aren't I? Mom's still here. We're still holding each other. Still getting through hard days. Together.

"I'm not going anywhere right now, Lizzie." Mom puts her hand over mine. Her gaze is soft and understanding, like she can read every thought in my head. "And when I eventually do, it means more to me than anything that you went for what you wanted. Reach out and grab for the things that mean something to you, rather than hold on to what you can control. You can't stop living life because it gets scary. You're the only one who decides if you're staying in one place."

I know she's right. But there's still so much doubt buried in the layers of me, pressurized from all those years of being suppressed.

"I don't know, it feels like everyone else is moving on with their life with babies and marriage and promotions and I'm in an alternate dimension. One where I'm trapped behind some stupid opaque wall on the other side of adulthood. Like I'm failing."

"If you're happy with your life, where's the failure? There's still plenty of time for all those other things, if that's what you decide you want." Mom pours herself a cup of tea, giving me some time to avoid direct eye contact. "You know, Lizzie, when your father and I got divorced, we were the first of the friend group to split. And everyone thought I was crazy, deviating from the life plan. Wanting to move back here and raise you kids mostly on my own. At first, I couldn't relate to the people who were still married and co-parenting. But you know what? We found other channels to connect. Getting married, buying a house, having a kid, getting a raise, that's not what builds happiness. That's not what determines adulthood. Growing up means figuring out how to make decisions that are right for you, without giving a fuck what other people think."

I almost faint when I hear Mom drop the F-bomb. But then, like the sunrise spreading across the horizon of my silly little head, it dawns on me. She's right. I had an idea of how my life would turn out, and it didn't go that way so I felt like a failure. But maybe the things that didn't happen, the things that changed, have given me the space to keep choosing new adventures. To choose what's right for me.

"Ugh. Can you stop being so logical and therapy-ey? It's making me feel better." I cough up a laugh.

Mom smiles. "I've learned a lot the last few years. Have to share some of it." She releases the mug she's holding between her hands and pats my back. "Go take a shower. Call your friends. You'll feel better."

"What if I don't want to feel better," I mumble into my palms.

"You will. I don't buy that all this hurt doesn't have something to do with Jessie, either. Talk to her." Leave it up to Mom to get to the root of things.

"Where do I even start?" My heart dive-bombs, thinking about Jessie. We haven't had a real conversation in so long, I don't even know where to begin.

"Start with a shower. I'll slice some cucumbers for those eyeballs of yours." Mom kisses my forehead and I already feel better. It's nice to not to have to pick myself up alone.

My mother's wisdom did not misguide me—the shower works wonders for my mental health. I sit on my bed with my hair wrapped in a towel, staring at my phone, and wondering if the steam's rejuvenating powers will give me the courage to be honest with Jessie.

The last messages with Jessie are inconsequential bits of chit-chat. There's not a single thing about our personal lives. I bite my bottom lip. What if I annoy her with my problems? What if she just wants to live her perfect dream life with Clark and his Excel spreadsheets and I ruin that?

Remember, Lizzie. You can't know what Jessie is thinking unless you ask her. I force myself to type out **Hey!** then wonder if an exclamation point is cringe.

It doesn't take long for three bubbles to appear. We used to tease Jessie endlessly for being a green-bubbled Android user. Once she and Clark joined a family plan, she shocked everyone by switching to Apple.

I shake my head, pivoting from this train of thought. I am trying to fix this, not point out every change that has occurred over the past few years.

Jessie: *Hihi. What's up?*
Lizzie: *Not too much.*

Aside from the fact that I'm accidentally catering your cousin-in-law's slash my ex's wedding, I think.

Lizzie: *How was the honeymoon?*
Jessie: *It was awesome. Now time to unpack and decompress from the wedding. The number of people who buy things that are not on the registry is insane.*
Lizzie: *Need any help unpacking this week?*
Jessie: *Hell yeah. Come over tomorrow?*

I take a deep breath. I'm nervous to see Jessie, but her home always felt like my home, too. Maybe being in that space together can close this rift between us.

Lizzie: *Sounds good. Lmk what time's good. Want me to bring anything?*

Jessie: *Chardonnay is your ticket in the door :p I'll text you time tomorrow.*

Lizzie: *You've got it*

I have to survive my work shift and a conversation with Zed about what went down. Maybe he'll decide I'm not qualified and fire me on the spot. More likely, he'll take me off the job.

After that, I'll have to go face Jessie.

Apparently, this is a day of reckoning.

By the time I walk into the greenhouse, Zed's in his office with the door half open. He's on the phone with his feet up on the desk, a mug of tea throwing steam next to him. He looks up and waves.

At least I'll never have to see Lionel or Faye again if I'm fired. That thought is almost enough to bolster me. I get to work so I don't go insane.

I go about my morning tasks, prepping a shipment for one of our largest clients, a landscaping company in Carver. I pretend my mind isn't spiraling with thoughts of Faye believing I'm crazy and Lauren admitting that I'm not the right fit for this job.

Zed walks over when I've finally made it to watering the hydrangeas. I stare into the rainbows dancing off the spray of water and take a deep breath.

"How's the day going?" He waits as I turn off the hose. The rapid shush of water slows to a drip. Anxiety balloons, filling up every inch of my insides.

"It's alright. They put too much milk in my morning coffee." I shrug, hedging. I almost wish he'd fire me and get it over with. Then I could start fresh, throw myself into motion building a new life somewhere else. It's not like I haven't done it before.

"Switch to tea! Unless you go British-style, in which case milk might still be a problem, lassie."

"I think lassie is a Scottish thing," I reply.

"Right ye are!" His accent is so bad, I laugh in spite of everything. I wish he'd keep it up for the conversation we're about to have. Bad news won't seem so horrible when delivered in a butchered Scottish accent.

"Anywho, Lauren called."

I fidget. "So, who's taking over the Everlast Wedding?" I try to sound casual but the words come out croaky.

He blinks. "Taking over? No one."

"What do you mean? We're going to drop it? You can't lose out on that money on behalf of me." It's one thing to ruin my own professional life, but I'd be devastated in the consequences leaked to Zed, too. "Tell them I won't touch a single thing related to the wedding. Or I'll tell Lauren I quit, if I have to." I can't live with myself if I have somehow ruined Zed's chances at a high-profile gig on top of everything else. The greenhouse needs this wedding.

"Lizzie, please relax. Try the breathing thing we practiced." Zed's big into breathing exercises. I oblige.

He continues. "We didn't lose the account. I explained to Lauren that you're a professional." He shrugs, like that should be obvious. "I told her you had it handled and as long as the couple was cool with it, you were still in charge." At first, I can't believe it. I wonder what I've done to deserve this much faith. But Zed looks at me like he knows me, like he doesn't doubt I'm capable of handling anything life throws my way. That belief warms me, like the sun peeking through holes in the clouds.

"If they're okay it, are *you* okay with it?" Zed asks.

I mean to say yes, I am okay with all of it, but what comes out is the truth.

"I don't know." I sigh and drag a hand down the side of my face, likely covering my cheek in streaks of dirt. "I could give two craps about Lionel's feelings. But if it's going to make Faye super uncomfortable–I don't want my emotional baggage to ruin someone else's big day. And she seems to love that jackass."

Zed chuckles. "I always knew you were a romantic. Of course, I won't pressure you into anything. But I know you would never jeopardize your job, or the quality of your work. It's an unlucky lot that you know the groom. And I know you can handle this. I have more faith in you than I do in Janet Jackson, the queen of my soul."

"I guess you're right."

"You know I'm right. Janet Jackson is a groundbreaking cultural icon."

I laugh in spite of myself. "Fine! You are right about Janet Jackson which means there's a ninety percent chance you're right about me."

"I think you should talk to the bride." He says this like talking to my ex's fiancé is no biggie.

"Really?" It makes sense. But I really, really don't want to. I don't want to face her, or share any part of my side of the Lionel drama with her. The idea of looking back at all of that and having to speak it aloud makes me feel pathetic.

"Do I have to?"

"No. But I think you should. For you."

"Fine, I'll think about it," I grumble.

"He's in a band, right?"

"Yup."

"Don't take this the wrong way, but maybe dress less like a groupie when you meet up with her." Zed gestures to my oversized band T-shirt and ponytail held by a neon yellow scrunchie.

"And I only say that because I literally *was* a groupie. Many moons ago, mind you."

I feel my lips turn up while I shake my head. It's hard to reconcile the crunchy, outdoorsy, modern-day Zed with a Zed that used to fawn over guys in pleather.

"Point taken. I'll try to be more bland. More soulless," I say.

"Right, you get it. Just temporarily, might I add. If you go bland on me long-term, I'll have to stage an intervention that features the song *Sexy Back* on repeat. And no one wants that." Zed nods, satisfied. He turns to walk back to his office.

"Hey Zed?"

"Mhm?"

"Thanks. For believing in me. You know, all that cheesy jazz."

Zed grins from ear to ear. "I think you're a gouda employee,

I'll always brielieve in you." He gives me a thumbs up. By the time he walks away, I am fully smiling. The damn puns get me every time. Thank the universe for Zed.

Before I even realize what I'm doing, I take out my phone to text Adam the good news. Then I remember I owe him an apology, too. I've been so consumed by the Faye/Lionel drama, I haven't had time to properly freak out about Adam. I pushed one crisis aside to deal with the others.

No combination of words sounds right and a text apology seems cheap. I think of the apology I've always wanted after being heartbroken; it would definitely involve some of those clear confetti-filled balloons (they're horrible for the environment, I know, but they're so cool) and some form of chocolate pastry. And the actual act of saying "I'm sorry," which was as difficult to drag from the men I've dated as it was to get tickets to *Hamilton* on Broadway.

I sigh, tugging on the hose for more slack. It's time to go water all the areas of life I've been neglecting.

20

The sky is lit burnt orange by the time I get to Jessie's. I've been here more times than I can count. This is where I dragged Jessie through learning how to play Ticket to Ride. Where I first danced to Taylor Swift's *Midnights* release. It's also where I ended up on the day I found out my mom was in remission. This home has held me through so much. So why do I feel weird about walking through that fairytale-pink front door that I helped paint?

I tug on the hem of my Metallica t-shirt to buy myself some time.

"Hiya, Lizzie."

In my distress, I failed to notice Clark trimming the edge of the grass on hands and knees. With actual scissors.

"Oh, um. Hi Clark!" I say, overly cheerful to make up for my jitters. "What do you happen to be doing?"

"Ah, touching up the grass. Life in the 'burbs, you know!" Clark chuckles. "Door's unlocked, let yourself on in."

"Thanks. Good luck with the grass."

Clark waves a hand and leans his face low over the lawn once more.

When I get inside, Jessie's not in the living room so I yell for her. I spend a brief moment wondering if I'll end up a character in a murder mystery. I love Clark and he is a genuinely wonderful person, but people also loved Ted Bundy. What if Clark has been fooling us all along, and used those lawn shears to murder my best friend?

As I'm trying to remember if I saw any flecks on blood on

the metal blades, Jessie yells, "In the bathroom!"

If all else goes to hell, at least Clark's not a murderer. I put the white wine I picked up on the way over in the fridge to keep it chilled. It's sweating from the short exposure to the heat of the evening on my walk in.

"You would not *believe* how constipated I still am from this trip. You'd think they put butt plugs in airplane food." Jessie walks down the hallway from the bathroom, looking tan and fit from the summer sun and endless walks up Italian hillsides.

"At least it's better than the food being full of laxatives?"

The shadow of something I can't read flickers across Jessie's face.

"Go sit in the living room and I'll make us some popcorn." I do as I'm told and let Jessie flit about. When I get to the living room, I debate where to sit. Since when does it feel like I'm intruding on my friend's life? A place I've spilled both wine and secrets looks different when I'm mentally on the outside, looking in.

As I debate where to sit, Jessie yells snippets of conversation from the other room. We talk about Clara's pregnancy (she's doing great), we talk about Jessie's miscellaneous friends from the wedding (they're doing great), we talk about my mom (she's great, really great).

"I hope you're hungry because I popped two bags' worth." Jessie sets a bowl of our favorite popcorn mixture on the table within both of our reach. It's slathered in butter and then drizzled with Hershey's syrup and caramel ice cream topping.

The smell is hot, sweet, and heavy with memories. We ate this popcorn after my breakup with Lionel. And the day after Jessie's first date with Clark. I sniff in the feeling of being young and bonded by hope for all the things we had yet to experience. It takes me a second to realize my eyes are watering.

"What the hell... are you crying Lizzie?" Jessie looks alarmed.

I need to get off the nostalgia train, like, now. "Remembering how much this popcorn has gotten us through. How many awesome and shitty nights." I try to lighten the mood with a chuckle, but it sounds like one of those rubber chickens is stuck halfway down my windpipe. Jessie narrows her eyes. I know that look. She's not going to let this go.

"Why are you being so weird? You haven't even asked me about the trip. I feel like I've barely heard anything from you since the wedding." The tension is thick in Jessie's voice. It's how she gets when she's considering whether or not to let herself be mad. She stares at me, twirling a piece of highlighted blonde hair around her middle finger.

I try to stare back, but I can already feel the pressure building behind my eyes. I don't want this to end to our friendship. I don't want Jessie to think that I hate Clark, or her decisions, or any part of her life. I'm not sure how to explain myself. Besides my mom, this is the person I am closest to. The person who has sat with me through every difficult thing. It's hard to untangle that ball of mixed up feelings; sadness, loss, jealousy, confusion. Happiness and joy for my friend are also mixed in there, snarling everything up. I take a deep breath, grab the mental strand of yarn closest to me, and start pulling.

"Why didn't you tell me Lionel was getting married?"

Jessie, my favorite loud-mouth, is very rarely silent. But I watch as she bites her lip and pauses.

"I felt like you were carrying a lot already," she says slowly. "It felt like the wedding was hard for you to get through with the Lionel stuff, and you had told me not to talk about it. I waited for you to bring it up, and then you never did."

"That's kind of bullshit." The words slip out, shocking me. Jessie goes wide-eyed. "You're my best friend. Didn't you think I needed to know something that would be shoved in my face at your wedding?" Irritation bubbles in me, a feeling I didn't expect to show itself in the first ten minutes of our conversation.

Jessie looks me in the eyes. "You're right. It was a shitty thing to keep from you. And I'm sorry. I found out a week before the wedding and I… I didn't want to drop that bomb on you and make you dread that day. I was selfish as fuck and I'm sorry. I get why we've felt so far apart." Her eyes sparkle with tears. I think of her sequined self, shimmering on her wedding day, of how much I love Jessie's shine, the parts of her that are so different from me. And I recognize the parts of us that complement each other so well, and how our friendship brings out the best of our strengths and counteracts each other's weaknesses. I can forgive Jessie, because although she understands me to my core, she is different than I am. And she isn't perfect either.

"I miss you." It's the core of truth amidst the chaos. I have to get through all the things I need to say, before I dam them up again.

"I feel like your life has changed so much. I don't know how I fit into it anymore. You're married and thinking about kids and you live in your own house and you use a meat thermometer. And I live in my mom's house and work at a plant shop and I'm in falling in love with someone who is moving on."

Jessie's eyes are saucers, but she remains calm. Her public persona may be a lot to handle, but Jessie is the rational to my emotional. Somehow, I forgot that in our weeks apart. I've been missing my counterweight.

"Okay, first off. I didn't realize you were insecure about being meat-thermometerless. I promise to buy you one for your birthday." In spite of my nerves, I sniffle out a laugh. Jessie smiles.

"Yeah, Lizzie, our lives are different but look," she scoots over on the couch so we are hip to hip and leans her head into the crook in my neck. "I don't know how my life will change, or how yours will either. But, like, we've always been different people. I wore a tiara to prom and you refused to wear heels because you read that book about stilettos being used to weaken women's ability to run away, for Christ's sake. We've still always been there for each other. I don't see why that would change now."

"I know. It just isn't like it used to be, you know?" The wave of change crashes over me again. It feels so true; like everything is shifting while I'm mired in quicksand.

"I get it. And I'm sorry, I know I've been shit to talk to lately. This wedding thing was all-consuming for a while. Honestly, it was fucking exhausting." She sighs. "I haven't fully felt like myself in a while."

I've assumed that Jessie was pulling away from me, that

things were off between us because her life is changing in ways mine is not. I've made this about me and never stopped to consider that it could have to do with Jessie's feelings about the changes happening to *her*.

"You could have talked to me. You can always talk to me." I bite my lip. How would she know that, though? I certainly haven't made it easy. I think back to every time Jessie sent me texts and I answered with a short quip in turn. I don't remember how it started, but my brevity must have been weird for her, too.

"Yeah, I know. It's just, I know that you and Lionel's breakup was devastating. And everything with your mom… I didn't want to throw my problems on you. And maybe I'm projecting, but we hadn't really talked about Lionel, so I thought you wanted to deal with it on your own. And that made me feel like I should do the same."

"I'm so sorry. I promise I always have room for you," I say.

Jessie places her hand on mine. We let our palms absorb each other's warmth.

"I know. I'll talk to you next time. I'll always have room for you too, you know. At every single point of my life. It doesn't matter where we live or if I have twelve babies. You're my forever person and nobody can change that."

It feels like my heart cracks down the middle. All the stuckness and sadness that I've felt over the past weeks finally finds its way out.

"You're my forever person too," my voice trembles.

"But you have to trust me to handle your shitty shit too, Lizzie. I don't know anything that's going on with your life right now. It hurts to be shut out." Jessie's eyes glisten. "I know how much your mom's treatment sucked. I was there when you were pretending not to fall apart for her. But you don't have to be fine with me. I can't help if you don't talk to me."

I've spent so much time trying to protect my friends from my problems, sparing them my ugly feelings. It's not life that's separating us, it's the wall I built between us.

"I know," I whisper. "I'm sorry. I didn't want to be the sad, lonely friend. I didn't want to bother you." It comes out a weak, tired admission. I've spent so much time minimizing my problems, wishing them smaller so I could focus on everyone else. All I've done is bottle everything up. It's impossible to move forward if I pretend the problems don't exist.

"Bother me? Seriously? Your feelings aren't a fucking bother, Lizzie. The last time you bothered me was when we went on that trip to Nashville, and I couldn't convince you to dip out of the Grand Ole Opry tour so we could go to boozy brunch instead. Oh, or when you made me *actually* peddle on the peddle bike on that trip. This reminds me, we should never go to Tennessee together again."

"Hey, that tour was cool and we drank mimosas after, just like you wanted," I shoot back. "But you're right. Not about Nashville! I haven't been open with you and I'm sorry. From now on, you're getting one hundred percent truth about the diarrhea parts of my life."

I'm not being left behind; I'm the one who stuck my ankles in the mud. Our friendship can grow in new, beautiful ways, once I pick up my feet.

"Thank god. Maybe some of your verbal diarrhea will inspire my actual intestines to get things moving," Jessie pats her stomach and groans.

"Now, can you please fill me in on your life? I'm tired of hearing second-hand info from Clara." She grabs a handful of popcorn, shoves it in her mouth, and waits.

We spend the next half hour recapping my past few weeks. About my role shifting at the greenhouse, about Adam, about the wedding and the shock of finding out it was Lionel's. I end on the fact that Zed thinks I should talk to Faye.

"Okay, I need some water. That was intense. But there it is, all my crappy crap."

"Shit! I wish I wasn't now related to that dick," Jessie says. "We already RSVPed no in case you're wondering; we're visiting Clark's mom that week. But now I wish I'd be there for *you*. Enough about Lionel, we'll figure that part out later. More about your new man meat. And his man meat. Spare no details."

"Adam is amazing." I sigh.

"And?" Jessie prompts.

"And he is so sweet." I return to the couch with a glass of

water and chug it.

"*And?*" Jessie makes her annoyance clear.

"And he's an incredible cook. He makes food seem like an art form. He's thoughtful and sexy and he has arms that you can hang off of, like a jungle gym."

"Okay, now we're getting somewhere." Jessie rubs her hands together. "So why can't you be with him forever and always?"

"He's moving. His sister died in a car crash a few years ago here, which is so terrible and heavy and obviously affected his view of this place. Basically, he can't be happy here because everything's connected to losing her." I swallow. I feel deeply horrible for Adam, and I know everyone processes trauma and grief in their own way.

"Oh my god. That's awful." Jessie's eyes well.

"Yeah. It's terrible. I could never ask him to stay in a place that makes him relive the worst loss of his life. But I am finally starting to feel like I belong somewhere. Being near Mom is important to me. Being near you is important, too. I don't want to lose you guys." I swallow the lump in my throat.

"First of all, you'll have us even if you move across the earth. But I get what you mean. And like, you merged your whole life with Lionel's and were going to change everything for him. And then he didn't do the same for you. It makes sense that you don't want that to happen again." Jessie says this easily, like she hasn't just exposed a fundamental truth my subconscious was set on ignoring.

"I hadn't thought about it like that but, yeah. You're right."

I've been in this situation before, and I centered other people instead of myself. I don't think I can do that again. I want one thing that I get to keep. I want one thing I get to choose.

"If you had told me all of this weeks ago," she gives me a pointed stare, "I could have told you that. And for the record, I think you also need to be fully transparent with Adam. He sounds like a big boy" (she winks) "in a lot of ways. Tell him how you're feeling and that there's no pressure. But it's not fair to keep him in the emotional dark, too."

"You're right. I'm scared and it sucks. Ugh, I both hate and love you," I reach for Jessie and she reaches back, until we are hugging across the couch armrest.

"I love you so much. I know you're scared, but you're a tough bitch, you know that?" I feel a tear from Jessie's face drop onto my knee. Which prompts me to immediately start crying.

"What's wrong with us?" I laugh-sob.

"So, so much." Jessie laughs back.

When Clark walks in, we're still hugging and crying. The alarm on Clark's face let me know we must look as emotionally raw as I feel.

"Hi Lizzie.. oh, uh… is everything okay? Do you need tissues?" He glances down at our glasses. "More wine? Whatever it is, I'll get it!" Clark's distress at two grown women holding hands and crying drags a snotty snort out of me. Which makes Jessie giggle in a way that turns into ugly hiccups. Pretty soon, our crying morphs into hysterical laughter.

Clark comes back in with tissues. He leaves them on the table in front of us and mutters, "More wine then," as he grabs the glasses and heads into the kitchen to top us off.

"I needed this so badly." Jessie sniffles and squirms back to her side of the couch. She flops back like a rag doll and blows her nose.

"Me too. Things have been weird with everyone." I sigh, but talking about it all has already made me feel lighter.

"With your mom?"

"No, not her. Mostly Adam." I try to let this sound light and easy. But I can see from Jessie's pinched brow that she's reads me for filth.

"What happened with Adam?" Clark asks as he walks back in, brandishing two glasses filled to the brim with white wine and ice cubes. I smile. He pours the way Jessie likes, heavy-handed.

This might be my new reality; Clark wanting to know things about my life. I never took the time to wonder if that could be a good thing, but I realize I like it. And I could probably use his advice.

"Well, I may have freaked out after finding out that the wedding we are catering is Lionel's…"

"Which Lizzie didn't tell me until *today* because she didn't want to bother us on our *honeymoon.*" Jessie rolls her eyes.

"Honey, Lizzie was trying to be thoughtful." Clark nods at me.

"Sorry! No more withholding," I promise again.

"Ugh, fine. I'll stew about this later. Continue." She waves a hand.

"I may have reminded him he was leaving, sort of harshly. And then he offered to make me soup and he was being so nice, but I was in meltdown mode. So I snapped. And I haven't responded to his texts. And we haven't had any real conversation since."

"Okay, first question. Are you over Lionel?" Jessie looks at me in the way only your best friend can, like she is probing my soul for the truth. "Yeah, I am." The admission is easy, and I finally know it's completely true.

"It's not the fact that it's Lionel that has me triggered, it's the whole marriage thing. The fact that another person who was a big part of my life is doing the next-stage-of-life, moving on thing."

"Yeah, but haven't you moved on, too?" Jessie asks.

"I guess so. It just feels… different. Like, I'm not getting married or buying a house or whatever."

"No, you're just changing careers and dating a hot chef and hanging out with your mom and kicking my ass in our Peloton challenge," Jessie rolls her eyes. "Lizzie, you do realize that your life is baller right? And you can do anything you want to do with your future, it doesn't have to be the life everyone around here lives. Fuck marriage. No offense, Clark."

"None taken." Clark puts his hands up.

"The hot chef may hate me now. What almost-thirty-year-old ghosts a guy she's working and sleeping with?" I frown.

"If a guy offers to make you soup in the summer, I think he could forgive just about anything." This from Clark, as he steals a sip from his wife's wineglass. She swats at his hand, but he switches the glass to his left and takes another gulp. Jessie sticks her tongue out, then smiles. I take back the anxiety-provoked murderer thoughts from earlier. I always knew I liked this man.

My question comes out small. "You really think he could forgive me?"

"Yes. Definitely. But only if you know what you want." Clark nods, confident in his declaration.

"Damn. When we get into our first real fight, I'm going to need you to have this much perspective." Jessie steals back her glass and raises it to him in a toast.

I am genuinely happy for these two and the life they built. They didn't end up together haphazardly. Jessie dated a lot (and I mean, a LOT) of duds before she found Clark. It was never going to be about checking off a box to move into the next phase of life. They found each other and made decisions that aligned with what they both wanted.

Maybe I could have that too. Mom's advice joins forces with Clark's. Life is too short to tiptoe towards my future. To be scared to lose the things that could make me happy. To crush the possibility of a love so big, it threatens to wash away all my doubt.

"I know what I want." I nod, the statement final and my voice clear as a bell for the first time today.

Clark stares at me, serious. This man takes nothing lightly. "Okay. Then let's cook up a plan to get your chef back."

21

Guarding the coveted window table at the coffee shop is a full-time task. But it's worth it, since it's the only spot with enough privacy that the entire cafe won't be able to hear me beg. Unfortunately, it's also the best spot for taking conference calls. Two work-from-home Millennials ask if I'm leaving soon.

"Sorry, waiting on a friend." Their lips draw thin, tight lines but they nodded politely. I see them eyeing me like prey from a table against the wall as I glance down at my Apple Watch. 8:56am. Faye agreed to meet here at nine. I pat down some fly-aways in my hair, which does nothing, thanks to the humidity.

I debated ordering a coffee so I wouldn't be sitting here protecting this table like a troll, but then I figured I should buy both drinks. After all, I was the one who asked Faye to meet up after Zed's pep talk. I'm positive I can't buy her affection (first and foremost because I could never afford it, judging by her family's home), but a peace offering in the form of coffee seems like a start.

By 9:05am I've officially deemed myself insane for thinking I could make it through this exchange without breaking into hives. Sweat pools under my armpits, despite my clinical strength deodorant working overtime and the weather being a drizzly 72 degrees. I have a glimmer of hope that maybe Faye's stood me up, a tiny revenge against her fiancé's ex who must surely be intent on spoiling her wedding because, come on, what are the odds that I'd be involved unless it was in the name of sabotage? If she doesn't show up, I am officially free to declare defeat while saying that I tried.

No such luck. Faye enters the coffee shop like a dream, layers of fabric flowing in the rainy breeze behind her as she closes a clear umbrella. Is she wearing chiffon? She's so flawless, it hurts.

I desperately want to win her over. Not only because my job hangs in the balance, but because she seems genuinely cool. It's confusing to feel this way about my former love's new partner.

I wave to her with what I hope isn't a crazy smile. I'm not sure how I'm going to disarm her when I can't seem to pull myself together.

"Lizzie, hi." She walks over and I notice that the restaurant volume has dropped at the entrance of this other-worldly woman and the ease with which she carries herself. Where I originally thought she was all soft edges and pixie light it's now easy to spot the intensity of her gaze, the skepticism she doesn't bother to mask. I have a feeling Faye has always gotten what she wants out of life because she's not afraid to ask, and that she follows a scorched-earth policy if people don't comply. I can't pretend that I don't admire that.

"Hey. Good morning. Would you, um, like a coffee? I waited," I say stupidly, gesturing to the empty table.

"Yes. An oat milk latte with an extra shot of espresso." She sits and I scramble up, all too happy to fetch her drink if it means I get a minute to collect myself.

I order her oat milk latte and a cold brew for myself (I am positive my nerves don't need the added caffeine, but I am powerless in the face of cold brew) and try Zed's breathing technique while they're being prepared.

I start to rehearse lines in my head like I did when I was Lollipop Kid #3 in our middle school play. "Faye, Lionel is a big lumpy dog turd and I would never want him or his late-night-video-game obsession back," I practice in my head.

Okay, maybe that won't work. Should I pinky-promise that I don't love him anymore? That the way he ordered pepperoni on his pizza then picked off all the actual meat (so it had just a hint of pepperoni flavor on the cheese) made me want to scream?

"Order for Lizzie!" I snap out of revelry. Here goes nothing.

Faye is distracted on her phone when I return to the table. She's probably texting Lionel about how she wishes she was anywhere else. She puts the phone down, grabs the latte with her perfectly manicured fingernails, and waits.

"Fancy meeting you here." I try for a break in the tension.

"You asked me to come."

"Yeah, bad joke. Look, Faye." I pick at my fingernails, cut short so dirt doesn't get trapped underneath. I sit on them to get myself to stop.

"I wanted to talk about my role in your wedding. You and Lionel's wedding. I truly didn't know you were the bride before I took the job."

"Yes, well. This is a big day and I can't risk anything ruining it. I am thinking of asking Lauren to work with a new team member. I could try to work with a different company but I do not think that will be possible, given the timeframe." She looks me straight in the eye, sizing me up. She is a nice person, but I'm sure it's hard to have sympathy for the girl (me) whose career and romantic relationship she's about to derail.

It's exactly what I expected her to say, but it still spikes my heart rate. I need to work this event with Adam. Aside from my career hinging on this event, it's also a key part in getting him to trust me again.

"I understand. And I know I was a little… odd, the other day."

I think about everything I decided to say during this meeting. How to establish my credibility and reassure her that my work won't be affected by the relationship I used to have with Lionel. Then I throw all of that in the trash and decide to give her honesty.

"Full Casper-the-Ghost level transparency, I kind of freaked when I realized it was your wedding," I say. "If I knew this was the scenario, I never would have put either of us in this position. But please believe me, this event is extremely important to me. This could determine my future at Green With Ivy and I don't want to mess it up. I have worked *really* hard to make things perfect and I want this to be the best possible day for you both." Every word is true, and to lose it all because of a rotten coincidence would give me big beef with the universe.

She takes a sip of her latte, then looks me in the eye again. Sheesh, this woman is great at maintaining eye contact. It makes me itchy. Or maybe that's the hives.

"I haven't told Lionel yet," she says.

"Really? Why not?" The surprise in my tone is authentic—I thought she'd run to tell Lionel the second I left.

"I wanted it to be my decision. He likes having the final say and… well, if I want to keep you on, then I'll keep you on. It shouldn't matter to him anyway." She shrugs.

Ouch. Whether or not she meant that to sting, if she's considering keeping me, I'll take it. I'll take a thousand tiny paper cut insults if she'll say this is a go. Because, for the first time I've allowed myself to admit, I need this to work out. I want Adam to succeed, even if it means my love life is doomed. And I do want to be the perfect florist of the world's most perfect wedding. I'm still not sure about stepping into a bigger role at the greenhouse, but I want to point to an accomplishment and say *I did that.*

"And it shouldn't," I say. "I am in a new chapter of my life and all I want, more than anything, is to give you a perfect wedding. I have been working on the arrangements and building the relationship with catering for weeks now." I can feel the slight edge of pleading. I am not above begging. If that is what the Frenchwoman wants, that is what she shall get.

"Hm yes, I think the caterer is a lovely relationship to have, no?" She quirks one side of her mouth up. I try not to squirm under her knowing smile. Does she suspect about me and Adam? Maybe she has some crazy Spidey-senses.

"He seems like he is cut from good, strong cloth," she adds. I breathe out. I hope she is objectifying Adam and his hunky frame and doesn't notice the blush spreading like wildfire across my cheeks.

"I think you deserve happiness, too." She nods graciously and although it might be for show, I feel a little prick of sympathy for Faye. I think she's a good person who is going to be stuck with Lionel, a grade-A shitty boyfriend, as her husband. I hope he's grown more in this relationship.

"Thanks, Faye. That means a lot to me."

"Listen, Lizzie. You can stay on. I trust you, and I do not think you would go to all this trouble if you were going to do anything unseemly. You are very good at your job."

The sense of pride washes over me, soothing the last of my nerves. I *am* good at my job. And it feels very nice to have the respect of someone who could easily dislike me solely based on circumstances.

"Thank you for the coffee. I must go get my hair done." She taps my knuckles lightly with her perfect piano fingers then takes the last swig of her latte and stands.

"Thank you so much, Faye. I appreciate it," I say, trying not to smile too much.

"Au revoir." She waves each delicate finger, one by one, and sashays out the door.

My body feels lighter, the possibilities making me buoyant. Or maybe that's the caffeine. Since I've been hanging out with Adam, I've become a caffeine lightweight.

"All yours!" I wave to the Millennials across the cafe, turning over the coveted table. I barely have time to scoop up my to-go cup before they mumble thanks and plop down, pop in their AirPods, and ignore me completely.

"You're welcome," I mutter. I am determined to ride this caffeine high until it fizzles out. I stroll out of the coffee shop into the day's gloom.

While walking strategically under awnings, I pull out my phone and text Adam for the first time since we learned the identities of the bride and groom. I try not to look at the five messages I haven't responded to that he sent over the past few days. I just wanted to make sure things with the wedding were ironed out before we talked. Plus, once these floodgates open, I won't be able to close them.

Lizzie: *Hey, you around?*

The three bubbles pop up almost instantly. My heart hits the ceiling. I have to fix things. I need to explain that, in my shock, I said things I didn't mean… The bubbles disappear again and my stomach plummets.

After another minute he replies *Got errands to run. What's up?*

I think about typing "I'm sorry I was such a confused asshole" but it doesn't seem like enough.

I can't find the words to explain how I thought my life would follow one trajectory until it nosedived into another. And how the shock of being a part of my ex's wedding threw me back into the spiral I'd been working hard to break away from.

Lizzie: *Talked to Faye. All good on that front.*

Adam: *That's great news. Never doubted you. She would have to be insane to let the most talented, dedicated florist go.*

My heart clenches with the desire to deserve Adam's kindness. Before I can think about how insufficient it seems, I text the beginning of an apology.

Lizzie: *I'm sorry I was so short with you the other day. And that I haven't answered you.*

He doesn't make me wait long for a response.

Adam: *Nothing to apologize for. You're right. I'm leaving and I haven't been acting like it. It wasn't fair to you. I'm really sorry.*

My throat constricts. This isn't going the way I wanted it to. *What did you expect him to say, Lizzie?*

Lizzie: *Can we meet up and talk about it, please?*

Adam: *Sure. Busy with work most of this week, but I'm free tomorrow afternoon. Come by?*

How is it possible that a man I've hurt, avoided, and attempted to crush my feelings for is so quick to invite me back in? I consider just how grateful I am for Adam. I ignore the part of my brain that tells me he's still not mine to keep. Not until I admit how I feel. Until I explain what I want and let him make his own decision.

Lizzie: *For sure. Only if I can feed you this time. Sound good?*

Adam: *The magic eight ball says yes. See you then.*

I smile to myself, the thought of seeing him tomorrow lighting me up like a Christmas tree. I sprint to my car. Not even the endless drizzle can touch me.

22

"What kind of food does a professional chef like?" Clara picks up a dragon fruit and squints at it as we stroll down the bread aisle. Once Jessie and I cleared the air, I should have known that we'd immediately make up for lost time by tackling a project. Cooking for Adam was Clark's plan to win him back, but it's Jessie who insists I implement it.

The mission is to find the meal that most clearly says (in Jessie's words), "I'm sorry I'm an idiot, please stay with me forever and P.S. let's bang." I think that's a lot to ask of a food product, but Jessie's convinced and she recruited Clara.

"You could make things easy on yourself and explore the frozen food aisle. Maybe that's his secret food kink, quick and easy. Sharp contrast to all his big fancy meals," Clara says. She leans heavily on the cart as she rolls through the grocery store. Her stomach is now straining her back, which is apparently a thing that happens when you carry the weight of another person in the front of your body.

"Are frozen spring rolls how you got pregnant?" Jessie shoots back.

"Dino nuggets, but close. Lizzie, bring them to Adam and ask if he'll tricera-top you," Clara deadpans. I sputter, feeling the iced latte dribble down my chin in an effort not to spray the nearby canned peaches.

"Clara, what the actual fuck is wrong with you." Jessie bends over her knees laughing. She reaches out an arm to steady herself on me as tears slip out of the corner of my eyes. I don't think I'll ever acclimate to the ridiculousness that is Clara.

"What! Don't you kids know how the birds and bees work," Clara shrugs innocently.

"I don't think dinosaur sex puns are the way to Adam's heart." I wipe the tears from my eyes and try to rein in the giggles that have left me breathless.

Clara's smile spreads across her face. "But they might be the way to his…"

"Uh, uh, uh that's enough. We are in *public*," Jessie hisses, gesturing to the teenager stocking shelves up the aisle. "Lizzie, how are you feeling about tonight?" She asks, probably to divert the conversation away from penis talk.

I take a beat to think. I could just say *fine* and move on, but I'm trying to give my friends unfiltered truth when it comes to my feelings.

"Honestly? I'm anxious. I'm worried he'll shut me down, but I'm also hopeful. It's like there are caterpillars crawling around in my stomach," I admit.

"Ew, that visual." Clara grimaces. To be fair, we did spend twenty minutes this morning talking about all the food and drink that's currently giving her the ick.

"I mean, I hope caterpillars are the precursor to butterflies," I rush on. "Like, if everything goes well, that inching along feeling will turn into fluttering."

"Well, whatever happens please know that I think you're a badass for putting yourself out there. It takes big, juicy, metaphorical balls to do that," Jessie says.

Clara snorts, her eyebrows quirking up. "Can balls be juicy?"

"Juicy balls sounds a little… sweaty for my taste," I fake gag. "How about a different adjective?"

"Yeah! Like bouncy. Or veiny. Or succulent." Clara pipes up. "Oh! Or luscious."

"Who needs luscious locks when you've got luscious balls? Someone should pitch this to TRESemmé. Lizzie, if you need an extra confidence boost just remember we believe in your big, luscious balls." Jessie beams at me while Clara nods, and even though this is a completely ridiculous conversation, my heart swells. My friends believe in me. My friends have my back. My friends aren't going to run away if things go to hell. Instead, they'll pour me a glass of wine, scream Lily Allen songs, and distract me with silly jokes. They won't shy away if I end up in a pit of sadness. They'll throw down a rope and help me pull myself out. I forgot how wonderful it feels to not sit in darkness alone.

"Thank you for helping. This is so much easier to handle because I have you. Whatever happens with Adam…."

As if I'd summoned him, my phone starts to vibrate with Adam's name. Nerves make my stomach plummet.

"One sec," I say to my friends and head to a quiet spot next to a S'mores display before answering. I take a breath and click to accept the call.

"Hey!" My voice comes out high-pitched. I wince.

"Lizzie." I was expecting him to cancel, but he sounds all wrong. He sounds worried.

"What's wrong?"

"It's Mrs. Carol. Nella, I mean. She had a heart attack." I can hear the strain in Adam's voice, how he's trying not to panic.

"How is that possible? She seemed fine when we were there. Is she…" my throat tightens, unable to utter out the last part of the question.

"She's okay now. I think. They put in a stint. They wouldn't tell me much. I only found out because she asked them to call me to bring her a few things. I am driving to the hospital now."

"Okay. Do you want me to meet you there?"

"You don't have to do that. I felt like you should know. And I needed to talk to someone. Needed to ground myself before I go into that hospital again."

The hospital where his sister was taken after the accident. In all his time living in this town, he'd never gone back there. I can't imagine the heaviness he feels, especially when the last person he visited there never left.

I could never leave him to face that reminder of grief alone.

"I'm coming. I'll be there in fifteen minutes."

"Alright." There's a sigh, and I may be imaging it but it sounds like relief in the exhale. "Lizzie… thank you."

"Of course. I want to be there with you."

I hang up. Horror must be etched on my face, because as

soon as Clara and Jessie spot me, they rush over.

"It's Adam. Our friend, the lady we are getting honey from, she had a heart attack and now he's going to the hospital to see her," I choke out.

When I start crying, they ditch our cart in the frozen food aisle. Jessie puts an arm around my shoulders and walks me out while Clara slips a twenty to the teenager, apologizing and asking him to put all of our stuff away. He looks terrified (maybe taking money from us is frowned upon) but he nods and lets us go. Once we are out of the fluorescent grocery store lights, I explain everything through tears.

We hop in the car, Clara pulling the hospital up on her Google Maps and Jessie rubbing my back from the back seat while I try not to hyperventilate. It's too quick of a drive for me to properly tame my own anxiety. Adam's not the only one who hates hospitals.

"Call us literally whenever you need us to come get you," Jessie says when we pull into the lot. "I'll turn my phone on ring, so you know I'm serious." Jessie's phone has been taken off silent maybe twice in our entire friendship. She leans out the back seat window to hug me.

"Are you sure you don't want us to walk you in? I've been getting poked and prodded here for months, I probably know everyone in case you need to slip past security." I know Clara is only half-joking, that she and Jessie would set aside any other plans for the day if I needed them with me. It soothes my panic a bit, knowing the lengths my friend would go to.

"Thank you. Both of you." I breathe. "Clara, I don't doubt your abilities to sneak me in anywhere. But I need to go to Adam. And I think I need to do it alone." I take a deep breath. "Love you, I promise I'll call." I reach across and squeeze Clara's hand with my left hand while I hug Jessie. Then I jog across the parking lot and through the sliding glass doors.

This place is every bit as sterile as I remember. It barely phases me as I turn the corner and scan the waiting room. Adam is slumped over in a chair, elbows on knees. I've sat like that before, when my mom wasn't around to watch. It's the pose of defeat, gravity pressing too heavily down for you to be able to stay upright.

I say nothing as I hurry over, but my yellow Vans announce my arrival, squeaking on the floor. Adam's eyes lift to meet mine. Before he can say anything, my arms are around his neck, squeezing life back into him. Wringing out the sense of utter devastation that accompanies the threat of loss. I know what it's like to have been there alone. I refuse to let anyone I care about go through that by themself.

It takes a second, but then he's hugging me back, arms around my waist, letting me carry some of the weight. It takes more effort than I thought possible to peel myself away, even though I'm standing and he's sitting and the hug would be awkward in any other scenario. I force myself to sit and put my hands in my lap. I'm afraid being in this waiting room, the helplessness of it, will dig too deep into the past. That it'll unearth too much hurt. I gently take his hand from his knee and lace it in mine. I place our intertwined hands between us, like twin arteries powering the same heart.

A nurse comes into the waiting room a few minutes later. "Adam? Mrs. Carol will see you now."

She must be okay if she can talk and request to see her guests, right? I clear my throat, which has gone dry. "Could you phone up and see if she'll allow me in as well? I wasn't able to notify her I was coming." They're the first words I've spoken since I got here.

She asks my name, nods, and disappears. We get the thumbs up and are led up an elevator and through a maze of fluorescent hallways to room 301. I watch Adam's composure steady. His face remains pale, but he's steeling himself so the person on the other side of the door won't sense his panic. It's devastating to see it happen in real time.

When we open the door, the room is quiet. Somehow, Nella got a room to herself, which seems like a tiny miracle. She looks small tucked between the rails of the hospital bed. But I let some of the knot of tension I've held in my stomach unwind when I see she's awake. I sense Adam doing the same. Nella offers us a groggy smile.

"Hi kids," she says. Adam breathes a sigh of relief at hearing her speak.

"Hey. How are you feeling?" I ask, giving him an extra second to relax his spine.

"I've certainly been better. But I'm still kicking, so I'd say that is pretty swell. Thank you for coming. Both of you." She reaches out a hand and Adam walks over in two strides and takes it gingerly, like he thinks he might break her.

"We were so worried about you. What did the doctors say? Can I get you anything?" Adam says.

Nella pats his hands. "The thing about getting old and worrying about getting old along the way? It catches up to you." She smiles, like this experience has taught her a secret to the universe.

"I always thought I could keep myself healthy and free of disaster if I planned it out. A house with no stairs, a call button for if I fell, water aerobics classes at the gym." My throat works, going dry at how familiar all that planning and worrying sounds. I've never realized just how much Nella and I were alike.

"You did the best you could to be prepared. There's no way you could have prevented this," Adam says, pushing his hair back. He looks too pale in here, like he's fading into a memory.

"You're right. I'm glad I was prepared, and using my call button sure got the medics there faster. But no matter what I did, I wasn't going to prevent this." She laughs, sadly. "In fact, they said stress is probably one of the reasons I'm in here to begin with. Waiting for bad things to happen caused the bad thing to happen sooner. I guess that'll teach me to 'chill out' as my granddaughter likes to say." She laughs. Her high spirits release more pressure from the room. I watch Adam's shoulders lower as he processes that she is okay.

We make small talk for fifteen minutes, until a nurse comes in and tells us it's time for more tests.

"I can come back with snacks. Tea. Puzzles. Do you still like Soduku?" Adam's eyes are soft, the gray-blue of doves' wings.

"Oh sweetie, thank you." Nella pats his hand. "My daughter is flying in now. She should be here tonight. Don't worry yourself. They said I have to spend the day here before I can head home."

I breathe a sigh of relief for Nella and her family, and give thanks for the speedy ambulance and the stent that allows them all to be together again. We say our goodbyes and promise to check in tomorrow morning.

After the door closes, Adam breathes out. The color is still drained from his cheeks, but a hint of rose blooms under his stubble.

"I'm so happy she's okay," he whispers.

"Me too. That was scary. How are you?" His face is still pale in the afternoon sun filtering through the window, his body tense as a telephone pole.

"I'm fine."

"Promise?"

Adam looks at me. Then he reaches for my right hand. He holds it in the palm of his left, giving me time to withdraw. When I don't, he entwines our fingers.

"Promise."

We walk down the hallway, take the elevator, head out to the parking lot, and hold hands until we reach his truck.

"I'll drive you home, if that's okay."

"You sure you're good? I can drive if you need a minute."

He hesitates, and then he nods. "Yeah. That sounds good."

I put my hand out to accept the keys, then walk around and climb into the driver's seat. Adam blasts the air conditioning. He leans his face forward into the stream while I adjust the seat and mirrors.

"Where'd you learn to drive manual?" He watches as I put the truck in gear, intrigued.

"My first boyfriend in high school. He had an old Chevy. It was when we'd first gotten our licenses, and since I didn't drink at the time, he wanted to make sure I could be the getaway car in case any party we went to got broken up by cops."

"He sounds like a charmer, making sure he had an out," Adam scoffs while he turns the AC off and rolls down the window. It's a bright, beautiful day, with puffy clouds floating across a blue sky.

"He was actually an okay guy. Not the most romantic person I've ever known, but nice. I think he has, like, three kids now." I shrug. That time of my life seems far away, like all that has happened between then and now has subtly shifted everything about me until I became someone new. I remember hearing that all the cells in your body change every seven years, until you're the same human composed of completely new pieces.

"Plus, now I still have a shot at one of my childhood dreams of being a Formula 1 Driver."

We pull onto the main road, Adam laughing. "Formula 1 was your childhood dream? Every other kid wanted to be a doctor or president or ballerina."

"I actually wanted to be one of the people who changed the tires," I say sheepishly. "They were always so efficient. I liked how those few seconds could change the outcome. That a small thing, when done well, could have a big impact."

"You're the most surprising person I've ever met." When I sneak a glance at Adam, I expect him to be grinning. Instead, he's studying me, the way I look at art. Like he wants to commit every bit of me to memory.

"That's me, an enigma," I give him a small smile.

His voice drops as he says, "Thank you for coming. I know it meant a lot to Nella."

"Of course."

"I didn't mean to interrupt your day. And I know this isn't a pleasant thing. But thank you, Lizzie. Being in that place was a lot easier with you there." Adam's facing me completely now, downy eyes turning darker.

"You didn't interrupt anything. My friends were helping me plan an extravagant dinner for you, so I could fully apologize," I say. I fight the flutter of nerves in my stomach. Damn caterpillars, going full butterfly.

He clears his throat. "You don't owe me an apology."

"Yes, I do. I've been so distant since we found out about the wedding. I didn't know how to process everything. I wasn't ready for Lionel to make a guest appearance in my life."

"You have nothing to apologize for. I get that you were with Lionel and now he's marrying someone else, and you have to be involved. It's a crappy situation. Plus, you were right. I am leaving and you're building something good here, I don't want to get in the way of that with something temporary."

My heart plummets, hearing him echo back the words I said when I was upset. And I'm still scared, but I manage to say, "What if… what if I changed my mind?"

"What do you mean?" Adam's voice is laden with questions neither of us are explicitly asking.

I throw on the blinker and pull onto a shoulder that abuts a field of long grass and wildflowers. I unbuckle and turn to face him, the wind dancing through Adam's window and leaving through mine, playing with our hair along the way. It bathes me in that woodsy, minty smell that is so purely Adam, it makes me smile. His eyes follow the movement.

"What if I want more than temporary?" I say in a soft voice. The vulnerability hums through my skin, and my heart steps out of my chest. It's a relief to speak the truth, even knowing my fragile heart might be smashed to pieces by the end of this conversation. Adam's eyes soften.

"What are you saying, Lizzie?" His voice is gentle, a caress. I want to cocoon myself in it. I want to wrap myself in the safe, reliable, caring essence of him.

"I want us to be together. I know the long-term situation would be a puzzle, but… but I want to figure it out. Being with you feels like this piece of myself that went dormant is coming back to life. Like the world expands when we're together. I don't care about Lionel. I don't care about distance. I am saying I want to do this, for real. Because I feel like you see all the dark parts of me, all the sad pieces I'm still welding back together, and you care about me anyway. I like you so much, and despite my terrible communication lately, I can't imagine not talking to you every single day. These last few days were torture, honestly."

I choke on the word *like* because what I feel for Adam is so much more than that. But in all of my admissions, I'm still not ready to admit to more.

Adam is quiet, but I watch a slow smile burn its way across his face. My heart somersaults when he reaches out to tuck a strand of hair behind my ear. He opens his palm and lays his hand on my cheek. The contact calms me, even as my pulse skyrockets.

"I just so happen to like puzzles." His thumb moves to stroke my skin and the electricity between us heats me to my core. There is so much unspoken potential hanging thick in the summer air. It's kindling, waiting for his words to set it ablaze.

"You are so beautiful, E. So smart. So fucking witty." Adam's dimple appears, and I think I must be melting. I'm gooey as Adam's apology brownies. "I love taste-testing with you, watching you moan over pancakes. I love watching you come back to yourself. There are no dark parts of you, only pieces of yourself other people didn't know how to appreciate. I won't make that mistake. I'll spend every day we're together making sure you realize that you're life-altering in every incredible way. So, let's do it. I'm in."

My heart feels like it might explode, the joy aches so sweetly.

"Adam, I…" I don't get the rest out, because his hands shift into my hair, tilt back my head.

"Please," Adam says throatily. Like he's a drowning man who's stumbled upon an oasis. "I've been waiting days to kiss you." I make a soft, breathy noise and then his mouth is on mine, tongue parting my lips. There is no more sound of cars whizzing past, or birds chirping, there's only the sigh that leaves him. When I bite his lip, he pulls me onto his lap. He bites my chin and moves his mouth higher to whisper into the shell of my ear, "Nothing on earth tastes as good as you do on my tongue."

"Not even an in-season apple pie?" I ask, voice breathy as he kisses down my neck. "I know the things you'll do for a crisp crust." If I don't try for levity, I may die from all this happiness.

"Nothing, Lizzie. I would change my entire world to have my mouth on you every day," he sighs into my clavicle.

A fire engine roars past, sirens screaming and reminding us that we're still on the side of the road. "We should probably go, before someone thinks we need checking on," I say reluctantly.

"Okay. Just one more minute." Adam lets his head rest over my heartbeat. I wrap my arms around him, pushing him into me. Holding on to the one thing I desperately want to keep.

23

I ring Nella's doorbell with one hand and balance a plant-adorned wicker basket full of goodies in the other. There's nothing more satisfying than putting together the perfect gift and I put a lot of thought and time into this one; it looks professional grade if I'm being honest. Floral arrangement may be my forte, but gifting is my passion.

I'm surprised when a child's face answers the door with a robust "hi!" It takes only a glance to recognize the features; a small nose, delicate ears. Nella's granddaughter looks so much like her.

"Hi, hello. I'm Lizzie. A friend of Nella's."

"Oh, Grandma told me about you! You're the plant girl." She nods enthusiastically at the basket in my arms. It's an apt description, especially since my Jeep is chock full of plants for Nella's window boxes. Zed comped them all for me because he is, undeniably, the best.

"Shelby, who is that?" A woman who I assume is Shelby's mother materializes behind her.

"It's Lizzie," Shelby says, as if that explains everything. Got to love kids.

"Oh my gosh, so sorry to keep you standing outside here." The woman gestures me inside. "Let me help with the door." She opens the screen for me, and I step into Nella's home.

"Thank you."

"I'm Maria. My mom says you were there that day at the hospital?"

"Yes, I was there with my… Adam." I cringe internally. *My*

Adam? That didn't come out the way I wanted it to.

"Thank you so much for being with her. I know how much it meant to have you two there. It's hard to be so far away as she gets older." Maria bites her lip and I can tell she's reliving how close she came to losing her mom.

I never know how to handle these conversations, and I'm not particularly keen on oversharing. But I lean into my instinct to open up, so that Maria feels comfortable doing the same.

"I understand. My mom had some scary health issues a few years ago. I couldn't stand to be away from her, either. It was an honor to be there with Nella. Please know I'll help out however you need." I reach out and touch her forearm.

Maria's eyes silver. "Thank you, Lizzie. Mom talked about how thoughtful you were, but it's so nice to meet you in person." I offer a soft smile. "Here, let me help with that." I hand her the basket and we walk towards the living room.

"Wow, this is stunning." Maria lifts up the basket to get a better view. It *is* beautiful. I filled it with things Nella might enjoy and need; cozy socks, a calming candle from Scentsational, a gift certificate to order delivery from a local pasta shop, a puzzle, and a ton of other goodies. I managed to weave a live pothos plant around the handle and crafted a mini bouquet clustered in a mason jar. "I wish I'd known about these gift baskets all those time I sent my friends flowers. This is so much more practical and thoughtful than your typical arrangement. Where'd you get it?"

"Oh, I made it," I blush. "I work at a greenhouse so that's where the plants came from. All the other goodies I shopped for locally."

"It's incredible. Mom's gotten a ton of flower deliveries, but this is way more her speed." Maria's smile is genuine, and warm pride flushes from my head to my toes at her praise.

We walk into the living room, where Nella is curled up under a crocheted throw that I'd bet she made herself. Shelby has returned to her side, and they're playing checkers on a small side table.

"Lizzie, dear! Hi!" Nella grins and gets up. She looks much more vibrant than the last time I saw her. I let out a breath I didn't realize I was holding.

"Nella, you look great." I walk over and give her a hug, careful not to bump the checkers.

"Having my girls here has helped tremendously. Shelby is a particularly great caregiver. She always puts just the right amount of ice cubes in my water, isn't that right sweetheart?"

Shelby grins at her grandma, nodding aggressively. "Gram drinks *a lot* of water. Did you know humans are made up of mostly water? It's in our blood!"

"That's true. We are nearly 60% water," Nella smiles, ever the teacher.

"Shelby, now that Gram has company why don't we take a walk to the park down the street? I bet the ice cream truck is there," Maria offers.

"Okay! We'll finish checkers when I get back, Gram!" Shelby kisses her grandma on the cheek before she runs to get her shoes.

"We'll give you a bit to hang, Mom. Lizzie, it was wonderful to meet you. If you ever want to make more of those baskets, I have a whole slew of people to send gifts to over the next few months. Does my mom have your number?"

"I've never made them for other people. But yes, she does. I could definitely put something together for you."

"A ton of my friends would love your work. I'll have Mom share your cell and get in touch." Maria smiles and goes to help Shelby apply sunscreen. I nod, wondering if she'll reach out. The idea of building custom gifts for her friends incites a tinge of nerves mixed with excitement. I turn to Nella.

"Lizzie, how are you? It's so nice of you to come visit."

"I'm doing great, thank you. The wedding is coming up quickly, so I've been super busy. But it's exciting, honestly. Adam wanted to stop by with me, but he had a last minute meeting with a potential client. I know he came by a few days ago, I'm sure he'll be stopping by again this week."

Nella's eyes light up at the mention of Adam.

"How is that partnership going with you two?" I don't miss the undertone.

"He's great to work with," I say noncommittally. Nella

smiles, like she can see past every barrier I try to keep up. I move the conversation in another direction. "I brought some flowers for your window boxes. I have a few different options. Would you like to see them?"

After Nella pours me a cup of hibiscus iced tea and assembles a plate of the cookies from her gift basket, we set up outside. Nella sits in a lawn chair, the flowers from my car unloaded before her.

Pink, purple, and white petunias dot the lawn along with inch plant, a light purple plant I brought to cascade over the planter's edges. I rip open a fresh bag of soil and tug the stuck-together planters apart.

"These are beautiful, Lizzie." Nella sighs. "Mateo would have loved the deep purple. Let's go with those, please."

"Sure thing," I say with a smile. I pull the purple and white pots towards myself and line them up the way I want them, tucking the inch plant in the middle. The pink will go back to Zed, although he'll probably tell me to bring them to my mom.

As I push gently on the flexible sides of the pots to loosen the roots I ask, "What was Mateo like?"

Nella's voice goes dreamy. "He was such a gentle soul. Quiet, contemplative. He loved mind teasers. He did all our gardening, although I'm not sure that man ever ate a vegetable in his life, starches notwithstanding." She chuckles, more to herself than anything. "He could be so stubborn. He was the love of my life."

I hear the tears in her voice before I look up, and regret bringing up this line of conversation. I wish I'd bit my tongue. "I'm sorry, I didn't mean to make you upset."

Nella laughs. "Honey, I'm not upset. After all this time, I still cry at the beauty of finding each other. We were so fundamentally different, and yet we built an incredible life together. We knew one of us would leave the other first." She shrugs. "We planned to be together until the end, and that means there was every chance that old age and life would come for one of us before the other. I'm not sad, because I'd do it all again. I'd lose him all over if it meant I got to have the lifetime's worth of love we shared."

It's not until a drop lands on my dirt-streaked jean shorts that I realize I'm crying, too.

"Can I be honest with you, Lizzie? Even if it's none of my business?" Nella asks, wiping at her wet cheeks with the back of one hand. Her wedding ring sparkles in the sunshine.

"Of course you can." I swallow.

"Maybe he's already told you this, but I think Adam is head over heels for you. The way he looks at you when you're not looking… it's how I'd look at Mateo if he showed up one last time.

"I know being at that hospital was hard on him. But with you there, he seemed like he could breathe. And when he came by a few days ago, you were all he could talk about. I don't think I've ever seen him so distracted. The boy nearly dropped a casserole. It was adorable." Nella smiles in that *I know everything so why bother lying* way that my own grandmother used to have.

I blink away the straggler tears while my heart plays hopscotch. "I think I may have some similar feelings," I admit. I should have expected Nella to note every change in Adam. And although she hasn't known me for very long, I guess I am an open book.

"But he's leaving, so it's complicated." I sigh. "He told you that, right?" I quickly add, hoping I haven't shared too much personal information on Adam's behalf.

"Ah, yes. He told me. Honestly, I understand needing a change but I don't think he needs to run so far away. I told him so."

"How'd that go?" I ask.

"He's stubborn, that one." She smiles sadly.

I give her the barest truth. "I already care so deeply for Adam, I don't want to hold him back. I think this is where I'm supposed to be, but his life is carrying him elsewhere."

"Hm. Well, I've always lived in this one place, so I'm not the best to offer advice about a big move," Nella says. She pauses, thinking. "But I do know a good deal about relationships."

"Those haven't been my strong suit lately. But I'm working on it."

"That doesn't seem true," she replies immediately." I've seen you show up for me. For Adam. I know that life is an adventure. But the people… those are the most important piece of the puzzle. Not only romantic relationships. People you trust, that you rely on, they won't leave you just because your lives go in different directions. What do you want for yourself?"

"I want to move in a direction that feels like *me*." The words leave my lips before I have time to think. I watch them hang in front of me. They're utterly, undeniably true.

'So, what feels like *Lizzie* to you?" Nella smiles softly, pitching me the hardest, easiest question.

What feels like me? Not being afraid to figure it out as I go, or to make mistakes. Building something new, something beautiful. I look down at the collection of flowers I've put together, think about all the new things I've done and relationships I've forged recently. I've discovered new passions, strengthened friendships, and built a life for myself that is filled with people and experiences I genuinely care about. This is the version of myself I love, the one who supports people, who tries new things, who makes choices without second guessing. This whole time I thought I was standing still, but maybe my growth has been below the surface. Maybe I've been expanding my sense of self, my life, by reaching my roots out in new directions.

"Gram, look what we found! It's so big!" I'm saved from answering by Shelby skipping across the lawn yielding a gigantic maple leaf. Nella's face turns to her like sunflowers to sunshine, beaming.

I focus on the plants around me, extracting them from their individual pots and arranging them together. I cover them in new soil and consider if replanting myself could feel like happiness, too.

24

The morning of the wedding unfolds with a picture-worthy sunrise. I've already been awake for hours by the time the glowing orb peeks out from the edge of the earth. Witnessing a sunrise in the greenhouse feels like watching a fresh version of the world unspool. I love being there when the plants unfurl, arms reaching towards sustenance and warmth.

I haven't seen Adam since I dropped off the herbs a couple days ago. He opted for the full plants, so he can pick the basil, rosemary and thyme fresh right before cooking and garnishing. He's been busy prepping and training up his catering team since then. I imagine this will be a crazy morning for him, too. Just because we aren't together doesn't mean I'm not thinking of him relentlessly.

I take a swig of the iced coffee that Nina shoved into my hands upon arrival, bless them, and turn back to my prep sheet. I highlight "review event timeline" since I've had that memorized since last week. Next up, the sub items under "Check inventory." I highlight vases, tools, floral tape, and O.S.B. (short for my coveted Oh Shit Box, which contains duct tape, twine, and everything I could possibly need to remedy any disaster on earth or in a spaceship). The only thing missing from inventory are the floral arrangements, which Nina and I will inspect before I load them up.

"How are we looking?" I jump at Nina's voice behind me.

"You scared me! Did you tiptoe over here? Be gentle, I am very fragile today." I put a hand on my heart.

"I could have clomped over here on horseback and you

wouldn't have noticed. You're in the zone this morning. Ready to look over the flowers?" Nina grins.

"Yeah, let's do it." I roll the highlighter away from the edge of the desk and stand up.

"Nice T-shirt." They nod at Blondie, smiling out from my vintage tee. Adam sent it as a good luck present this week. Even if we haven't had much free time to spend together, his thoughtfulness has crumbled the rest of the walls I had built over my heart. That man will be my undoing.

"Thanks. It was a gift."

"From your tasty boy toy? That was a chef pun for you, in case you missed it," they say.

"From my *colleague.* Who happens to also be my *friend.*" I know I'm being defensive, but if it's that obvious to Nina, does everyone see it? Even if I've admitted my feelings to Adam, I'm hesitant to tell the world that Adam and I are more than friends before the wedding is over.

"Okay, I can respect that."

I sigh. I am so tired of keeping things under wraps, and I know Nina would never judge. They've watched me cry over dead plants and spilled coffee. I think of the flowers, unafraid to open themselves up to the world every day. I think of Jessie telling me that good friends make space for all parts of us.

"You're right. It's a weird thing. I'm trying to make sure today is perfect. I keep thinking if I stress about the wedding, maybe I won't have to think too much about Adam. And how it's going to end up."

"How's that working so far?" They sip their own coffee, giving me space to talk.

"Not great, if I'm being honest."

"Doesn't seem like it."

"I'm worried I'll see how good he is at his job today and it'll make me want to melt into a puddle. And then I'll try to chain him to a bedpost or something to keep him here. Not in like, a sexual way," I add, the mention of a bed making my cheeks burn.

"I could see how that's challenging. Although I've never experienced that myself. Derrick's electrical wiring jobs are not exactly a turn on." Nina smirks and I chuckle.

"But honestly," they continue, "I'm intrigued to meet this colleague friend of yours. I need to see if he lives up to the hype. If you aren't in love with him by now, I'm pretty sure Zed is. The custom tea mixes he's been bringing by have Zed swooning."

"They have a bromance to a level which I never previously thought possible."

"Truth."

I'm happy that Nina and their grounding presence will be with me through today; I'm not sure how I could face this alone after my last time on those perfectly manicured grounds went so horribly wrong. At least today, there shouldn't be any surprises. Today, I have a list. I throw an extra highlighter in the Oh Shit Box with a flourish.

Everything is smooth, up until we arrive at the venue to find the front gate very clearly locked. I press the buzzer like we did last time, but no one answers. After three tries and ten minutes, I am starting to panic.

"Maybe it's broken?" I chew at my thumbnail. My schedule did not account for a delay.

"Maybe all the butlers are busy shining people's shoes," Nina says, looking at the towering hedges as if we might drive the van through them.

I give Lauren a call, but her phone goes to voicemail. I'm not surprised; I'm sure she's also busy getting everything in order. I flip open my binder to the page of contact info. I would never bother the bride or groom on a day like this. The next contact on the list is Natasha, mother of the groom. Excellent.

I was never close with Lionel's family, since they lived on the West Coast. I might be able to get away with pretending not to know the cousins I met once on a trip to California, but there's no way his *mother* won't recognize me.

I borrow Nina's phone, since I'm sure my number is still buried somewhere in Natasha's contacts, and I don't want to shock her with a phone call from her son's ex on his wedding day. I have no idea if Lionel told her I'm involved; I'm betting no. Communication was never his strong suit.

On the second ring, a male voice answers.

"Hello?"

"Um, hi. Lionel." Shit.

Nina mouths LIONEL, their eyebrows lifting to their hairline. I nod.

"It's Lizzie. I'm outside. With the flowers. We're having issues with that gate… will you let us in?"

"Lizzie. Hey, hi. Yeah, sure thing. I'll be right out."

Nina and I have a couple minutes to prepare, during which I silently mouth *fuck* and try not to panic while Nina squeezes my hand. None of my visions of today involved me interacting with Lionel directly.

I'm back to faking calm, cool, and collected by the time Lionel himself opens the gate. He waves us in and closes it behind us. I stop the car, not because I want to talk to him but because it would be rude to drive away and ignore the unfortunate reality of his existence.

Lionel walks to my driver's side window. "Lizzie, hey. Sorry about the gate thing. The buzzer guy wasn't there."

If I've ever wondered if the groom goes through the same hours-long preparation on wedding day, Lionel is proof to the contrary. He's wearing sneakers and I deduce that he is at least lightly buzzed, based on his gait and lightly slurred speech.

"No worries. Hey, I'm sorry if my involvement made anything awkward for you or Faye. Thanks for agreeing to keep me on," I say.

"Oh, no problemo. Faye was kind of weirded out, but I know your work and obligations come before feelings or whatever. You're the most by the book person I know. You'd never go off script. I told her that."

His words should irk me. I imagine the way they would have cut me in the past. But now they just feel like a reminder of Lionel's one-dimensional view of people, and how little he ever truly knew me. I feel nothing but a slight spark of happiness that I am not the one who will be stuck with this man, for better or worse.

"Thanks, I appreciate that," I say, and mean it.

"Hey Lizzie?"

"Yeah?"

"How's your mom doing? I'm sorry about how that all went down." Lionel, who I've seen stand in front of crowds of thousands without batting an eye, looks flustered. And although I want to revel in it, I want this momentous chapter of my life to be closed. I want reconciliation. I want Lionel to move on and I want that for myself, too.

"She's doing great," I say with a grin. "Honestly? Staying with her was exactly what I didn't know I needed." The rightness of that statement lands in me like a stone settling in water.

I offer him a truth that I didn't know I had in me. "I'm happy for you, Lionel. I'm glad things worked out the way they did. Faye seems lovely."

"She is," he beams. "Right on, Lizzie. I'm happy for you, too. Being a badass business lady." Lionel waves and climbs back in his golf cart. It isn't until he zooms away that Nina says "Badass business lady? What a dweeb."

I snort a laugh, and we are back to focusing on the big picture.

The rest of the day goes off without a hitch. I'm so busy that I don't have time to worry Lionel's family or friends will see me. A few do, and although they must find it strange, they don't say anything. So I don't either.

After setting up the altar and lining the walkway with fresh flowers, the last pre-ceremony task is to deliver the flowers to the wedding party. Nina's on her way to the carriage house with the boutonnieres, which means I'm responsible for the bouquets.

I don't see anyone outside of the bridal suite, so I knock softly. When the door cracks open, excited chatter spills out in a variety of languages. I'm surprised when I realize that it's Faye herself who has opened the door. Her friends are preoccupied watching each other get hair and makeup done and don't notice my arrival.

"Lizzie, hello."

"You look beautiful," I say without thinking. It's true. Faye's dress is flowing, her hair in an intricate updo complete with a tiara. She looks like she's stepped out of a fantasy novel.

"Thank you." She gives me a demure smile.

"I came to deliver your bouquets. Then I'll get of your hair." I lift my arms as proof, offering out the boxes I carried in from the van.

"Please, come in." Faye steps aside and I place the first round of bouquets on the side table. Faye's friends finally notice me, and although they are clearly intrigued (I'm sure they've heard the drama) their smiles are kind.

I lay out the arrangements. When I'm done, I walk to where Faye stands in the hallway, chatting with Lauren. Lauren gives me a hurried hello before wandering off, presumably to make sure everything is picture-perfect.

Faye turns to me. "Okay, that's it," I say. "You'll want to wipe the bottoms of the bouquets down once you take them out of water so they don't drip, I've left some hand towels for that. I'll be back later this evening to dissemble the features and collect the vases."

Faye's eyes find mine. "I would like to say thank you."

"You're welcome. Everything looks amazing. I hope you have a perfect day with the perfect flowers." I hold the eye contact, feeling like this is an important moment for more reasons than my career. I *do* want her to have a perfect day. I want everyone to find love and embrace it, without complication. I want for others what I've only recently realized I also want for myself.

"Not just for preparing the flowers. But also for being respectful and persevering, even within the circumstances. You are a very nice person." Faye nods, agreeing with herself as the words fall like confetti around me.

Happiness blooms in my chest, spreading like bright yellow food coloring in water. "Oh. Well, thank you. This is extremely important to me. And I think you deserve to be happy. I am glad you two found each other." I should probably say I wish for Lionel to be happy, too. But a girl's only got so much grace to give.

"Thank you. Now, I have to check on my friend's makeup. She has a penchant for smoky eye that does not work with my vision. Goodbye, Lizzie." Faye nods again, and then slips back into the realm of hairspray and laughter.

Nina and I leave after we set up, and I take a hot shower and a nap before I head back for clean up. I wake up to a text from Adam:

Adam: *Things are heating up over here (in a good way). Can't wait to see you later.*

I throw on my usual t-shirt and leggings combo and make my way back towards the estate to pack everything up. Time to finish this.

By the time clean up duty ends, my hair has come half unpinned from its bun, curly pieces breaking free and tickling the sides of my face. I blow them out of my eyes and check the final items off my list.

The relief of this day, this challenge, being over is palpable. My brain is tired, but my body is wired from the mix of late-afternoon coffee and success. I've never been more grateful for an hour of sleep than the nap I took between drop off and pick up.

The guests are happy, everyone is drunk and tired, and all of the serving equipment has been dutifully packed into the van.

Adam informs me that three glasses have been broken, which is apparently fewer than usual. Despite the commotion and cheers of OPA!, no bare feet were harmed.

Adam sent the rest of the crew home, so it's just the two of us packing up. The company that handles the linens has long since stripped the tables. Even the remaining guests have moved indoors to continue the party.

"I think that's everything," I say cheerily, doing a final check before setting down my list. After Nina and I packed up the last bubble-wrapped vase, they loaded up the van and left to drop everything at the greenhouse.

"Nightcap?" Adam asks. He smiles at me, hair disheveled and shirt rumpled. He looks exhausted but deeply content.

I bite the inside of my lip. "What if we get in trouble?"

"What if?' He cocks an eyebrow, a challenge issued. It's not much of a risk, considering no one is paying any attention to the two of us cleaning in dirty aprons. The only concern is being alone on a moonlit summer night with a man I can't seem to resist, who currently smells intoxicatingly like mint and woodsy aftershave. Shouldn't he smell as sweaty as I feel?

I take a breath. I said I'd be more open in this new dawn of my life, didn't I? The pull of the full moon and the ocean that I've heard but not been able to touch all night win out. "Let's do it."

Adam smiles and gives me the *one second* gesture. He walks to the truck and returns with a backpack. We slip off our shoes at the top of the wooden stairs and climb barefoot to the beach below in silence. The tide's up and the moon is so bright it looks like you could cross its ribbon of a path to the horizon. As we pad down the grooved steps, our hands brush.

My first footstep onto the cool sand melts the tension. We get halfway to the water before we plop down, both too tired to care about sandy pants. The waves swish softly, an endless rhythm that drops my heart rate. I made it through. The wedding is over, Lionel is married, and my life didn't implode. I feel strangely calm, like I'm floating on that endless trail of moonlight.

I hear a pop and a minute later, Adam hands me something in the dark. It's a tiny plastic cup of champagne. I smell it and the bubbles tickle my nose.

"Thought you could use your own celebration. You're going to make a great business partner, Lizzie." Adam clinks his cheap cup against mine and we sip. The bubbles tickle their way down my throat and I recognize this feeling as contentment, as time ticks on but I am happy to stay exactly where I am.

I'm not hiding in memories or pumping the brakes on the future. This happiness is here and now. I feel time unravel, opening space for a potential future I've been too afraid to let myself consider.

Adam is silent beside me. A soft breeze pushes his hair to the side and the warm glow of the moon reflects off his eyes. He looks the way I feel; peaceful. And even though I am terrified that what I'm about to do will ruin the moment, I'm more frightened of what happens if I let this feeling go. Because it's not the moonlight, and the ocean, and the bubbles. It's the person beside me who asked me to take a breath and experience this with him. My colleague who has become a friend, a support system, someone I know is always in my corner. I'm not just happy because I made it here. I am happy because I am here with Adam.

He's leaning back on both hands when I wedge my cup of champagne in the sand and reach my left hand out to cover his. The feeling of skin on skin sends electric signals to every part of my body. He pulls his gaze from the ocean to look at me. It's too dark to read his expression, but he leans in. I do too.

The first kiss is gentle, soft as moonlight. When we pull back in the dark, I almost believe I've imagined it. Until he leans in and kisses me again. This time the kiss is hungrier, sealing us together. The wind whips the rest of my hair free, and I feel him smile against my mouth.

"What's funny?" I whisper. I feel a little drunk, but since I've taken two sips, I know it has nothing to do with the champagne. The bubbles in my head mirror the butterflies in my stomach and the shivers of desire everywhere else. I've wanted this man for so long, and here he is laughing at me again. Instead of making me feel terrified, I'm exhilarated. I want to join in.

He turns away from me to rummage in the bag by his hip. "Hold on! I brought you something."

I make a horrified face. "If you pull a condom out of that bag, I swear to god, Adam…"

He looks back at me, feigning offense. "Really, you think I'd produce a condom with this much flourish? I do have *some* subtlety." He resumes rummaging.

"Ta-da!" He turns around, triumphantly wielding *something.* It's hard to make out at first, but once I recognize it, I laugh. It's a hair tie.

"Thought you might need one of these."

He dangles it towards me encouragingly and I take it. The plain black hair tie has a tiny piece of paper taped around it, fluttering in the wind. I pluck it off. It's hard to read in the darkness, so I hold it close to my face.

To have and to hold the hair of my favorite wedding date

There's nothing I can think to say that won't make me cry, so I close the space between us instead and almost knock Adam over as I scramble onto his lap. I press my nose to his nose.

"Thank you."

"For the hair tie?" That goddamn dimple is threatening to ruin me.

"No, for generally being the best person I've maybe ever met. And also for your Probsty dimples." I poke said dimple experimentally, then put my other fingers on his face.

"I thought we were past that." I feel the heat of him blushing in the dark.

"We'll never be past that." I lean in and kiss him without holding back, without over thinking. I kiss him the way I've wanted to since we stood in the warm belly of the greenhouse, sizing each other up. We kiss until I've forgotten all about getting in trouble for trespassing and am more focused on how I can get Adam out of his pants.

"I think we are out past curfew," I break away to whisper.

"You truly are such a rule follower." He starts kissing my neck and there's probably no rule I wouldn't break to ensure his mouth stays on my skin tonight.

"But you're right. Want to come over? I know it's been a long day, so I understand if you want to head home."

"I'd love that. But, only if I get to wash the smell of lavender out of my hair. If your shampoo and soap happen to be lavender scented, count me out." He grins.

"You're safe. I respect flowers, but I do not own floral-scented toiletries."

"Alright, let's get a move on then. I hear a hot shower calling my name." Adam holds my hands and we counter-balance each other so we can both stand in the shifting sand. He packs his bag and slings it over his right shoulder, then tucks me under his left arm like it's only natural that we stay wrapped up in each other. Warm joy melts me deeper into his side as we take the steps together, the wooden stairs creaking under our combined weight.

"Maybe we should have worked more closely today. Being in close proximity to you feels pretty stabilizing."

"I would have dropped at least three trays. Broken a thousand glasses," he smiles.

"No way! You're always the picture of suave. Like you've got your shit together."

"Lizzie, every time I'm with you I feel like I am trying so hard, I must look like the biggest bumbling idiot," Adam says without shame.

My cheeks flush. It's elating to know Adam feels the same way I do.

We're silent for the last stretch by the houses, afraid someone might hear us and break the spell of our magical post-wedding night. We make it to the truck unbothered. I expect Adam to go around to the driver's side, but he rests his palms on the frame so his arms are on either side of my head. There's space between our bodies, but it feels like we are the only two people on earth, locked together.

"I feel like I am on fire every time I'm around you," he whispers in the dark, like it's a secret.

"All I've wanted to do these past few months is spend time with you. To listen to you talk about flowers. Watch your fingers flutter when you get excited about something. You know how many times I wished I could hold your hand?

"I love feeding you delicious things that make you smile. I'm sorry if I sound creepy. I know you were in a weird place with this wedding. And that we don't know what the exact future looks like for us. But I couldn't let tonight end without saying that."

"I wouldn't have been able to get through this wedding with anyone else. Thank you. For being an amazing colleague and friend and… well yeah." I cut myself off because what else *is* he to me? He kisses me again, pinning me against the wind-cooled metal. My fingers twitch to touch him. I put my hands on his chest, then pull away when my pointer finger meets something sticky.

"Looks like you got down and dirty today" I lift my finger to show him the jelly smeared on it. His smile turns wicked as he gently grabs my wrist and sucks the finger into the heat of his mouth. He licks the jelly off me, and I am liquid.

"I think it's time to get cleaned up." Adam kisses me again before he opens the passenger door. I have so many things I need to tell him, so many plans stewing in my mind. But it's been a long day and I want to make sure this conversation happens when I can say exactly what I need to say.

We listen to boygenius on the way home and I keep my hands to myself, afraid to freak him out while he's driving. But when we get back to his house and the car is in park, there is tumult in those gray eyes.

"Come inside. You can shower while I make us dessert," he says low and thick.

"Aren't you tired of cooking?" I swallow.

"For you? Never."

"Okay," I say breathlessly. I fully lose the ability to form coherent thoughts when he leans over the seat and tastes me. He comes around to open my door, then intertwines our fingers and gently tugs me inside.

We hold hands in the kitchen and giggle about one of the bridesmaids who tooted while walking down the aisle (it was cruel to laugh, but impossible not to).

"Always a farting bridesmaid, never a farting bride," I shake my head sullenly, stifling my laughter.

It isn't long until Adam pulls me towards him by the waist and starts to kiss me in a way that makes my legs wobble. He pushes me up against the kitchen island so I can feel all of him, flush against me.

"Hi there," I try at nonchalance.

"Hi." His voice is rough. He is looking at me like I'm something prized and delicious.

"You're looking at me like I'm a truffle. Like a very expensive, sexy mushroom."

When he laughs, it shakes both of our ribcages.

"You have all the delicious things in the world to pick from and you're comparing yourself to a mushroom."

"Well, we don't have mushroom here, do we?" I gesture to the complete absence of space between us and can't contain my smile.

He leans in. His breath is warm as it tickles the delicate shell of my ear. "You're perfect, you know," he whispers, tucking back my hair.

"Not so bad yourself." I kiss him slowly, let my tongue explore and graze over his teeth. Then I push out my arm to give us some space. I take in the burning desire heating his face.

"Now, let me shower. I remember mention of desserts?" I shimmy off the island while Adam adjusts himself and nods.

"Towels are in the closet. I'll grab you some clothes. I will heat up leftovers?"

"Anything but broccoli sounds perfect." I give him a kiss and bite the bottom of his lip just hard enough to hurt. There is something so gentle in his offer to clothe and feed me, something that wrings out every ounce of doubt. I can't wait to tell him exactly how all in I am, no matter where he goest.

"If you aren't back here in fifteen minutes, I am coming in there to check on you. And that's a promise."

"Set a timer. I'll look forward to it." I wink, and head to the bathroom. I should probably take a cold shower to cool the heat in my veins. Instead, I step in and let the warmth embrace me.

25

The weeks after the wedding feel like emerging from a cocoon I didn't realize I was trapped in. Even as I revel in the success and what that means for Adam's business and my job security, there's a sense of wanting *more* that makes itchy. I am ecstatic that things went well, that I did Green With Ivy and Zed proud. Adam's gotten three inquiries from wedding guests, and even if he won't be around to fulfill them, it's nice that his talent's being recognized. The greenhouse is buzzing, literally and metaphorically. Nina and Zed made me cry when they bought me a cake covered in flowers and sang a congratulatory jingle.

But part of me wants to cast off this version of Lizzie and step into the next iteration of myself. I want to try. With Adam. With my career. To embrace this version of me who is curious about the world instead of scared of it. I want to feel and share everything, instead of keep it all locked inside.

For the first time, I see this wedding as a stepping-stone on a new path I haven't considered yet. I'm ready to shake the dirt off my Vans and take a step in a new direction.

That's why I asked Zed for a meeting. As I step into his office in the early morning, the fan doing nothing to combat the late summer humidity, I wait for my confidence to waver. But it doesn't.

"What's up, busy Lizzie?" Zed smiles up from his newspaper. I didn't even know they still delivered those anymore. Zed lays down his sweat-smudged copy. I take a breath.

"I think I want to start my own business." It tumbles out of me and lands between us. I expect the statement to take up too much space, or float away. Instead, it lingers. Solid, true, right. When he doesn't answer right away, I begin to worry. Zed's done so much for me, and I don't want him to think I'm ungrateful...

"Lizzie, that's terrific." He's beaming. "I always knew you were meant for big things. And I think that's the most decisive statement I've ever heard from you. So, what's the plan Stan? How can I help?"

I open and close my mouth once, a fish out of water. I'm not sure how it's possible that I'm surrounded by so much support. My soul is floating, buoyed by Zed's confidence in me.

"Um, well I haven't totally thought it through. But I think something in the curated gifts world. I do know that I'd like to take some time to figure it all out."

"Let me know how I can help you. And if you want to work in floristry here while you plan, I'd be happy to keep you, flower child. You did such a stellar job on the Everlast Wedding, I'll be able to keep Nina on full time if they agree to it. I might need your help convincing them, come to think of it. Make sure you talk up how much fun you had with your many highlighted lists." Zed, still smiling, walks over to pat my shoulder.

"You're not upset?"

"That I won't get to see you regularly? Of course. But I know what it's like to feel called to something. I would never get in the way of your dreams, kiddo. I will help you any way I can."

"Zed, I don't know what to say."

"Say that you'll take my place as the understudy for Chris' family's next virtual Shakespeare production and nothing more." He gives me a wink. "We'll do an event debrief this week and build in time afterwards to talk about how we can manipulate your schedule here. Sound good?"

"It sounds amazing. Thank you, Zed."

"You're welcome, Lizzie. Daisy says congratulations, she thinks you're going to be paw-fectly awesome at whatever you choose to do. Isn't that right, baby cat?" On cue, Daisy brushes against my legs and purrs.

"See? She's proud of you." Zed scoops her up and sets off

to fill her food bowl.

After the workday ends, I text Jessie and Clara in the group chat. Clara says she'll let James know I am out on the job offer.

Clara: *Good. Your ass is too hot to be eaten by an office chair all day.*

And to think, I was worried about letting her down.

I can't wait to break the news to Adam. I want to absorb his reaction in person, to share my excitement and fear and desire to build something that feels authentically me.

I know Adam will shower me with reassurance and motivation. But I also know that I'll need as much support as I can get. Which is why I don't second-guess myself as I stop by Scentsational on my way home.

Ginny looks up at the chime of the doorbell and waves. I browse the store while she finishes up her conversation with a man holding a toddler.

Once they leave with arms full of lotions and creams, Ginny wanders over. "Hi, sorry about the wait. Lizzie, right?" Ginny beams at me, and I'm impressed by her recall. I wonder how many people she meets every day, and how many of them (like me) she inspires with her story.

"Hi! Yes, Lizzie. I know this is kind of weird, but the last time I was here with my friend Clara, you told us about starting your own business." I clear my throat and go on. "It's something I just started thinking about and, well, I could use some perspective. I was wondering if you'd like to talk about your experience over coffee? My treat. Whenever you're free."

"Oh my god, of course. It would be my pleasure. I wish I had more people to talk to when I was deciding to do this thing for real."

"I appreciate it. I don't even know where to begin and to hear from someone it worked out for would help."

Ginny gestures to my phone. "Let me give you my cell and we'll plan something." She continues while typing in her number, "The shop's closed on Tuesdays, so that's probably most flexible for me. And kudos to you for asking for help. My parents thought I was nuts when I told them I was leaving my nine to five to open the shop. Having a community who knows your struggle is huge." Ginny's approval energizes me. The fact that she doesn't think I'm strange for reaching out to a relative stranger dissipates any tension. It's nice to ask for help for a change.

"I've never thought it could be a possibility for me but… it just feels right, you know?"

"I do know." Ginny nods. "Bring your ideas to our meeting if you want, I'll help you workshop them. Or you can rapid-fire question me. I'll make sure to keep the stress of first year sales and the incident also known as *the great flood* brief. Because once I was over that hump, the rest of it's been awesome."

I leave Ginny's with a coffee date set for Tuesday and the feeling that I might burst with potential. I stop at a bakery and pick up tiny celebratory cakes, one chocolate and one strawberry cream, Adam's favorite. He doesn't know it yet, but today is cause for celebration. The feeling of rightness I have—it's like finally stepping into myself.

When I get to Adam's, I let myself in with the spare key. This small piece of metal unlocks a future I haven't let myself imagine before now. A life where Adam and I brainstorm new recipes, compete in board game nights, and fall asleep to summer thunderstorms with the windows open. Daydreams swirl as I unlock the door. It's exciting to look forward to life's changes, instead of dreading them.

I slip off my shoes and make my way down the hall, balancing the cake boxes. Adam's in the kitchen, ingredients for the pesto he promised me spread out before him. When I step closer, I realize he's on a phone call with AirPods in, back to me. I place the cakes silently on the counter and though every part of me wants to wrap my arms around his waist and squeeze him from behind, I decide to be patient. As I lean over a chair to wait, he continues his conversation, ignorant of my presence. I've just reached into my purse to dig out my phone when he says, "Yeah, that sounds good. It's a deal. It'll just be me signing. Tell them I'll send over the down payment next week."

My stomach drops. Signing? Down payment?

"I can come inspect in person if you need me to. I'm in over my head, everything is happening fast and I need space. I want to move quickly."

My heart jumps into my throat. I know things between us moved quickly, but I was sure Adam wanted this to work. I imagined his dream of moving away solo might be replaced by pieces of our future together, until he started to envision a new picture.

At the very least, I thought there would be a conversation. One that went something like *will you come with me?* Or *I'll wait for you, we'll do this together.* I never imagined it'd be *moving quickly* or *needing space.* Once Adam told me how he felt for me, I truly didn't think I'd be left behind. Again.

Gosh, I am so, so stupid.

I'm living a sick version of Groundhog Day after falling in the same trap. The pressure in my chest is intolerable, building until I'm sure my body will fissure, cracking every part of my heart in the process.

Adam's done nothing wrong. But it doesn't stop me from shattering. Even if I was willing to go with him, he probably wants a clean slate. A fresh start. Away from anything that reminds him of this place. Away from me.

The reality burns a hole through me. So, this is what devastation feels like. Lionel hurt me, but I also never felt like Lionel understood me. Adam sees and admires my complexities in a way so few people have. He helped me step into a more complete version of myself. Adam was a slice of sunlight that I desperately wanted to bask in forever. It's hard to breathe through the hurt.

Before he hears me, I slip my phone back into my purse and pad to the front door. *Don't cry, don't cry.* I just need to make it to my car, and then I can give in to this disappointment that's threatening to eat me alive.

I can go to Jessie's. I can call Clara. Mom will cancel her Pilates class and watch movies and eat gooey chocolate chip cookies with me. I can fall into a safety net of the people who love me.

I grab my shoes instead of stopping to put them on and slip out the door.

The stifling heat of summer is a slap. The inside of my head feels as heavy as the stagnant air. I promised myself I wouldn't spiral. And yet, I've gone and derailed my life all over again.

A rush of cold air greets me when I open the driver's side door, remnants of air conditioning spilling out. It's a brutal reminder that it only took a few minutes in Adam's house to change everything. As I start to slide into the driver's seat and leave the heartbreak behind me, I hear a shout. "E! Hey! Lizzie! Wait!"

26

One thing about me; I am terrible at stealth mode. I've never regretted being the least sneaky person on earth until now, watching Adam run down his porch steps towards me. He clearly heard my hurried exit. I close my eyes.

"Lizzie, what's wrong?" The normally composed Adam sounds frantic. He reaches me and glances down at my one bare foot still outside of the car, burning on the pavement. I pull my second foot out of the car, drop my sandals and slide them on, buying myself time before I have to look at him. I'm not ready for this conversation. If only I'd been a little quieter.

"Are you okay? When I turned around, there were boxes on the counter, but you were gone. You'd never abandon cake without a good reason." He tries at a smile while his eyes scour my face for an explanation.

Oh right, the cake.

"Yup, I'm just peachy. The peachiest. Just call me cobbler, that's how peachy I am," I say thickly. I finally open my eyes and give him a wobbly smile. "I just misunderstood."

I don't want to cry in front of him. But, like having to pee after a road trip and finally pulling into the driveway, I was so close to being in the solitary confines of my car that I can't keep the dam from breaking. I consider running away, but my lack of sneakers makes it difficult to full-out sprint. "It's my fault. I got the impression that things between us were different. That your plans had changed. Anyways, you know what they say about assuming." I certainly feel like an ass.

"What are you talking about?" Adam's tilts his head, eyes

swirling gray and blue with worry. He steps closer, the smell of the woods enveloping me.

I put my hand out to keep him a step away. "You're leaving, and I get that," I say softly. "I can't spend more time wishing my life lined up with anyone else's. I need to come to terms with doing things on my own."

He keeps reading my face and I see the moment when he finds the answer he's looking for. His face softens. "You heard me on the phone." It's not a question.

"Yes. And I knew you were leaving once the wedding was over, and our plans to make a future together were vague. I just, I thought maybe things had changed. That you'd stay or we'd move together. But yeah. I hope your new place is awesome. And closer to a farmers market, like you've always dreamed." I try to joke, but the tears finally win. Adam steps towards me, but I don't want platitudes. I want to rip off this Band-Aid of hurt. I still have great parts of my life to focus on. I still have other people to share pieces of life with.

"Lizzie, I'm not leaving."

"Adam," I sigh through tears, "please. Go back inside and I'll go home."

"No, I mean I'm not moving. I'm not going anywhere." He takes a step towards me. I don't back away.

"Wh… What?" I sputter. "But I heard you talk about buying a new place."

"I finally committed to leasing a dedicated space for Clásico," he says. "No more using my entire upstairs as storage, or my kitchen as the main prep space. Things are going to grow quickly thanks to the new referrals from this wedding. I was going to tell you, but I didn't want to take away from your wins." The fist around my heart unclenches. I remember how to breathe, but the tears continue their slow roll down my cheeks.

"E, please don't cry." Adam lifts the hem of his t-shirt and, heartbreakingly gentle, uses it to wipe them away. "I thought once my stuff was moved, maybe you could use one of the rooms as a new office space. If you want. I think you should follow your dream, and I want to be here to help." The summer sun glints off his tousled hair. He's so earnest, hope rises in me like helium. Adam isn't asking me to change my life, he's asking to be a part of it. And the way he's looking at me says this is more than temporary.

"Can I hold you?" He asks.

I nod and am immediately wrapped up, pressed against him like he can't stand for there to be any space between us even in the sweltering heat. He rubs a hand along my spine and I melt.

I don't want to question him, because I want *here* and *together* to be the reality. But I would never ask Adam to stay somewhere that hurts him. I already love him far too much for that. "Don't you want to start fresh somewhere new? A place free from constant reminders of loss?"

He continues to hold me, pulling back only enough so I can see his face.

"I think I've realized that my sister is going to be with me wherever I go. Leaving this place won't ease the pain of losing her. And honestly, Megan would like the idea that I am building new memories somewhere that still feels connected to her. She would have loved you, you know. The two of you would have teamed up and given me hell." He smiles sadly, remembering his sister in a way I haven't yet seen. Like her spirit can still be a part of his life, even though she isn't physically here anymore.

"Do you want to know what I wished for on that Thai place's chalkboard?" He asks, soothing and gentle. His eyes hold mine, a silent promise. *I've got you. I won't let go until you tell me to.*

"No," I sniffle. "I want your wish to come true. It won't if you tell me, remember?"

"Don't worry. I think if you're part of the wish, you get to know about it, penalty free." His left hand comes to rest on my cheek, stroking.

"I wished for you to be happy. You said you'd written a whole bunch of things on that chalkboard, but none that you remembered. You seemed so hopeful that this time would be different. I promised myself I'd do anything to make your wish come true, E."

"But you don't know what I wrote," I say, confused. I know he didn't have time to ready hastily scribbled dream that day at lunch.

"It's kind of embarrassing, how much I thought about you after that lunch. How talented and fierce and so goddamn attractive I thought you were. I wanted to know you so badly, to know what you wrote so I could help you find whatever it was." He takes the hand from my cheek and runs it through his hair. "Shit, this is embarrassing. But I went back on a work trip into the city and figured it out. I looked for your handwriting; it's all over the chalkboards in the greenhouse. I knew you used blue chalk and where you were standing, because I couldn't take my eyes off you that day. Honestly, I haven't been able to think of anything or anyone but you since the day that we met.

"I fell in love with you in a million ways, for a million reasons, but seeing you show up for everyone else… you never stop believing in the good, Lizzie. I saw a glimmer of it the first day at lunch. All I could think was I would give anything to show you that you're worth staying for. That I love every single complexity of yours, every thought, every pun, every joke that slips out of that pretty little mouth."

My heart swells. *I fell in love with you* reverberates through my entire body. It warms me, like stepping into bath water after being out in the cold. Adam took time to understand me, went to lengths to find out what was important to me. He sees and loves all parts of me.

"You wished for life to make sense." He looks at me, the blue in his eyes a color that's been painted onto my soul.

"I'm staying. I know *my* life makes sense when I'm with you. If I got to write a new wish, it would be that you feel the same. I'd hope life with me makes sense for you. That you want to build a future together the way that I do. That you want *me* to stay. Because I am so fucking ready to show up for you every day. I want you to be my first taste-tester, always. I want you to teach me everything you know about plants and 80s hair bands. To wake up next to you. I want you to be the one to beat me in board games, even if my friends never let me live it down. Will you let me do that? All of it?"

This contentment threatens to swallow me whole. Like a door to part of me I'd closed off has finally unlocked. Like a key sliding into place.

I take a breath and find my voice.

"I thought you were an arrogant prick when we first met," I start. "Cactus pun intended." I watch his lip twitch. "But you're one of my favorite people to be around. You are so genuinely, unnervingly nice, Adam. And thoughtful. And did I mention that you also happen to be really, ridiculously good looking?" I watch the dimple grace his cheek and smile in return.

"I love you. So much already. And it's scary to say, and I don't want to freak you out, but I do, I want to try this. I want so many things when it comes to you. I want it all." Adam squeezes me to him, and I nuzzle into his collarbone.

I rest my cheek against his chest. "I came here to tell you that I'm leaving the greenhouse," I say into his shirt.

"What?" Adam looks down at me, joy and confusion etched into the lines in his brow.

"I have some new ideas for the direction I want to go with my work. I'm open to different versions of the future. To living different places, to trying out self-employment, to being more vulnerable. But every version of the future I want to build includes you."

His smile is the most stunning thing I've seen all day. And I work in a place filled to the brim with flowers.

"I love you, Lizzie," Adam whispers into my hair. "I'd go anywhere with you. I'd do anything for you." I smile into his chest and wrap my arms around his neck. I'm not ready to let go. I probably won't ever be.

I'm finally choosing the kind of life I want, one that's uniquely mine. There are so many changes on the horizon, and I can't wait to embrace them. I've always loved a sunrise, after all.

27

Mambo Number 5 thumps through the speakers, the bass matching the pounding of my heart. It's two o'clock in the afternoon, but Jessie, Clara, and I fly around the DJ like spinning tops. After an hour and a half of Clara's mom's mandated baby games, everyone seems *very* relieved to have escaped to the dance floor. Although, I admit, it was fun to watch an assortment of one hundred people in costumes perform to win the *Best Dad Joke* trophy.

Clark and Adam have gone off in search of refreshments. I imagine they're discussing the merits of flood insurance or something as thrilling; Jessie and I found out that those two nerd out hard during our double date last week.

I glance to my left at Jessie, and try to match the pace of her kickball change. Damn she's quick, even in her mile-high Sexy Patrick Star heels and fishnets. And, miraculously, she has breath left to talk. Clark dressed up as a rock (as in, the rock under which Patrick lives), which is so hilariously, perfectly Clark that Jessie didn't even try to get him to dress as a more exciting member of the Bikini Bottom community.

"I still think you should have come as SpongeBob and made Adam dress like Squidward. We could have done a four-way costume!" Jessie sulks.

"And think of all those tentacles," Clara winks on my right. Her baby bump is… well, bumping. She said her spawn (her words, not mine) was looking forward to "sloshing around in there."

"Well, I think this costume suits me better," I quip. "You

look a-Dora-ble, by the way." Clara is dressed up as Dora and her partner, James, is Backpack. When I asked why he didn't dress as Boots instead, she scoffed. "Backpack has a thousand times more swag than Boots, Lizzie. And if I don't get laid after my own party, then what was the point?" Apparently, my friends have a thing for men dressed as inanimate objects.

I glance over at Adam, who's showing Clark something related to the stock market or orthopedic shoes on his phone. Although he ignored Clara's request to go shirtless, he does make a pretty charming (and gigantic) Sully. He looks up and meets my gaze, like he knows exactly where to find my eyes, even in a sea of pipe cleaners and Party City getups. His smile lights me up from the top of my fake eyeball headband down to my green tightsed toes. Turns my personal version of Mike Wazowski is enamored with his hulking, hairy friend.

"Clara! Can I steal you for a second, *please.*" Clara's mother materializes behind us, exasperated. She is wearing Mickey Mouse ears and not a single other piece of costume paraphernalia. I wonder if she could have predicated that Clara's ideal baby shower would require two different frozen margarita dispensers and a fog machine.

After the two of them walk away, Jessie narrows her perfectly microbladed eyebrows. "I would have bailed on Clark to match outfits if you wanted, you know. The men might be temporary, but our friendship is forever. You're stuck with me. Non-negotiable. You're the jellyfish to my SpongeBob. The Brave Little Toaster to my Security Blanket. The HIM to my Mojo Jojo."

"I don't think those last two are technically *together*, but I know that," I laugh. Jessie takes that as an invitation to trap me in the tightest bear hug of all time before I can answer.

"Promise?"

"Yes. Promise. Can't. Breathe."

"You already couldn't breathe from the dancing," she says to the top of my head, since the heels give her about six inches on me, and gives me an extra squeeze. "Whatever happens, it's us forever, bitch." Even though we are at a standstill in the middle of the dance floor blocking other people's dance moves,

I don't care. I let Jessie wring out any of the remaining fear of change that occasionally creeps up.

"I'm so happy you're finally setting out on your own new work adventure. And I'm so pumped to live vicariously through you. If you run out of time for me because you're so busy being a hashtag girl boss, I'm going to throw a we-just-ran-out-of-Burnette's level meltdown, bitch."

I should have known I'd never live down the one time we ran out of alcohol when Jessie visited my college dorms. When your party-minded friends come to visit, stock up on everything. Lesson learned.

"Don't be silly, you've always got entree into my life any time." I wink.

"If that was a pun because you're now dating a chef, I'm going to scream." Jessie makes a sour face, even though I know she loves it.

I laugh, but the back of my throat grows tight. Some of my new life goals are uncharted territory for Jessie, my mom, my friends. The beauty of creating our own blueprints makes me emotional. I love the idea that, through each other, we get to experience a thousand different versions of life.

"Enough being sentimental, it's time to *dance*." Clara bumps her way back into the circle in her pink crop top and frilly yellow socks and everyone whoops. She backs it up on us.

"Jessie, we can also *help* Lizzie, you know. We won't snap in half if we have to paint a wall or something. Plus, I'll already be working on the launch strategy, right?" Clara beams at me while wiggling around. She's insisted on giving me marketing training while I build my brand and work on logistics.

"Very true. We'll be so annoyingly in your shit, hyping you up to everyone we know," Jessie says.

"Please, I want you there for all of it. The good, the bad, the ugly. And you know I will always carve out time for the people I love. Mom will kill me if I miss even one Pizza-zaz night. It's the one break she takes from eating organic. I've got to give her a reason to slam some Oreos and gobble Funions."

"Speaking of organic, how did the big move go?" Clara does a spin move before refocusing her energy on my answer.

I didn't necessarily plan on moving in with Adam so quickly but since I spent most of my nights at his place, it just made sense. I expected things to feel like they were moving too fast, but they didn't. It turns out I'm growing into a person who trusts her feelings and instincts instead of trying to match my life to arbitrary timelines.

"Things are great. We're currently peeling wallpaper in the room that will be my office. That part's torture. But I've got some IKEA mega-bookshelf plans in the works that'll be worth it."

"I am terrible at building furniture. I always lose those little wooden pegs. But I will bring wine and good chat," Jessie promises.

"Well, if we're talking about getting pegged, count me in."

"CLARA!" Jessie and I shout in unison.

Clara just laughs. "Come here." She scoops in Jessie with one arm and me with the other, and gloms us all together in a group hug, her bump tucked in the middle of our embrace. In this moment, I can see our shared future so perfectly; dinners with all of us passing around the baby, Jessie cracking jokes, Clara leaning in to whisper about the orgasmic quality of Adam's food. Adam smiling across the table, enthralled by Clark's new lawn management techniques. A world in which our separate lives are perfectly different yet lovingly intertwined.

As we unravel from the hug, the men return.

"Your drinks, ladies." Adam and Clark are impressively balancing a handful of colorful beverages.

"Thanks. Wow, look at the stability of those hands," I say to Adam as he doles out drinks. "If I've got a green thumb, shouldn't you have sausage fingers as a chef?"

He wiggles each finger individually. "Not sausagey in look, but sausagey in spirit."

"You know," I say, "you delivering me a beverage feels sort of familiar."

He hands me a margarita and leans down to whisper, "I thought about ordering you a Sex on the Beach, but I figure we can cover that base later." I blush and look up to meet his eyes. They reflect all the love, admiration, and desire I feel when we're together.

"I wouldn't change a single thing about that night. Or this moment." I link my arms around his neck, balancing the drink between them.

Adam kisses my forehead. "I am very thankful to that fruity drink and ensuing poisoning for bringing us together."

"Me too." I sigh and lean my body into his, breathing in the forest essence that is Adam.

"Okay lovebirds, get over here and do the Stanky Leg with me or I'm calling party foul!" Clara yells from the middle of the dance floor.

Despite it being midday and Clara's grandmother sitting at the edge of the dance floor near us, Adam kisses me shamelessly before saying, "Let's get stinky."

He grabs my hands, and we head into the dance circle to break it down. I don't need this extra giant green eyeball to see that these people are my happiness. These people are my forever. Even as I watch my boyfriend dance with a human rock and Clara pretends to strap her husband on like a real-life backpack, my life makes perfect sense.

28

"You alright in there?" Adam taps on the door, checking to see if I'm still alive.

"One more minute!"

I zip myself into a funky dark purple jumpsuit I found at my new favorite vintage shop up the street. I should have gotten ready hours ago, but I was worried I'd get dirty while making last-minute preparations. No matter how clean I try to be, I always manage to collect smudges. Now I'm late to my own party.

"Okay, set!" I open the office door and step into the forest green hall of Love It or Leaf It. "How does it look?"

The murmur of voices filters down the thin hallway, and I'm suddenly nervous. I bite my lip, but Adam steps into my line of sight before I start to panic.

"Shit, you look spectacular, E." He looks down at me like he wants to eat me. My blood boils.

"Be careful, or I'm going to have to help you out of that outfit sooner rather than later." I flush from my head to my fingertips, then tell myself to cool it.

"Thanks." I reach out and touch that beautiful dimple for good luck.

"Are you blushing?" He teases.

"Nope. Must be the lights." I point up at the Edison bulbs that run the length of the ceiling.

Adam chuckles before kissing my forehead and scooping me into a hug.

"I'm so proud of you," he whispers into my hair. I let myself soak it all in while the tinkle of laughter floats to us. Adam's gentle love wraps around me like a weighted blanket before the happy mayhem of the day begins.

He sets me down again, but it still feels like I'm floating.

"Thanks, I like it too." I twirl so the bell-bottom legs flare out. "I couldn't have done this without you."

"That's not true. You may have struggled hanging some of the taller plants, sure. But you were always going to accomplish whatever you chose to do. Whether I was here or not." He kisses me again, this time on the lips, and takes my hand. He's right. But it sure has been a hell of a lot easier with his support and affinity for power tools.

Together, we walk down the hallway to the front of the shop.

Disco ball planters spin in the windows, throwing rainbows in all directions. The light shimmers over the people who have made the trek to Love It Or Leaf It's grand opening. True, it's only twenty minutes away from Windstone so it's not too bad a drive, but I am still deeply grateful for the effort.

The shop – my shop – creates specialty gifts that include floral arrangements paired with local products. We get our fresh flowers from Zed and our collections feature local goods like small-batch honey and soy candles. We offer a wide variety of hand-selected items to celebrate every type of accomplishment, from births and engagements to writing a novel or running a marathon. Organic running gels, baby bibs (I love you from your head to your toma-toes being my favorite), plant propagation stations; we can create a custom celebration basket for every occasion. I've loved creating a space that celebrates people's individuality.

Ginny has been especially helpful getting through all of the paperwork and recommending people to build out the shop. She chats with Bob in the corner, whose bee collection recently doubled when he acquired Nella's bees. Nella couldn't make it, since she finally moved to live with her daughter, but she sent a beautiful note. It's pinned to the cork board behind the register, where we'll encourage guests to pin up their own stickers, mementos, or scrawled wishes.

It's been a daunting venture, opening my own store. But Brett's marketing classes paired with Clara's expertise are helping me build confidence in my brand. It helps that I have plenty of experience handling financials and balancing Zed's books. I wave to Zed and his husband, Chris, who gives me a thespian's bow from the crowd.

I look around, taking it all in. I see myself reflected in the decor, the thoughtful touches, and the Soft Rock covers playing in the background. I'm nervous, but I'm bolstered by the bone-deep sense of rightness I feel every time I step into this space. Adam smiles, reveling in my happiness. His love seeps like rain into every one of my pores, watering my soul.

Adam's parents hang in the corner with my mom, who's been chatting them up about the benefits of her new step aerobics class. As I'm about to greet everyone, the door chimes. My heart warms, a lightness spreading through all of my limbs.

Jessie and Clark walk in, trailed by Clara. She's carrying the newest addition to our friend group, baby Greg.

"Lizzie!" Clara and Jessie yell in unison, like they've been practicing it. The force of them almost topples me, both of my friends smushing me in a group hug that only ends when baby Greg squeals from the middle of it all. When we pull back, he squirms in Clara's arms and reaches for my dangling earrings.

"Here you go, Clark. This is either good practice for the future or a reminder to use birth control." Clara turns around and plops baby Greg into the arms of Clark, who doesn't look as alarmed as I'd expect. On the contrary, he acts like having a baby shucked off on him happens on the regular, making funny faces until Greg cracks a smile. I turn my attention back to Jessie as she says, "Oh my frickin' god, look at you!" She grabs my hand and twirls me around. "You look gorgeous, this is absolutely your color. Hi Adam. You look nice, too." She goes on tiptoe to kiss Adam's cheek. He greets my friends and then excuses himself to check on his parents.

"I second all of that. This place is incredible, Lizzie. I am so beyond excited for you, you beautiful fucking unicorn." Clara squeezes my hand.

It's comforting to know some things never change. Clara's

language never toned down after pregnancy turned into an actual human child. She slipped seamlessly into the mom role, foul mouth and all. I'd bet Clara's commitment to only ever being herself is why Greg's the most chill baby I have ever met.

"Thanks, all of you. I'm so happy you're here." They've seen me cry over this place and heard enough about my imposter syndrome over the past year that I wouldn't have been shocked if I scared them off. It turns out, once I open the tap to my feelings, they're impossible to bottle up again.

"Of course we're here! This is truly insane. Look at your dream come to life!" Jessie presses the side of her face to mine, and I wonder if her makeup will leave an imprint. "I want to be you when I grow up. So proud of you, babe."

"Seriously, Lizzie. You are an inspiration," Clara says. "Now what's a girl gotta do for a glass of champagne? No more designated driver lifestyle for me, thank you very much." I point towards the front counter, laden with snacks made by Adam and champagne uncorked by yours truly.

"Watch the baby!" Jessie calls over her shoulder to Clark as they wander away to pour themselves some bubbly.

As I look around, my heart goes full Grinch mode, growing three sizes. This is a life I chose. A life I worked for, and compromised for, and cried over. Where a thousand tiny things went wrong (accidentally ordering the wrong pattern of wallpaper almost broke me) and nothing came easy, and things aren't perfect but they're *mine*.

The support from Adam, my mom, my friends, my new small business community has gotten me here. I've learned that, even as problems arise and things don't go according to plan, your people will never go away.

After some more mingling, I pick up a wick cutter from a side table and tap it lightly against a champagne flute. Everyone turns, a room full of smiling people I would do anything for, and who I know would do the same for me.

"First of all, I need to say thank you. Thank you for being here. Thank you for helping this dream grow into an actual, tangible reality. Every single one of you has made this possible. I am so honored to know you. This has been one of the most all-consuming, magnificent projects of my life. And so much of that has to do with the people I've met who helped build this place. I'm so proud that every product on these shelves has a local connection. I'm so honored to help people celebrate the achievements of the people they love.

"This place is about love, connection, and community. I hope these gifts serve as a reminder that the people who truly see you and support you are always with you. Cheers!"

Everyone raises their glass and salutes this fresh start, the unexpected joy I've found. I know the hard parts aren't over. I know there is more work ahead, that I'm just stepping onto the next stone of this path. Life is going to morph and evolve, but the thing I've realized that makes it a lot easier? I can embrace it. In fact, change can be kind of awesome.

A chorus of "Cheers!" echoes back. I watch all the people I love smile, laugh, and clink glasses, the chiming crystal an exclamation mark on a beautiful beginning.

Acknowledgements

Writing a book is unequivocally my most taxing labor of love to date. I've learned that a novel is a piece of your soul that exists outside of your body, which makes sharing this extension of myself both terrifying and thrilling.

My long list of thanks starts with you, the reader. In a world that continues to move towards impersonal interactions and AI art, people who support real human beings' work give me renewed hope. Publishing a novel's been my dream since I was a kid penning stories in a spiral-bound notebook covered with frolicking horses. Thank you for supporting a former horse girl's dream.

"Self-publishing" is certainly a misnomer. This book would not exist without the family that cheered me on, the friends that believed in and inspired me, and my ever-supportive partner, who regularly looked me in the eye and told me to cut it out whenever imposter system reared its ugly head.

Books have always been my happy place, and that love of literature was inspired by my family from the get-go.

All the thanks in the world to:

My dad, Brian, for immersing his ten-year-old in the works of Shakespeare by passing them off as bedtime stories.

My mom, Kelly, for taking me to the library and encouraging me fill my room to the brim with pre-loved *Goosebumps* books.

My grandparents, Martha and Ken, for never being upset when I chose to consume a book rather than a meal at the dinner table.

My grandparents, Jeannette and Jimmy, for endlessly

encouraging my dreams.

Erin, for always believing I'd become a published author, even when my faith wavered.

Alex, for letting me sit on the truck bumper and read in the sunshine.

My siblings, for teaching me to navigate the ridiculousness of the world with humor, grace, and the occasional expletive.

And the rest of my family, who are my constant cheerleaders and whose enthusiasm for this novel helped me make it through many rounds of edits. I love you.

There's no better partner than George (in my obviously unbiased opinion), a statement that rang particularly true while writing this. Giving your partner the space/time to write and edit in a house bursting with energy (did I mention we have two attention-seeking cats and a puppy?) is an act of love. If that wasn't enough, he makes a mean iced latte and always made sure I was properly caffeinated.

I'd be remiss not to thank the world's greatest writing group, Writers With Cats, not only for cheering me across the finish line, but convincing me to start.

The core of this novel is friendship, which is only proper. My friends are everything. The love, compassion, and empathy found in Jessie, Clara, and Lizzie are an amalgamation of all the people I love. I hope I did justice to the joy found in experiencing life with your favorite beings; it is a direct reflection of the happiness and fullness my friends bring to my life.

An extra shoutout to my beta readers, co-editors, and endless compliment-givers, Angelique and Melissa. And to Jill, whose shared love of romance novels helped brainstorm several key plot points.

If I could make one chalkboard wish for you (and share it, penalty free) it would be this; I wish you a life brimming with soul-deep friendships, helpful hair ties, and deliciously good books.

About the Author

Kate Murphy, a Massachusetts native currently based in northern Mexico, has an affinity for puzzles, puns, and toaster strudels. A lover of compelling narratives, she gravitates toward stories featuring memorable protagonists with world views that challenge societal norms.

When she's not immersed in fiction, you can find Kate playing board games with her partner, George, or hanging with her cats, Pico and Luna, and her dog, Pepita.

You can get in touch with Kate via email at katemurphywrites@gmail.com or on Instagram @Metakated.

A Perfect Arrangement is Kate's debut novel.